The heavy metal door leading down to the boiler room wasn't locked. He looked for the big I-beam that ran the length of the basement ceiling. The perfect spot for the show.

So the little buggers came here for an education, did they. Well, he'd give it to 'em in spades. Wasn't this his finest lesson? Maybe this was what he wanted to teach 'em from the beginning.

His hands worked fitfully until the hangman's noose had taken shape. He took out his nicely printed note and read it over again with satisfaction. "The last rational act of a man . . ."

Also by Gaylord Larsen
Published by Ballantine Books:

AN EDUCATED DEATH

THE 180° MURDER

Gaylord Larsen

BALLANTINE BOOKS • NEW YORK

 Published in the United States of America by Ballantine Books, a division of Random House, Inc., New York, and simultaneously in Canada by Random House of Canada Limited, Toronto.

Library of Congress Catalog Card Number: 87-91472

ISBN 0-345-34201-1

Manufactured in the United States of America

First Ballantine Books/Epiphany Edition: September 1987

To A.O.

. . . evil people tend to gravitate toward piety for the disguise and concealment it can offer them.

—Dr. M. Scott Peck,
psychotherapist

Prologue

Once he decided on his course of action, his thoughts crystallized. His headache gave way to a new, giddy feeling of relief and release that convinced him of the rightness of it all.

The last rational act of a man trapped in an irrational world. That had a good ring to it. He said it over and over in his mind as he went about his business.

The rope was tucked up under the spare tire. Whenever he visited a building unfamiliar to him, he would look for places where he could do it—a hot water pipe or a sewer line strong enough to hold the force of two hundred falling pounds, and a ledge or something high enough to jump from.

Maybe Woody Allen thinks about suicide every day, but does he do it? That's where you separate the men from the boys. The true believers from the . . . true believers.

He smiled at his private joke, closed the trunk lid, and gave an enthusiastic tug at the hemp rope to test its strength, as if his arms could somehow duplicate the kinetic energy generated by a free-falling psychologist. Then he started off toward the Faulker Building with a heroic stride. He wouldn't form the hangman's knot until he was safely inside the basement. Somebody might see him and get the right idea.

Forget Hemingway and his "misuse of the gun" crap; the rope was the only way to go—complete, majestic. Give them something to contemplate during Chapel quiet time.

Oh, no, no. That was the wrong thing to say. Too many other kinds of memories came in with it. His Aunt Ella was singing in his mind again, almost as loudly as before. He thought he'd lost her at the dentist's.

I danced on a Friday and the sky turned black.
It's hard to dance with the devil on your back;
They buried my body and they thought I'd gone,
But I am the dance and I still go . . .

He started humming loudly some nonsense melody, just to stop the sound of the old lady's song, and, to his surprise, it worked. Good-bye, Aunt Ella.

He laughed aloud and automatically reached for the pulse beat on the inside of the left wrist. It was fast. No time to stop and count it, but it was fast, all right. All the symptoms were in place. Still no sexual thoughts, though. As a trained professional, he knew all the signs, but he was powerless to do anything about them, even if he wanted to. It was as if he was watching a television rerun. Something that had already been completed, and he was only watching it now to catch up on some of the clinical details.

He unlocked the side door to the old stone building with his stolen master key. As he swung the big wooden door back, he caught the dim reflection of a scowling face in the little wire mesh window. He smiled at it and it smiled back. It wasn't the face of death, he told himself. It was the face of release. Of victory over . . . memories.

Oh, God, no. Not memories. He wasn't doing all this because of memories. It was the principle of the thing. They had to understand that. The missionary's kid had nothing to do with it. He was a big boy. He knew what he was doing. The whole mess was built into him from birth.

"It wasn't my fault. . . ." somebody using his voice shouted.

The head was pounding again, and he stopped and gripped the stairwell railing.

Calm and quiet, now. Calm and quiet. Just hold on a little longer and it will all be history. No more headaches, no faces, no more voices . . . He wondered how they'd done that. It had to be a "they." The whole thing was put together too well for one person. He had to hand it to them. They did a beautiful job. They knew him like a book.

"Touché, my unknown friends. You almost played the game better than I did. You thought you could destroy me philosophically, didn't you? But you can't, you see. I'll have the last laugh."

The heavy metal door leading down to the boiler room wasn't locked. He pushed it open with his back and flicked on the light, at the same time looking for the big I-beam that ran the length of the basement ceiling. The perfect spot.

So, the little buggers came here for an education, did they? This would be his finest lesson. Maybe this was what he wanted to teach 'em from the beginning.

Ten, eleven, twelve . . . thirteen turns around the loop, then bring the end through and pull it all tight. His hands worked fitfully until the hangman's noose had taken shape. He made a long toss of the noose over the beam. Well, what do you know? He made it on the first toss. Another omen, if he ever saw one. Now lower it to a dramatic angle and tie off the end on the short, sturdy stairwell railing. There. It'll allow a long enough fall to snap the spinal cord, yet will be close enough to the door to give 'em a good shock when they come in.

He took out his nicely printed note, along with the roll of Scotch tape, and carefully taped his final statement to the railing. He read it over again with satisfaction. "The last rational act of a man . . ." Yes, that's fine. All the words spelled correctly.

Remember to relax the neck muscles on the jump. Don't want the agony of dangling there, strangling. Who knows how long that would take. Want a short, sharp snap.

He teased the near end of rope until the noose end began swinging. When it swung close enough, he reached out and grabbed it, then slipped the loop over his head and brought it up snug, as if he were adjusting his Sunday tie.

Time to do it. Not to think about it, but to do it.

His plan was to climb onto the tubular railing and then to jump directly under the spot where the rope hung over the I-beam, but as he tried to get onto the railing, his leather soles slipped on the slick metal. He tried to regain his balance with his arms, but only succeeded in minimizing his chance for a "short, sharp snap." He lost his fingertip grip, first on the railing, then on the cement stairwell. Then his body, at the end of the rope, swung pendulum-like gently out over the old furnace, and the noose tightened smoothly across his windpipe, closing it. On the first swing back toward the stairs he made a halfhearted attempt to hook a toe onto the landing, but it was no good.

Oh, no. Now the coroner will know he suffocated and

not . . . the other way. How long . . . how long? Don't struggle. Let it happen.

Oh, God in heaven, why couldn't You have been real? It could all have been so different.

Lungs burning . . . but the pains . . . not too bad. He was surprised. The pains weren't too bad.

He saw the missionary's kid, sitting in the classroom, smiling at him. How could that be, when neither of them was dead yet? I'm sorry, kid. I didn't know what I was doing. . . .

The body twisted and swayed for another seven minutes. Then it was still. As still as the stairs, the furnace, the dirty old basement. And just like the rest of the physical universe, the little tableau continued its journey through time and space without the slightest acknowledgment that the troubled spirit of Dr. Alexander Hacchi had ever been there.

Chapter One

"Let me remind you all that Trinity University is a Christian institution," President Rollins intoned. It was the third time in the last fifteen minutes he had used that phrase. Two faculty members at the conference table rolled their eyes heavenward and shifted restlessly in their chairs, but Dr. Rollins plunged forward on his intended course: He had a responsibility—they all had a responsibility—to the students and to the God-fearing parents who had entrusted them to the university's care.

Dean Kitteridge, the elderly head of the Social Science Division, cleared his throat and slowly got to his feet.

"Thank you, President Rollins, for visiting our division meeting. I'm sure we all—"

"Now wait just a minute, Dean Kitteridge." Rollins was not about to be silenced. "I've been beating about the bush, I know, so I may as well come out with it: I am wondering if the Social Science Division has the best interests of this university at heart."

This curt comment brought all thirteen division members to the alert. "The Hacchi fiasco has put this institution on an emotional roller coaster, and the ride isn't over yet. It's been two weeks since Hacchi died, and we still have students going into counseling."

"Dr. Rollins, we know," Kitteridge interjected. "The counselors are in our division. . . ."

The president jabbed the air with his finger, a mannerism left over from his football days. Rollins had been an all-American linebacker and then a successful coach before moving into Administration. He was very popular among the powerful alumni, but his background did little to endear him in the hearts and minds of the teaching staff. Unfortunately, when he got excited, he had a habit of returning to the mannerisms that had aided his successes on the gridiron. The locker-room pep talk approach was not transferring well to the Social Science conference room—a problem he didn't seem to notice.

"I can't help but feel that if Dr. Hacchi had been more carefully evaluated before he was hired, this entire matter could have been avoided. We're all sorry about his demise, I'm sure, but I, for one, was never convinced the man belonged here. He wasn't a team player."

Harry Bishop, the nervous little economics professor, was on his feet, sputtering. "Now see here! Are you saying that Alex Hacchi wasn't qualified? Why, he was one of the finest scholars this university will ever see!"

This was exactly the kind of confrontation Kitteridge was hoping to avoid. "Sit down, Harry, please." Kitteridge reached his long left arm across the flustered Miss Merkle and got Bishop back into his chair.

"Dr. Rollins," the dean said calmly, "we followed standard hiring procedures with Dr. Hacchi."

"Yes, well, I think our standard hiring procedures might be in need of revision," Rollins challenged. His comment generated a buzz of dissent, for hiring new faculty members was, by tradition, handled in part by the Social Science Division. It was one of the last areas in which the faculty still exercised influence, and they were not about to relinquish it peacefully.

Kitteridge knocked on the table with the head of Miss Merkle's walking stick. Everyone quieted except the president, who was still in good voice.

"As for this new man you have in mind, I want to meet with the selection committee before the matter goes any further."

"Dr. Rollins," Kitteridge said, "the committee made its final decision yesterday."

"You'll have to put that decision on ice for the time being," Rollins snapped.

"I'm afraid that is impossible."

The old paneled board room turned suddenly silent, but the air crackled with energy. The president brought himself up straight, then smoothed back the wavy white hair above his ears. All who knew him recognized this was his way of biding time while he gained composure and thought about his next move.

"Explain yourself, Dean Kitteridge," Rollins said at last.

Very carefully, Kitteridge gave the walking stick back to Miss Merkle, then looked his president in the eye. "Mr. Bradley is already on his way down from Berkeley. I called him myself yesterday."

"Is this your idea of academic cooperation?"

"We have every intention of cooperating fully with Administration, President Rollins," Kitteridge said in his soft, conciliatory way. "I assure you, our actions have been most deliberate. However, since we already are into our fourth week of the new semester, we need a full-time replacement as quickly as possible. I'm sure Ms. Reed of our committee notified your office."

Hillary Reed nodded her pretty brunette head to back

up her dean, but Rollins waved his finger again, indicating that a discussion of what memos he might or might not have received was not pertinent.

"You're missing my point altogether, Dean," Rollins said. "I'm concerned about maintaining the quality of this institution."

"We all are, Doctor. But I would ask that you give this young man a chance. I read his dissertation and was very favorably impressed. The committee feels very strongly he will be a great asset to Trinity. He has a magna cum laude standing in the Berkeley Psychology Department."

"Berkeley!" Rollins snapped. "I wonder if anything good could come out of Berkeley."

The scriptural phrasing did not go unnoticed by the dean, but he chose to ignore its implications. He wove through more verbal sparring until the sound of distant bells mercifully broke up their meeting. Rollins, just to show he would live to fight another day, said sourly, "This is strictly a replacement assignment. Your Mr. Bradley will be up for careful review at the end of term—and I intend to take an active part in that review."

The president realigned his broad shoulders and marched from the room, and Kitteridge slumped into his chair with a sigh.

"Oh, dear," volunteered Miss Merkle. "Your poor Mr. Bradley. I should not like to come to my first teaching position with *that* kind of welcome."

The teachers not on their way to class gathered around Kitteridge to assess the damage.

"Who does Rollins think he's kidding?" exclaimed Harry Bishop. "Why didn't he come out and say only born-again parrots need apply for teaching posts at Trinity?"

Kitteridge scowled. "That's not entirely fair, Harry.

The president has problems you and I never have to deal with. Fifty percent of our outside financial support is church related.''

Orville McCaully, who looked exactly the way a philosophy professor is supposed to look—elbow patches and all—peered over his dusty glasses and asked, ''When's this young hotshot of yours supposed to arrive?''

Kitteridge checked the watch in his vest pocket. ''The committee is meeting him at the Quad flagpole at four-thirty. Care to join us, Orville?''

McCaully declined with a gnostic shrug. ''No, thanks. Doesn't sound like he'll be here long enough to get acquainted.''

''Oh, dear,'' Miss Merkle had to say again.

Chapter Two

Four-thirty came and went without any sign of the hotshot from Berkeley. When the three other committee members started looking to Kitteridge for an explanation, he began picking up the loose McDonald's wrappers that had blown across the grassy Quad. This demonstration in humility touched the other professors, but not enough to give the elderly dean a helping hand. Kitteridge had been at Trinity since its humble inception as an institute for the preparation of foreign missionaries, and while it might have been appropriate for instructors to perform janitorial duties back then, the younger faculty members weren't about to do so now.

The University campus was located on a beautiful site, a gently sloping foothill setting that granted some spectacular views of the Pacific Ocean off some three miles to the southwest. The mature trees and manicured shrubbery gave the place a sense of permanence, making the school look more Ivy League than Southern California.

It was a beautiful setting, that is, if the viewer had no architectural sensitivities, for each building appeared to have sprung up in its own era with no sense of its surroundings. The Faulker Building, four stories of

Midwestern dust-pink stone, was the oldest. Its three south-facing gables, labeled "God the Spirit," "God the Father," and "God the Son," attested to the University's spiritual roots. The building still looked as substantial and monolithically foreboding as it had seventy-five years earlier when it first had been dedicated to the work of the Lord. Never mind that the top two floors had been declared unsafe for occupancy by the county's Earthquake Preparedness Board, and that a running battle had been going on for over a year with other county authorities who wanted the entire building condemned. And never mind that its once honored position as the most prominent structure on campus had since been usurped by the sprawling Science and Technology Building, its sandy-yellow bricks set in the sterile, geometrically correct designs of the fifties. For some reason the S and T, as it was known, was just as impersonal and almost as foreboding as the old Faulker Building.

Next came the signs of the sixties, when an infusion of government and institutional monies had paid for a series of buildings in a Spanish motif, complete with terra cotta tile on each roof and stucco walls made to look like white adobe. Very practical for the climate, but after several tourists mistook the buildings for a California mission, the University's board of directors decided they had made the place look "too Catholic," and a series of ill-advised attempts to camouflage them took place, leading to new brown roofs and a profusion of bougainvillea covering most of the graceful breezeways.

But the crowning effort toward the unusual had to be reserved for the Prayer Tower. A certain God-fearing businessman in Des Moines, Iowa, had left the bulk of his estate—generated from thirty-five thriving hardware stores—to the University, with the stipulation that the tower be erected. It looked like a cross between a water tank and the rotating restaurant in Seattle, Washington. And in an attempt to curry favor with the student body, it had been painted the school colors, crimson and white.

One didn't have to be an allegorical poet to recognize that Trinity was struggling to locate its own soul.

After fifteen minutes of waiting by the flagpole, the two young male committee members began making noises about papers to be graded and errands in the village to be run before dinnertime. After they left, Kitteridge sat down on the flagpole bench next to the fourth committee member, Hillary Reed. A high California haze had moved in, cutting into the benefit of the late afternoon sun, and this in turn cooled off the coastal land, allowing a March breeze to move in off the ocean. Sitting shoulder to shoulder helped to cut the coolness a bit.

"You can take off, too," he told her. "There's no point in both of us waiting."

"I'm beginning to wonder if we've done the right thing," Hillary ruminated. "One of us should have gone up to interview this Mr. Bradley personally."

"Don't fret. He's probably had car trouble."

"But what do we know about the man, really? He's had virtually no teaching experience."

"He's had two semesters as a teaching assistant under old Finnigan at Berkeley," Kitteridge said.

"Being a T.A. is hardly the same as being responsible for your own lesson plans and carrying the ball all by yourself."

"Dr. Finnigan assured me he is very resourceful. What's really on your mind, Hillary?"

"Oh, I don't know. . . ." Hillary turned up the collar of her stylish jacket and looped a hand through Kitteridge's arm. He was one of the few people with whom she could sit like this without getting talked about. "I just don't want any more crises. Last semester Alex Hacchi's behavior had us all on the verge of hysteria. I think we are entitled to a nice quiet semester for a change."

Kitteridge chuckled sympathetically, but didn't say anything.

One white and two gray seagulls flew in from the west, made lazy loops around the flagpole in search of dropped french fries they might have missed on their last sortie, then headed back out to sea.

"Has it occurred to you how similar in background the two men are?" Hillary asked. 'Both psychologists, fairly young, both single. Hacchi was raised by an elderly aunt, and Bradley was raised in foster homes."

"Oh, really?"

"It's in his application. Don't you read the personal stuff?"

"I guess I missed that."

She squeezed his arm. "You old fox. You don't miss anything."

Kitteridge hauled his heavy briefcase onto his lap and snapped it open. "I want to show you something." A manila folder labeled "Bradley" was lying on top of everything else. He rummaged through it and came up with a newspaper clipping. "Here. From the *San Francisco Chronicle*. That was the first I'd heard of him."

Hillary held the two-column article in both hands because of the breeze and read: " 'Oakland psychologist fingers bomber.' Oh, yes, I remember reading something about this," she said.

"Bradley worked with the Oakland Police Department as a forensic psychologist. The police asked him to do a psychological profile on the bomber they had up there two years ago. Look here." Kitteridge couldn't resist pointing out some of the goodies in the article

" 'He predicted the bomber would be a man born in Eastern Europe, in his mid-fifties, who probably lived with an invalid mother or maiden aunt. He would wear double-breasted suits and rimless glasses.' He divined all that from the notes the man left around and the types of bombs he planted. Can you imagine that? And when they caught the guy—read here—he was right in almost every detail, right down to the invalid aunt and the double-breasted suit."

"Very impressive," Hillary responded, without sounding impressed. Then she looked at him narrowly. "So you think we need such skills here, do you?"

He smiled, retrieved the clipping, and put it away before answering. "He's a very talented man, very close to completing his Ph.D. I think it's important Trinity seek out people who are at the top of their fields—whatever their specialties."

"If he's so good, why is he accepting a position with little ol' Tri-U? And don't tell me it's because of the fantastic salary schedule."

"Maybe you'd like to ask him that question when he gets here."

"Well . . ." Hillary glanced at her wristwatch, then got to her feet. "Right now, I have two hungry children who are going to be throwing tantrums about their dinner if I don't get home. Give me a call if anyth—"

She was interrupted by the sound of a German auto in pain. They both turned and watched as an old Volkswagen van came chugging up the graceful drive that circled the Quad. The vehicle looked as if it could have been in every peace march ever held on or near the Berkeley campus. It was crammed to the windows with boxes and suitcases, and on the roof were two long parcels wrapped in tarps. The van mercifully whined to a stop about forty yards from Hillary and the dean, and the driver hopped out.

"Oh, no," Hillary murmured at the sight of him. "Comes the lamb to the slaughter."

But, in truth, the tall stranger looked more like a lion than a lamb. He had a full head of wild yellow hair and an unkempt rusty beard. He wore a grease-stained T-shirt and chopped-off Levi's. He waved a friendly hand toward them and called, "Hello there! You must be the welcoming committee. I'm Jason Bradley."

Hillary whispered into Kitteridge's ear: "I take back everything I said about his being like Dr. Hacchi."

Kitteridge ignored her and did a smooth job of introductions, just as if Bradley had appeared in a three-piece suit. Bradley showed his dirty fingers, explaining why he couldn't shake hands.

"My top gears went out on me. I've been driving in second ever since San Luis Obispo. Sorry to be late."

"Looks as if you're pretty well loaded down," Kitteridge remarked.

"Yes. All my worldly goods."

"What's that on the rack, Joseph's bones?" Hillary asked.

"Joseph's bones? I don't follow . . ." Jason frowned.

"Don't mind Hillary," Kitteridge said. "She's only testing your knowledge of Scriptures."

"Ah, I see. Joseph's bones . . . But I'd hardly call traveling Coastal Route One a trek across the desert." He gave her a big smile.

"My analogy needs work."

Jason patted one of the tarpaulins on top of his van. "These are my kites. I'm a hang gliding enthusiast. You ever hang glide, Ms. Reed?"

"Not on your life," she scoffed.

"It's a great sport. I'm looking forward to testing the

ocean cliffs and the foothills around this area. That is, if Dean Kitteridge doesn't work me too hard!''

''Oh, we'll manage to give you a few free hours,'' Kitteridge said. There was a quiet moment as the three eyed one another, then Kitteridge went on, ''I had thought there would be a little time for me to show you around a bit, but I think that can wait until tomorrow. Do you have a place to stay?''

''I saw a motel back on—''

''Nonsense. You come home with me. My wife and I will be happy to put you up until you get settled.''

Jason was impressed. ''That's very kind of you. I'll get a bite to eat and cleaned up and . . .''

''No, no. You come to dinner. I told Angie I'd probably be bringing you.'' Kitteridge rubbed his hands, either in anticipation of the houseguest or to keep warm. ''Tell you what. I have my pickup in the faculty lot. I'll go get it and swing by here so you can follow me. That'll give you two young people a chance to get acquainted.''

Kitteridge was gone before either could object.

''His pickup?'' Jason asked. ''Spry old fellow, isn't he?''

''Yes, he's a marvel.'' Hillary looked Mr. Bradley over at close range. She thought there might be a rather attractive man under all that hair, but she wasn't too sure. ''You think you'll like Trinity?''

''Yes, I hope to. I wouldn't have come, otherwise.''

''I think you'll find it quite a change from Berkeley.''

''How so?''

''It's a church-related school. We do things a bit differently here.''

''Oh. I'm not much for campus politics, if that's the problem.''

''Poor boy. You probably still think being a college

professor has something to do with educating young people."

He gave her a slow look. He didn't know quite what to make of her. At thirty-three, she was only two years older than he, but there was a good city block showing between their life-styles.

"What's your area of specialty, Ms. Reed?"

Hillary declined to cooperate. "What's your best guess?"

"Well, let's see. . . ." He took the challenge with a smile and looked her over. "Social Science Division, small liberal arts school, dresses nicely—all color coordinated . . . slacks . . . how about Women's Reentry Program, and maybe Marriage and the Family?"

She looked wary. "You read that someplace."

"Yes, I did."

"You saw our college catalog."

He laughed. "No, I read it right here." He pointed at her mouth with his one clean little finger.

"I didn't say anything about Women's Reentry."

"Yes you did. Kitteridge punched the title of 'Ms.' when he introduced us. That tells me women's rights and all. The reentry programs on most campuses are traditionally the hotbeds of that sort of thing."

"I take it you don't approve."

"Oh, please, I just got here. Do you have to pigeonhole me so soon?"

"That seems to be what you are doing to me."

"You're absolutely right. I'll keep my mouth shut."

She planted her hands on her hips. "How'd you know I teach Marriage and the Family?"

"It's kind of a goofy shot in the dark. You sure you want to hear?"

"Yes." She folded her arms in front of her as if waiting to be impressed.

"Well, the young ladies who come to most of these private schools are working toward their M.R.S. degrees, which makes for an abundance of Marriage-and-the-Family type classes. And just because I liked the irony of it all . . ."

"Irony?"

"Yes. You're wearing a gold necklace with the names 'Timmy' and 'Valerie' showing, which leads me to believe you're a mother. And then," he pointed to her left hand, "there's no ring."

She quickly pocketed her hands.

"And that tells me, divorce," he said softly.

"That's cruel. How do you know I'm not a widow?"

"There's much too much hostility in the tone of your voice, especially to be directed toward a male you hardly know. Probably a few barbs left over. No, I'd say you've been through a pretty messy divorce."

"So that's what you call ironic—a divorcée teaching Marriage and the Family?"

"Yes, and at a Christian school, too. Tsk, tsk."

"Mr. Bradley, I think you're rather rude."

"Yes, I guess you're right. But since you apparently came out here with the intention of testing the 'new boy on campus,' I thought I might as well give you a little show. Sorry if it stung a bit."

Kitteridge pulled up in his beat-up yellow pickup and honked.

"I think he wants me to follow," Jason said. He opened the van's squeaky front door. "May I drop you someplace?"

She stepped clear of the van for fear it might suck her in. "No thank you."

"Ms. Reed, I'm sorry we got off on the wrong foot. I hope we can still be friends," Jason told her.

"I don't see why not. With my shortcomings and your penchant for detail, we should hit it off very well."

He laughed and slipped behind the wheel. The van sputtered to life and chugged off after the pickup.

Hillary scowled after them and twisted her fists in her pockets.

"So much for my quiet semester."

Chapter Three

Dean Kitteridge rapped on the half-open door of Jason's basement office and poked in his head. "How are you settling in, young man?"

Jason took his feet off his desk and stood up. "Just fine, Dean. Come in and sit down."

Kitteridge hid his astonishment at the sight of Jason, who was now clean-shaven except for a blond mustache and dressed in a tie and a dress shirt and jeans. "I don't know as I would have recognized you."

"Well, the full beard looked slightly out of place around here."

"I hope it was a comfortable adjustment."

Jason stroked his throat. "Still a little drafty."

Kitteridge folded his long legs and dropped into the only other chair in the room. He held out a pair of washed and folded socks. "I believe these are yours. The wife cleaned them up a bit."

"Please thank her."

"No problem. Angie said it was like old times, having someone about the place to pick up after."

"Was I that bad?"

Kitteridge laughed and looked around the cracker box of an office. "Classes going okay?"

"I think things are falling into place. Oh, by the way, I asked the custodian for the keys to this filing cabinet." Jason tapped the two-drawer file tucked in next to the small desk. "He said you have the keys for it."

"Yes, I do. I wanted to talk to you about that." Kitteridge took a set of keys out of his pocket, but he didn't hand them over. "This was Dr. Hacchi's office, you know. A lot of his papers are in there. Don't know exactly what to do with them. No family . . ."

"You want me to box them up?" Jason offered.

Kitteridge frowned and walked over to the small window. From this level in the S and T Building one could see only the bottoms of some shrubs and a bit of grass that had turned a winter-brown.

"I was thinking you might be interested in looking over his papers. He taught in your discipline, you know."

"Okay. Not a bad idea."

Jason silently watched the dean. He was a big man with something on his mind, and he looked a little like an aging animal in a cage too small for his frame. Kitteridge came back and sat, facing Jason.

"You are aware that Hacchi kept thorough notes on his calendar there. Have you had a chance to look them over?"

Jason thumbed the daily reminder calendar in front of him. "No, I haven't. You feel I might learn something from them?"

"Just a thought. Well," Kitteridge was on his feet again, "I must be off. Another administrative council session. Goals and objectives and all that. Let me know if I can be of any help."

"And the keys . . ." Jason hinted.

"Oh, yes." Kitteridge looked at them in his hand, as

if he were reluctant to give them up. "We're kind of tight about keys around here. Don't lose them."

He tossed them to Jason.

"Okay, I'll remember that."

Jason watched him go off down the corridor and tried to figure out what this little meeting was all about. Not a word about Jason's course outlines or study plans, but there was definitely something on the old-timer's mind.

Jason didn't have time before his ten o'clock class to do anything about the file drawers, but he started thumbing back through the desk calendar pages.

In a small but very legible hand Hacchi had noted things to do, student appointments, meetings, etcetera. In the right margins were check marks. Apparently he checked things off as they were accomplished. Nothing very unusual.

Jason thumbed ahead to see what the entries were like just before Hacchi's death. He knew Hacchi had committed suicide on the twenty-seventh of February, but his handwriting for that day was just as confident and expressive as before. Next to the nine-thirty time line of the morning of the twenty-seventh Hacchi had written two reminders to himself: "Pick up slacks at cleaners" and "Dental appointment." Both notes had been checked off. That was curious. Why would he bother to run errands in the morning if he was planning to hang himself in the afternoon? Okay, maybe the cleaners. He wanted to pay his debts, get his house in order. But the dentist?

Jason was jolted back to the present by the sound of the tower clock chiming ten. He grabbed his briefcase and headed for class.

Chapter Four

The class was Introduction to Physiological Psychology. Jason had already taught a session of the same class at eight o'clock that morning and everything had gone well.

He plopped down his briefcase, leaned carefully on the corner of the teacher's desk, and watched the students' eyes as they filed into the room. This was all part of his calculated effort to appear friendly and approachable. A few students caught his glance and smiled back, but most of them were withholding judgment on the new arrival and came in wearing bored expressions.

For the most part the students looked about the same as those he had taught at Berkeley. Maybe these kids were a bit tidier and smoother of cheek. Or was that only his imagination?

After a quick head check against his roster, he began the hour with an old standard psych joke about how people who take psychology classes are usually in need of clinical help themselves. It got a fair response.

Next, while he was pulling the video cart from the corner of the room into viewing position, he gave a brief introduction to the tape he was about to show them. It included plenty of outrageous case studies, he explained, designed to whet their appetites for the semester ahead.

Jason had showed the tape to the earlier class, and had rewound it carefully before pushing the unit into the corner where he had assumed it had been sitting, undisturbed. During the nine o'clock hour the room had been used by an English teacher who thought visual aids for the classroom were a sign of intellectual, if not moral, weakness, so there was no reason for Jason to think his tape was not in the VCR where it should be.

He suggested the class take notes for later questions, then turned on the monitor and punched "play." He sauntered toward the back of the room, where he planned to sit and get his new attendance sheets into his three-ring notebook. When he was halfway down the aisle, he heard two girls gasp. Then a boy with a cracking voice yodeled "Holy cow." That was followed quickly by the shriek of another girl.

Jason looked at the class. All eyes were riveted on the monitor—all eyes, that is, except his.

On the TV tube, in living color, a young couple in the buff was sprawled across a double bed in the middle of a very active sexual encounter.

Jason hustled back up front and switched off the monitor, then stopped the tape. He whirled about to examine the sea of faces.

"Okay, whose bright idea was this?"

Nobody moved. The few faces with smiles on them quickly sobered up. Most of the students found something else to do with their attention. If Jason was hoping to spot a culprit in their midst, his opportunity was slipping away.

He got the tape out of the machine and looked at it. It had no label or identification—probably some cheap X-rated video a student had gotten hold of somewhere.

"This is the wrong tape."

Well, of course it was the wrong tape, dummy. What did he say that for? It only acted to break the tension.

A comic in the room cracked, "It looked okay to me," and the place erupted in snickers.

Jason could feel his naked cheeks heating up. He knew he was handling the situation poorly, but he couldn't seem to stop himself.

"Joke time is over. Now, does anybody know where the correct tape is?"

Nobody moved. Jason did a cursory search of the room but found nothing. He returned to his briefcase and hauled out the giant text for the class, along with his notes. Fortunately, he had taught the class as a teacher's assistant twice before, so he quickly began lecturing in full voice and high gear. He threw at them all the ten-dollar psychology words he would think of, and he knew plenty. Nobody knows the jargon like a fourth-year graduate student bearing down on his Ph.D.

By the time class was over, the atmosphere in the room had changed. It was so sober and quiet the class could have been a memorial service for the departed Dr. Hacchi. And in a way, it was, for no doubt more than one student wished for Hacchi back. Jason had put the fear of God into the class by showing them how tough Physio-Psych could be. Half the students left shaking their heads, and a good portion of the rest went out shaking their writing hands to get rid of their writer's cramp.

For his part, Jason heaved a heavy sigh of relief and headed for the University swimming pool. He had found that when he needed some space between himself and his troubles, the solitude and rhythmic exertion of swimming laps helped to clear his mind. He introduced himself to the student attendant, got assigned a locker and some gear, and was soon pushing off into the cool blue water.

By the time he had swum a quarter of a mile, he had begun to view the video episode with a little perspective. Okay, so somebody played a joke on the new teacher. So what? Why hadn't he rolled with it? He should have laughed at the situation and let it go at that. Why did he get on his high horse and give those poor kids such a bad time, expecting them to absorb as much in one lecture as he usually covered in two weeks?

It was true he was at a religious school, and he still didn't know the ground rules. How would the University react to having a pornographic tape shown in class? Surely they would understand—wouldn't they?

One reason Jason had gone into psychology was to find out more about himself. He thought he had a pretty nifty ability to get along with people and to think quickly on his feet. And here he had let the students get his goat the first week out. Good-bye, Mr. Chips.

Jason didn't have to wait long for the University's reaction. When he returned to his office after his workout, he found a neatly typed message on his office door from President Rollins: "Please see me in my office before twelve-thirty, today. This is important."

On the way over he formulated a letter in his head. It was to be addressed to the teacher placement office up at Cal Berkeley.

> Dear Mrs. Sparrow, Perhaps you remember me. You were kind enough to help me with my application for the teaching post at Trinity University. Now it appears I must call upon your good services once more . . .

Chapter Five

Miss Elsie Berkaw wore a pince-nez on her long, aristocratic nose. Jason didn't know they were still in existence, but it seemed fitting for Miss Elsie's dour demeanor. She was the executive secretary to the president. It said so right on the nameplate on her tidy little desk.

She looked Jason up and down like a federal beef inspector after a hoof-and-mouth disease scare, then announced: "The president is running a little late with his appointments, Mr. Bradley."

Judging from her attitude, Jason's fame had preceded him. He wished he had taken the time to change out of his jeans. He paced a bit, looking for conversational devices. The large grandfather clock in the corner of the room caught his eye.

"Beautiful old clock, there," he said.

"Yes. It belongs to President Rollins. He collects them."

The pendulum action of the clock was extremely slow, one cycle every five seconds. It seemed to taunt the nervous teacher.

"Tempus doesn't seem to fugit here, does it?" he asked. "So I think I'll take a chair."

Miss Elsie eyed the nearby waiting-room chair. "I'd leave it right where it is, if I were you."

"Good thinking," he agreed. "In that case, I'll sit in it right where it is.

"How long have you been with the University, Miss Berkaw?"

"Thirty-two years."

Jason said warmly, "I imagine you've seen a lot of changes in that time."

"I certainly have." She lightly caressed the top of her IBM Selectric and wistfully looked out the window. "We don't get the same caliber students we used to in the old days."

He leaned forward to enjoy the view with her. "Lovely campus."

"Yes-ss." She sighed. "But you should have seen this school before the Warren Court."

Jason found himself nodding, then shaking his head in confusion. He considered asking Miss Berkaw her feelings about AC-DC's latest album, but then chickened out.

She turned her attention to her typewriter, indicating her period of reflection was at an end. Jason took a seat in an uncomfortable chair and had started thumbing through an old issue of *Campus Life* when there were two quick beeps on the intercom.

"Dr. Rollins will see you now," Miss Berkaw said. "Go right through the double doors on your left."

Well, of course, old dear. They were the only other doors in the room, except for the one he came in by. He opened the right one quietly and pushed on in.

He found President Rollins in his paneled office standing in front of a small wall mirror. He had his suit coat in one hand and was busy brushing the collar and shoulders with a long whisk broom. Apparently the full head of wavy white hair came with a case of dandruff.

"Sit down but don't get too comfortable, Mr. Bradley," Rollins said, slipping back into his coat. "I have a Chamber of Commerce meeting in fifteen minutes."

Jason did as told.

"What's this I hear about your showing porno stuff in your class? If you tell me it's part of your study plan, then I'll have to tell you some of our own 'facts of life' at Trinity."

"Dr. Rollins, do you mind if I tell you what happened?"

"That's why you're here, Mr. Bradley."

They had met only briefly in the hallway Jason's first day of teaching, sort of a hello and good-bye thing. Rollins hadn't been any warmer then than he was now. Jason plowed ahead with his explanation, but before he could finish his story, President Rollins abruptly asked, "You were with the Oakland Police Department?"

"Yes, sir. I was assigned there as a forensic psychologist."

"Why did you leave?"

"The federal grant monies ran out, so I went back to school to work on my doctorate. And here I am."

"Yes," Rollins responded, pointedly failing to match Jason's attempt at cheerfulness. "Here you are."

With that detour ended, Jason got back to the class problem—but he kept feeling as though this were a locker room session with his football coach after he had dropped a pass in the end zone, and he wondered why.

Rollins, meanwhile, was looking over a pink phone message he had on his desk. When Jason stopped for breath, Rollins read from the note: "Your class was Physiological Psychology 2B? That's lower division. Freshmen and sophomores. Holy crud."

"It was somebody's idea of a joke on the new teacher. . . ."

"Listen. You're responsible for anything that goes on in your classroom. Or don't they teach responsibility up at Berkeley anymore? You should have checked the . . . dang tape before you started."

Jason wished Rollins would let loose with a few swear words to relieve some of the pressure he saw building up around the man's neck. It didn't seem natural to hear a barrel-chested two-hundred-and-fifty-pound Type A man saying "dang."

Jason attempted to placate his chief administrator by showing his great sorrow. "You can be certain that this won't happen again," Jason assured him. "I'll keep very tight rein on all my AV aids."

"There have been altogether too many of these kinds of pranks going on around here lately. They've got to stop."

This was news to Jason. "How do you mean?"

"Find out who pulled this on you and put a stop to it."

Jason frowned and rubbed his face where his beard used to be. "Dr. Rollins, I've already made a big enough fool out of myself over this. If I start running around trying to pinpoint who pulled this stunt, any chance I might have for some decent rapport with my students will go right down the tubes. Is it all that important?"

He rolled his eyes. "You'd know how important it is if you sat in this chair for one day. You're on probation here, fella, and you're not off to much of a start. I'll draw up a letter about this porno thing, and I'll sit on it for a spell. If you don't come up with anything, the letter goes in your file. I think that's fair enough."

Fair enough for whom? Jason wondered. It didn't

sound fair to him. He was still looking for rebuttal material when Rollins checked his pocket watch, then snapped his lapel to shake away imaginary dandruff and headed for the exit as he talked. "I like to think we're a team around here, Mr. Bradley. That's what makes a successful university. We all do our part. Keep us posted, won't you?"

It wasn't really a question; it was an order. Jason watched the president disappear through his private entrance, then he sat in place and listened to the two grandfather clocks in the room click their seconds off.

He wondered if he was being singled out by the president for rough treatment. He wondered why he had majored in psychology.

He wondered what the Cheapskate's Luncheon Special of the Day was in the cafeteria up at Berkeley.

Chapter Six

The Campus Police office was at the rear of the Student Union Building, out of view of most of the campus activity, but nice and close to the service area and the parking lot where the little brown prowl cars and the ticket scooter were kept. Jason asked the bright-eyed student aide at the desk if the duty officer was about. Before she could say anything, a desk chair squeaked in a smaller inner office, and a gravel voice called, "Yo."

A heavyset man pressing retirement age with a vengeance waddled into the room and said, "I'm Officer Ryan. What can I do for you?"

Jason introduced himself and said, "I was wondering if you folks had a fingerprint dust kit."

"Yeah, as a matter of fact, we do. What's the problem?"

Jason put his briefcase on the counter and took out the videotape that had been the cause of his problem.

"Being the new teacher on campus, I think I've been the butt of a practical joke. This was substituted in my classroom for one of the educational tapes."

Ryan chuckled. "They're at it again, are they?"

"What do you mean by that?"

"Oh, we had a rash of stunts pulled last year. Things

got a little out of hand. I thought we'd taken care of it by putting Animal House on probation."

"Animal House?"

"You know, like in that movie. It's one of the fraternity houses across the street from the Tower." He looked to his aide for help. "What was the house called, Mimi?"

"Beta Rho," Mimi said with a smile.

"Yeah, Beta Rho. I get all those Latin numbers mixed up. What have you got here?"

He started to reach for the tape, but Jason held it away. "This is what I'd like to dust. I've only touched it here in the middle, when I took it out of the machine. I'm hoping there might be a usable print or two on one of the smooth surfaces of the plastic housing."

"It would have to be a thumbprint if we're going to do any comparing," Ryan said. "We only do the right thumb for ID purposes on the students. But I'd be willing to give it a shot."

The crack about the "Latin numbers" didn't do much to fill Jason with confidence in Officer Ryan's forensic abilities, but there didn't seem to be any alternative. He set the VHS tape down on edge while Ryan got out what looked like a country doctor's satchel.

Mimi hurried up to the counter. "Oh, let me watch! I've never seen fingerprints found before."

"You sure you know how to do it?" Jason had to ask.

Ryan growled back at him, "I wasn't thirty years on the L.A.P.D. for nothin', I'll have you know."

He took out a brush device that had a squeeze bulb on the back of it and started pumping air across the tape. There didn't seem to be anything coming out of his atomizer device, but soon white patterns started to appear across the black plastic.

"Well, one thing's certain," Ryan barked. "Nobody tried to wipe it clean. Let's see what we have here."

He took out a small circular fluorescent lamp with a magnifying glass in the middle of it and got the tape adjusted under the light. After dusting carefully with the brush and turning the tape back and forth for a minute he announced, "Well, praise de Lawd. I think we got enough of a right thumbprint to nail somebody."

"Let me see," Mimi exclaimed, rushing into viewing position.

Ryan slapped her arm abruptly. "Kepa you hans off da evidence, my little chickadee."

The thumbprint was right on top, about where one would normally put a thumb to hold a tape. Under the light the white-powder traces stood out nicely against the black background.

"How do you know it's a right thumbprint?" Mimi asked.

"The size, for one thing. And you see that swirl of ridges, how it goes off to the right? That particular type of print is called a loop, and when it tails off to the right that way, it's almost always from the right thumb. And I can see at least five points of recognition. You only need four to hang a man in this state."

Jason smiled and rubbed his hands together. "Now then, can we run comparisons?"

Ryan scratched one gray sideburn. "Counting our part-time students, we got eight thousand cards to go through. You got three months to spare?"

"No computers?" Jason asked.

Ryan shook his head. "That's for the big boys. It would take money and time to have our prints computerized. You want to press formal charges?"

Jason's hopes sagged. "No, I don't think so."

"Well, I'll tell you what." Ryan smiled. "Things are

quiet around here. It might be fun to nail this bird. In my spare time I'll start pulling the student prints with loops in them. That'll cut the quantity down by two-thirds."

Jason shrugged his shoulders, unable to think of anything better.

"You leave the tape with us for a while," Ryan said. "We'll get pictures of the thumbprint, and then I'll pull it off with Mylar tape so's we can mount it."

Jason left Ryan and Mimi to their fun and headed across campus in the direction of the building marked Audiovisual Services. The structure appeared to be an original Quonset hut that had been thrown off the island of Guam for being an eyesore after World War II. Mercifully, it was hidden behind shrubs and trees so as not to further confuse the architectural mix.

Jason walked up the ramp to the Audiovisual Building and found a little Mexican woman adding water to the six-volt batteries of her blue electric delivery cart.

"Hi there. I'm Jason Bradley."

She pushed back her Dodger baseball cap for a better look at him, then grunted. "Oh, yeah, you're the new Dr. Hacchi, ain't chew? Room two-eleven. I'm Annie. Did you bring back our tape?"

"I need to talk to you about that," Jason said. "It seems to have disappeared between my eight o'clock and ten o'clock classes."

Annie capped off her batteries and looked at him disapprovingly. "You're supposed to hang on to 'em when we check 'em out to you." She sighed, as if to say, "These stupid teachers," then said, "Come on in. You'll have to fill out a lost report."

Inside, behind the long, narrow counter were rows of metal shelves containing brown and green sixteen-millimeter film cans and some wooden shelves holding video tapes. Two students dressed in wraparound smocks were rewinding films in the back.

Annie gave Jason a form to fill out. "Put down where the tape was when you last saw it," she said.

"That's easy. It was in the machine when I left the room at five minutes to nine."

"You left it in the machine?"

"Yes. I take it I wasn't supposed to."

She didn't answer immediately. Then Jason noticed she had a radio in the breast pocket of her jacket and was listening through the plug in her ear.

"Bad accident," she announced.

"Oh, really?"

She nodded. "Truck driver pinned under his semi."

"Here on campus?"

She shook her head. "Outside of Ogden."

"Ogden. Is that near here?"

"No. Ogden's up in Utah."

She took the form from him and started filling it out for him. "There's only fifteen video carts. We got to use 'em just about every hour in the mornings."

"You mean that video unit was used in another classroom at nine o'clock?"

"Could be."

"But the cart I used at eight was still there exactly as I had left it when I came in at ten. How does that figure?"

"Yeah, well, sometimes we do."

Jason blinked at her. She didn't seem to be able to give a direct answer to a direct question. He tried again.

"The cart I had at eight o'clock—was it or was it not used elsewhere during the nine o'clock hour?"

"Well, that's our problem, you see." She touched her ear-piece again. "The ambulance is there now."

"Up in Ogden?"

She nodded. He decided to lean against the counter and bleed awhile before he would rise and fight again.

Apparently things were quieting down up in Ogden. Jason watched Annie write rapidly across the form. He craned his neck to follow along and wondered why he couldn't make sense of what she wrote. Then it dawned on him. There were no verbs.

"Don't you think you should insert the words 'was lost' right about there?" Jason suggested, pointing at the spot where Anglo-Saxons liked their verbs.

"What for?" she wanted to know. "That's what this already is. A lost report."

"Well, listen," Jason said, exasperated, "I'm running late for the Mad Hatter's tea party. Can you tell me if you or any of your helpers touched the cart between nine and ten o'clock?"

Annie's big brown eyes were going slightly walleyed again.

"More trouble in Ogden?" he asked.

"No. San Bernadino Freeway."

Well, at least it was closer to home. Jason was about to give up hope of making any progress when, quite unexpectedly, he had the uneasy feeling that he was being observed. Then he realized the activity in the back of the Quonset hut had stopped. He felt certain it had stopped just about the time he had asked about Annie's helpers touching the cart.

In an effort to see what was going on back there, he quickly ducked his head in order to peer through the shelves of film cans. As he did so, a pair of eyes turned away from his and a rewind machine started up again.

Rather then pressing the issue, Jason decided to get back to Officer Ryan and his friendly little kit. He thanked Annie and told her he'd let her know if the tape showed up.

"Yeah," she grunted. "Have a nice time."

"Nice time?" he echoed.

"Ain't chew on your way to a tea party?"

About halfway down the ramp he decided she might be right.

Chapter Seven

The afternoon was taken up with mundane tasks, such as getting his van out of the repair shop and more school business. One of Jason's classes called for a workshop experience for his students, so he spent an hour at the county mental health facility meeting the staff and coordinating details for his students' work-visits. The University's School of Medicine already enjoyed a close relationship with the county hospital and the Mental Health Center, so most of his arrangements were routine.

Rescuing his transportation took a little longer. With a bill of four hundred and sixty dollars outstanding, the garage people ran a check on Jason's MasterCard and didn't like the looks of his credit balance, so he had to endure the embarrassment of the manager's calling Dean Kitteridge for verification of his employment. Kitteridge was kind enough to come down in his yellow pickup and talk with the repair shop people personally. He seemed to know half the people in the little town of Almaden, and his word went far.

By the time Jason had finished his dinner at a local sandwich shop and gotten back to his apartment, he had almost forgotten the video matter, but it all came back to him, like garlic from a bad meal, when he saw the blinking message light on his Phone-Mate. He listened to Officer Ryan's voice. He sounded very excited and wanted Jason to call him at his home as soon as possible.

Jason had a pretty good idea what Ryan would say. After his strange visit at the AV Building he had asked Ryan to check the thumbprint they'd found on the tape against those of the AV student staff. Apparently the officer had struck early pay dirt.

Ryan wasn't home when Jason called, but about half an hour later they finally made their connection. The old cop sounded more like a rookie than a thirty-year veteran.

"We got it! I got a match without question."

"One of the AV workers?" Jason asked.

"Yeah, you were right on the nose. And listen to this. Guess where this guy lives!" Not giving Jason time to guess, he rushed on, "He's a senior, living at the Animal House. We got him dead to rights."

"Whoa, not so fast," Jason cautioned. "Since he works in AV, there could be a completely innocent explanation for his thumbprints appearing on that tape. What I'd like to do is approach him kind of low key and talk. . . ."

"There's more. The guy's a communications major. He helps out with the AV productions. I think he *made* that tape. And I think we can actually prove he shot it with one of the school's video cameras."

"Wait a minute, wait a minute." Things were moving too fast for Jason's after-dinner mind. Officer Ryan was clearly better acquainted with the tape than Jason was. "You mean this kid from AV shot the thing?"

"Right."

"Where would he get actors to . . . Listen, what little I saw looked like the real thing."

"It probably *was* the real thing. I figger he hid the camera in a bedroom where he knew there was gonna be some action."

"Oh, brother."

"And he caught 'em in the act."

"Oh, no." Jason closed his eyes and watched President Rollins patiently whisking dandruff from his suit coat.

"The AV kid's name is Barry Peterson," Ryan was saying. "I went by the fraternity around six, but he was already out for the evening."

"You did? In uniform?"

"Yeah, sure."

"I wish you hadn't done that. This kid's college career is at stake. I was hoping to talk to the boy privately. I'd hate to be responsible . . ."

"I think it's a little late for that. The fat's in the fire."

"Does Mimi know about the matchup?"

"No. She left long before I got it."

"Let's keep this under wraps for the time being, okay? I want to talk to the boy. If the whole thing has to come out in the open, it may be a lot better on him if he comes clean on his own."

"Okay," Ryan said in a sad tone. "What do you want to do?"

"I'll see the kid in the morning."

"You better make it early. He's got a Production workshop class that meets at seven-thirty."

"Boy, you don't let any grass grow under your feet, do you?"

"I wasn't thirty years on the L.A.P.D. for nothin', I'll have you know."

"Oh, yes. I remember."

* * *

Jason slept surprisingly well that night, in spite of his troubles. He had gone to bed marveling at the fine line between student and teacher—a fine but such a cruel line. A short time ago he had been a rowdy student himself. Now, suddenly, he was called upon to be an authority figure. He didn't like the switch very much. It was still troubling him in the morning, and perhaps in an unconscious act of defiance, he walked out his front door at six-forty-five without his new tie.

His apartment was only a half block from the Quad and the Animal House. As he rounded the corner, he spotted Annie's blue electric cart cutting across the Quad at full speed. He checked his watch. What was she doing on campus at this hour?

Then he noticed the two black-and-white police cars double-parked in front of the fraternity house. He broke into a trot. Annie got to the entrance about the same time he did.

"What's going on?" he asked her.

She pulled between two parked cars and bumped the front wheel of her cart up onto the sidewalk. This time she had a different radio, apparently one designed to pick up police calls.

"I ain't sure. I was at breakfast," she answered.

Jason started up the front steps of the two-story stucco building. The place looked more like a run-down apartment building than a frat house. Rather disappointing after the big buildup. The front door was locked. Through the glass he spotted a uniformed officer standing in the small lobby. Jason rapped on the glass and the officer poked his head out.

"You from the Medical Examiner's office?"

"Medical? No, I teach—"

"Sorry. Nobody allowed inside during the investigation."

"What investigation?" he asked, but the officer was already closing the door.

Jason went back down toward Annie, hoping she had gotten a bulletin on her scanner. For the first time he noticed she had a hand-printed sign taped to the front of her cart. "Are you lost? Ask me," it read. Apparently she meant to be a help to new students. He wished them luck.

A small crowd of joggers and other early-morning types had started gathering, probably attracted by the sight of the two police cars. Just then, an ambulance came around the corner and pulled up behind the police cars.

"Bad news," Annie announced. "Real bad news. When those guys don't blow their sirens, that means they don't have to rush no place."

Both attendants got out, pulled a heavy-duty gurney from the back, and started up the steps. The policeman inside held the door open, saying, "It's about time you guys showed up!"

A pair of plainclothes detectives shouldered out the door. Between them was a thin, pale kid dressed in pajamas and a bathrobe that had dark red stains splattered across the front.

"Blood!" an onlooker announced.

The boy was handcuffed from behind, and the police had firm control of him as they lowered his head and got him into the backseat of a squad car. But in spite of his obvious predicament, the boy had a slight smile on his lips. He also had several blotches of pink showing up on his otherwise pale complexion. Jason had seen those symptoms before—on mental patients near exhaustion or under extreme anxiety.

"Do you know him?" Jason asked Annie as the police car drew away.

"I've seen him before, but I don't know him," she said. Then she turned and looked back up the stairs to the fraternity house.

"But I know *him,*" she said.

Another student had come out of the building. He had a round, puffy face and his eyes were red and wet from crying. He couldn't seem to get enough oxygen into his system. After several gulps he sat down on the steps and held his head.

Annie went up to him. Jason held back, but wanted to be able to hear what was said.

"What happened, Harold?" she asked him.

"He's dead," he answered, as if surprised. "Barry's dead."

"Barry Peterson?" Jason blurted.

The boy nodded. "He was stabbed in the night. Stabbed by somebody. I can't believe it."

"Who was it they arrested?" Annie asked, but the boy was in no condition to answer.

The front door was pushed open once more, and the attendants from the ambulance eased down the steps with their loaded gurney, moving as carefully as they could. It was wrapped tightly under a thick red blanket, but it was still easy to tell from the loose residual movement that life had left the body of the Peterson boy.

After the ambulance had driven away, most of the onlookers started drifting their separate ways. Annie sat on a step behind Harold and rubbed his shoulder in a rather awkward manner.

Jason suddenly felt cold. He looked to the east and saw that the sun, on its low-winter arc, had momentarily disappeared behind the Prayer Tower.

Then, for no apparent reason, he found himself reading, over and over, the sign on Annie's delivery cart: "Are you lost? Ask me. Are you lost? Ask me."

The words were beginning to mock him.

Chapter Eight

After Jason had finished his ten o'clock class, he headed for his office, where he found Dean Kitteridge waiting for him. The old fellow looked terrible. About ten years older than he had at the garage the day before.

Jason poured two cups of coffee from his trusty Mr. Coffee machine and loosened his tie. "I might just as well have canceled my class today. The students have an attention span of about five minutes."

"No, don't do that. It's important we keep things going as close to normal as we can."

Kitteridge put the coffee aside and started to pace in the small cubicle. Jason knew better than to talk to someone under stress about anything other than what he had on his mind. He sipped his coffee and waited.

"I've been down at the police station all morning," Kitteridge stated. "Do you know anything about the Tye family?"

Jason shook his head. "Is that the boy they arrested?"

"Yes. Matthew Tye."

"Did he offer any explanation?"

"As far as I know, he hasn't opened his mouth. His parents are in Thailand—agricultural missionaries. I thought someone should be with the boy, although he wouldn't see me." He was silent for a moment. "I used to room with his grandfather, on the top floor of the Faulker Building, back when it was a dormitory. We were going to evangelize the world in our lifetime. Did you know that? He's gone now . . . the grandfather. . . ."

He looked at the clock Jason had mounted on the wall in front of his desk. "It's after eleven—am I keeping you from class?"

"I'm free till one-thirty."

Kitteridge looked at his own wristwatch. "My watch must have stopped."

"No, it's probably correct," Jason explained. "I keep this clock ten minutes fast. It helps me get to class on time."

"Oh." Kitteridge smiled. "The tricks we have to play, even on ourselves."

Kitteridge fell silent again and seemed ruminative. Jason tried to get him back to his topic. "The rumor is that the police have already arrested the boy on a formal murder charge. Is that true?"

"Yes, it's true," Kitteridge said grimly.

"They must have a pretty tight case to move so early."

Kitteridge finally sat down, exhausted. He pushed up his glasses and rubbed his eyes. "Matthew Tye was found with the knife in his hands sitting by the body of Barry Peterson. It was four in the morning. Nobody else was up. That is, not until some students heard the Peterson boy groaning and came out in the hall and found the two of them there."

"And Matthew has offered no explanation?"

"He hasn't opened his mouth."

"Maybe he's in shock," Jason offered.

"Are you a Christian, Jason?"

The question came as such a surprise it caught him off guard. "I, ah, well, I. . ."

"Never mind. I didn't mean to embarrass you." Kitteridge gave Jason's knee a reassuring pat. "I just feel that when things like this come along, it helps. It helps."

Kitteridge started polishing his glasses as if his life depended on their being spotless.

"Young man, I have a confession to make. I haven't been entirely honest with you. I chose you to replace Dr. Hacchi primarily because of your background and experience in doing psychological profiles."

Kitteridge's glasses were finally clean enough. He put them on carefully, but he was just as careful not to look Jason's way.

"Perhaps I should not have done it. If you want an apology, then I apologize."

"I don't think there's any need for that. I needed the job."

"Good. Good. I'm glad to hear you say that. And I have no doubt you will be a splendid teacher, if you put your mind to it."

"Thank you. But I'm not so sure our illustrious president shares your confidence in me."

"Yes, I know. That's a problem we can work on another day."

"Psychological profiling is a very meticulous and time-consuming process," Jason ventured, getting back to the topic at hand. "How did you think I could be of help on a university campus?"

Kitteridge shifted in his chair. He wanted to pace some more, but held himself in place. "Dr. Hacchi's death was all hushed up much too quickly. It was as if one day he was here, alive and functioning normally, and the next day he was not only dead but also a non-person. The University seems overanxious to erase his memory."

Jason nodded. "You think President Rollins was behind the rush to condemn Dr. Hacchi?"

Kitteridge smiled. "Let's say he is a very good steward of the interests of our board of directors."

"There was a suicide note, wasn't there?"

"Yes, of course. But why would he do it? There's no earthly reason that I know of. Don't we owe it to the man to find out? Oh, I know suicide is considered a sin, and I realize Hacchi's death reflected badly on the school's philosophy. One of our scholars who upheld the faith shouldn't have taken his own life and all that. But the matter should have been investigated. I was hoping you might get curious about your predecessor and perhaps supply some insight. . . ."

Jason recalled his own questions about Dr. Hacchi's death because of the man's notes on his desk calender, but kept his reservations to himself.

Kitteridge gave a brisk slap on his knees with both of his large hands as if to announce a new subject.

"But that's all water over the bridge, or under the dam, whatever they say. Now I come to you with a more pressing problem. Could you look into this situation with the Tye boy?"

"What do you mean, 'look into'?

"I mean talk to the boy. See if you can do anything for him. I think he refuses to see me because I'm too close to his family. That puts off some of these difficult youngsters. See if you can find out what really happened. Find out what was going on inside his brain.

Maybe there are some mitigating circumstances. Maybe, for all we know, he didn't do it."

"Well, certainly, I'd be happy to talk with him. Have the police indicated anything about a motive for his wanting Barry Peterson dead? Matthew Tye had the opportunity and the weapon. If the police feel they have a prima facie case, they must have come up with a motive."

"No, I have no idea."

Jason rocked back in his chair and thought. "Did you know I was over at the fraternity house this morning?" he asked.

"No, I didn't know."

"I was trying to see Barry Peterson before he went to his first class. I got there about the time they brought Matthew out."

"Why did you want to see Barry Peterson?"

"It's a bit complicated. We haven't discussed the porno-tape matter yet, have we?"

"I heard about it." Kitteridge smiled. "You handled the situation about as well as could be expected."

"Well, President Rollins got it into his head that I should try to nail the culprit. I was going over to see Barry Peterson about it when the roof fell in. You see, there is some evidence to indicate Barry may not only have switched the tapes in my machine, but also actually may have made the sex tape in the first place.

"The thought occurred to me that one of the participants in the videotape may have found out who made it and gone in search of revenge."

"Could the man on the tape have been Matthew, do you think?"

"I just saw a few seconds of the tape," Jason said,

"and the man I saw was blond and muscular. Isn't Matthew dark-haired and rather slight?"

Kitteridge nodded. "He bears a strong resemblance to his mother. His dad's a big burly chap. He was on our championship football team, along with President Rollins."

Jason went on, "I figured the police might be interested in that tape, so I called Dr. Rollins this morning to see if I could release it to the police. You know what he said?"

"I have a pretty good idea."

"I suppose I can see his point. The press would have a field day with that tape." Jason scratched his chin thoughtfully. "I'm in no position to go tattling to the police against the president's wishes. But still, it bothers me. What do you think we should do?"

"I don't think it would hurt anything if we sit on it for a while," Kitteridge said. "After all, we'd feel quite badly if we released the tape, and then it turned out it had nothing to do with the mur—the death."

Kitteridge got to his feet. "Thank you, Jason, for agreeing to see the boy. It makes me feel better. He's alone and . . . well, thank you."

He turned in the doorway for one last thought that had brought a smile to his face.

"You know, it's strange how the Lord works. Here, you came to us for what I thought would be one reason, and now it turns out to be for another purpose altogether."

Jason frowned after the departing dean. He hadn't said it aloud, but he wondered what the Good Lord had been doing with His time at about four o'clock that morning.

He picked up the dean's untouched cup of coffee and poured it back into the pot.

Chapter Nine

Jason got on the phone and proceeded to ferret out the local ground rules regarding visitation rights. By a quarter to twelve he learned he couldn't interview a prisoner without the permission of his lawyer. Matthew's lawyer, it turned out, was the next warm body in line in the Public Defender's office, a fellow by the name of William Darrow. He must be a world beater. Jason reached Mr. Darrow just as the lawyer was leaving for lunch.

"Yes, Mr. Bradley, what can I do for you?" He sounded very young, but was making a valiant effort to live up to his name.

Jason explained his connection with the University and asked for permission to see Matthew.

"I can give you permission, all right, but he won't see you. He wouldn't even see me if he could help it."

"Have you talked with him?"

"If you can call it that. The only time he opened his mouth, he announced he would waive a preliminary hearing, and he wanted the earliest possible trial. Can you beat that? If you have any influence with the kid—"

"I've never met him."

If Darrow was surprised, he didn't sound it. "I've tried talking to him about plea bargaining and other options. He just sits there with a Mona Lisa grin on his face. He seems to think the whole thing is a game."

"Sounds like you have your hands full," Jason said. "I'll see what I can do when I talk to him."

"He's not gonna see you."

"Oh, I think he will. Will you call the jail and put my name on their list?"

"Okay. Maybe you got a magic wand or something."

Jason tried to spend some time preparing for his afternoon class, but found his attention span was no better than that of his students. So many questions kept bobbing into his mind. Why had the police moved so quickly? How had a lawyer been assigned so early? And why the little dig that Dean Kitteridge managed to get in about "these difficult youngsters"? Had they been smoking corn silk behind the barn?

In the cafeteria line Jason noticed the loudest noises he could hear were the rattle of silverware and the bumping of heavy cafeteria plates. The students, normally brimming over with chatter, had turned mute as zombies. Suddenly the loudspeakers cracked into life and a message, as if from On High, boomed out over the cafeteria: afternoon classes had been canceled so the students could attend a special Chapel assembly arranged by the administration and something called the Christian Endeavor Club.

Jason got a salad and looked for a spot near the north windows that looked out on the Topa Topa Mountains. After scanning the cloudless sky for several seconds, he spotted a hang glider riding the white stretch of sky below the blue and just above the earth's rolling gray-brown horizon. A speck in the distance only a kindred spirit would notice. Too far away to distinguish the type of kite or the quality of the pilot, but it gave Jason a lift just to watch the lazy figure eights being etched over the land. Freedom.

He came abruptly back to earth when he felt another cafeteria tray bump up against his own. It belonged to Hillary Reed. Meat loaf, mashed potatoes, and gravy.

"What are you doing over here by yourself? Don't you know we have a faculty room?"

"Just daydreaming, I guess. How do you manage to keep your slim figure, eating like that?"

"This is my main meal of the day."

He rearranged the small table to make room for her.

"Dean Kit just caught me in the hall," she began. "He asked me to take a look at that tape of yours with you."

Jason was appalled, but said nothing.

"He feels I know more students by sight than anyone else. He wanted me to try to identify the—what's the matter?"

"Do you know what's *on* that tape?"

"Why, Mr. Bradley, I do believe you are blushing. How refreshing. Yes, I know what's on the tape, but I feel we are mature enough to consider the material as detached professionals, don't you?"

"I suppose so." He pushed the lettuce leaves around in his bowl searching for signs of a shrimp.

"It's a tough job, but somebody's got to do it, eh?" She tried to coax a smile out of him, but he wasn't cooperating. "I thought men were turned on by visuals. I guess *Playboy* is just wasting its time."

She had a vocal technique that seemed to bestow each sentence with hidden meanings. Jason was in no mood for games.

"When do you want to see it?"

She checked her watch. "I've got to scoot home in a minute. I have some baby-sitter problems. Then I'd like to drop in on some of the Chapel service. Would three o'clock in my office be okay? I can arrange to have a VCR there by then."

"Fine."

He gave up on his salad and pushed it away. "How often does this Chapel business happen?"

"You mean canceling classes? It's the first time, to my recollection. Of course, as far as I know, this is also the University's first murder."

"You know how many college students were murdered in this country last year?" he asked.

"I have no idea."

"Eighty-seven."

"Meaning, I suppose, that it is hardly justification to suspend the educational process. But I think you'll find Chapel instructive in another way. Better stop by the service this afternoon."

"I plan to."

He looked out over the sea of tables and chairs. The cafeteria was about half-filled with laconic students. "I also get the uneasy feeling that there is something weird going on behind the quiet facade of this place. Do you ever have that feeling?"

Hillary was working on her "main meal" and didn't bother to reflect. "You're just new to everything."

"Did you know Dr. Hacchi well?"

She stopped in midchew. "What's that supposed to mean?"

"Must everything have a hidden meaning with you? I'm simply trying to get a line on the man. You must have known him."

"Dr. Alex Hacchi was a very strong-willed and self-centered person. He had all the answers to the world's questions, and you had better not bother disagreeing with him. If you did, he had an acid tongue that could put you in your place in a hurry."

"Really? I was under the impression from Dean Kitteridge that he was, well, a part of the born-again establishment around here."

"There were two Alex Hacchis," she explained. "Or at least one with two faces. Which one would you like? I can serve them up equally well."

Jason watched her nervously disassembling the meat loaf on her plate. He had a feeling her answers were supplying him with more heat than light. Had she been burned by Dr. Hacchi's acid tongue? Or had he just run into her hostility toward men again? He found himself with a strong yearning not to find out the reason for her vehemence.

"My, my, what a splendid-looking couple the two of you make here, chatting away, silhouetted against our beautiful mountains!"

Jolly Miss Merkle was approaching them, smiling. Since she needed her cane to balance against her short left leg, she had to carry her tray with one hand. She set it down next to Jason's to rest her wrist. Mixed vegetables, plain yogurt, water with no ice, and Sanka. Must be a home economics teacher.

"My, what a perfectly lovely day. I'm Betty Merkle, Home Economics." She extended a plump feminine hand with her little finger arched.

Jason stood up and took her hand. "Jason Bradley. Nice meeting you."

"I do hope you are going to like it here, Mr. Bradley. I hope you will become a part of our happy little family."

"Thank you for the thought. Won't you join us?"

"No, no, don't let me interrupt you two. I just wanted to tell Hillary that my girl can't be at her house until two this afternoon. I'm running a baby-sitting service here, it seems! You see, Mr. Bradley, my girls have to observe children in the home environment. Part of their classwork for Child Care and Development."

"Two o'clock will be fine," Hillary said, rather remotely. "By the way, Betty, I was just telling Mr. Bradley about Dr. Hacchi and his split personality. Anything you'd care to add?"

Miss Merkle's jovial expression turned sour. "I should say not. Let's not ruin a perfectly good lunch with the mention of his name."

Miss Merkle picked up her tray and marched off in a limping huff.

When she was safely out of hearing range, Hillary laughed. "That about sums up Hacchi for you. He brought poor Betty to tears on at least two occasions that I can recall. He said she didn't belong on a university campus. Called her our 'resident nanny' and a 'gimpy Pollyanna,' among other things."

"He sounds like a real sweetheart."

She snorted. "You're welcome to him, my friend."

The campus chimes started their twelve-thirty tolling, and Jason used them as an excuse to leave. Hillary Reed made him very uncomfortable. Perhaps it was the conflicting signals he got from her. She was an attractive woman, a sharp dresser with just the right eyeshadow and a hint of some very seductive perfume. But the knives always seemed to be out. She seemed to be operating on a higher plane than anyone else, and her comments were designed to remind her listeners of that fact. He wasn't looking forward to three o'clock.

* * *

The county jail was a relatively new building, and valiant efforts had been taken to make the place appear pleasant and livable. It didn't work. Pastel walls and oil paintings of seascapes could not hide the fact that this was a jail, and that those within it were locked away from society.

Jason found the visitation desk and introduced himself. A creamy-skinned mulatto in a lavender blouse bearing a pin that read "Deputy Grosser" asked him to wait until she phoned the "subject." After a few minutes she called Jason back to the desk and told him Mr. Tye would not see him.

Jason took some notepaper from her desk and wrote out the following:

> Matthew Tye—
>
> I am a new teacher at Tri-U, here for the express purpose of having a short visit with you. If you refuse to see me, I will have no alternative but to tell what I know about you to the authorities. I'll wait here for fifteen minutes.
>
> —Jason Bradley

He folded the note over once and gave it to the deputy.

"Would you see that he gets this? I'll wait out here."

She read it over and smiled. "You think you're pretty smart, don't you?"

"No, not smart. Just experienced."

"Wanna bet it don't work?"

They exchanged smiles. Jason said, "I'm a poor man. I'll bet you a cup of coffee."

"We get our coffee free around here. How about a candy bar?"

"Make it an Almond Joy, and you got yourself a deal."

She called in another deputy and gave him the note with instructions to deliver it right away. After he'd left, she said, "It takes him three minutes to get back to the cells. Let's synchronize our watches."

Six minutes and thirty seconds later Jason was being ushered back to the maximum security visiting area. He entered a small room with wire mesh glass windows on three sides and a telephone on the small counter next to a steel chair. In a few minutes Matthew Tye appeared in the little room opposite, already dressed in jail dungarees. He looked around suspiciously, then finally sat down and picked up his end of the phone line.

"They probably have someone listening in on anything we say here, mister."

"Oh, I doubt that," Jason said. "Prisoners are allowed confidential visits."

For several seconds neither of them spoke. Matthew was looking over Jason very carefully. The young man's complexion had improved, but his skin was very pale, as if he had been in jail a year instead of a few hours.

"What do you teach?"

"It's not important. I'd rather spend our time talking about you. You have friends who are very concerned about—"

"I'll just bet you would," Matthew broke in sarcastically. "What were you planning to tell the authorities?"

"What do you think I was going to tell them?"

Matthew pointed at Jason through the glass. "You're a shrink, aren't you? I recognize the patter. 'What do you think I was going to tell them?' " he mimicked. "You guys oughta develop a new line."

"You're close. I'm a psychologist."

"Of course! You're replacing Hacchi, aren't you? I shoulda known. And you're coming here to *help* me, aren't you? My, my, will wonders never cease?"

"Don't you think it's possible I could help you?"

"I think you guys oughta do something about the suicide rate in your own profession before you go around telling other people how to live."

Jason chuckled. "I guess you got me there."

"Oh, no you don't." Matthew's lip curled. "That ingratiating act won't work. You think you're gonna humble yourself so I'll loosen up. It's not gonna work. I read the book."

"You think I'm here to expose your deep, dark secrets?"

"Mr. Bradley, I don't know why you're here." He looked off toward a corner of the ceiling, trying to project boredom.

Jason waited half a minute, then asked, "How about telling me what happened at four this morning?"

Nothing.

"Dean Kitteridge asked me to see you. He thought perhaps someone outside the circle of family and friends might be able to help more."

Matthew leaned back in his chair and propped one leg over the other knee. He kicked the suspended foot in a casual manner, but the speed of the wobbles was a bit too brisk to be genuine.

"Have your folks been notified yet, Matthew?"

"Oh, no, you don't. You're not hanging that albatross around my neck. I'm twenty-one, the master of my fate. You're not dragging them into this."

''They're certainly going to find out one way or the other.''

''You don't know a damn thing about me, do you? You just bluffed your way in here, didn't you?''

''As a matter of fact, I know quite a bit about you, Matt. Do they call you Matt?''

''No, they call me mud.''

''Now you see what that tells me? You have very low self-esteem. That could be dangerous.''

''It could be baloney, too. You know, it's a funny thing about psychology books. Psychologists always turn out to be the heroes of their own books. You ever notice that? Beware of the philosophies that make heroes of men, Mr. Bradley.''

''Thank you. I'll remember that. Your father the missionary tell you that?''

''No. Life taught me that. It's a dandy teacher, life—if it doesn't kill you first.''

''Now that I know what your philosophy is not, how about telling me what your philosophy is?''

''Okay, you go first.''

''Huh?''

''You show me yours and I'll show you mine.'' Matthew smiled unpleasantly. ''What's the matter, Mr. Bradley, no guts? Let me guess yours, shall I? I think it's only fair, since that's what you came to do to me. I'd say you're not a born-again Christian. No, if that were your line, you would have gotten the Lord and the cleansing blood of Christ into the conversation by now. No, I'd say you're an original Hacchi man—the way he was three years ago when I had him in class, blazing that trail of psychiatric truth and light through the tangled web of superstitions and taboos that plague this troubled world. Give me a good couch and enough time, and I shall psychoanalyze the world.

"But what happens, Mr. Bradley, when the world doesn't jump to your tune? Suppose you make an incorrect assumption. Suppose one of your concepts is fallacious. What then, Mr. Bradley-psychologist? You gonna go down to the basement and hang yourself, too? Or are you gonna think up another philosophy so the world will beat another path to your doorstep? It shouldn't be too difficult. There are plenty of suckers for anybody with answers to the tough questions. They don't even have to be good answers, just answers. Because the questions are so demanding: What's life all about? Is this all there is? What must I do to be *saved*? Saved, Saved, Saved?"

Jason held the earpiece away from his ear so Matthew's tirade wouldn't blast his head off. The boy had worked himself into a lather, and his blotches were returning. He calmed down and even managed a nervous laugh.

"How'm I doing, Mr. Bradley? Recognize anything?"

"Yes. I think you got me nailed."

"Nailed to the tree, Mr. Bradley? No, no. You have the wrong metaphor. Set your sights lower."

"Now that we have me taken care of, how about yourself, Mr. Tye? What do you believe in?"

"Why, Shirley MacLaine is my guru. Didn't you know that?"

"Shirley MacLaine? The actress?"

"And the writer, Mr. Bradley. She's a little long of tooth, but I understand from people with an eye for such things that her legs are still very nice. *And* she's very big on synchronicity. Mysticism, Mr. Bradley. That's where the future lies."

"*Your* future, Matthew?"

"I'll stake my life on it." This turned out to be a

great joke for Matthew. He put down the receiver in order to hold his sides while he laughed.

Jason's palms were sweating.

Matthew sobered up and returned to his bitter persona. "Mr. Bradley, hasn't it occurred to you that I'm no dummy? Hasn't it crossed your mind yet that I'm following the only course of action open to me? 'Tis a far, far better thing I now do than I have ever . . .' "

"Listen, Matthew, did you kill the Peterson boy?"

He smiled. "At this point, it really doesn't matter. So long, Mr. Bradley. Come back and see me again sometime, after you've sharpened your rapier."

Matthew got up and disappeared from view before Jason could react. He felt as if he'd just finished a brisk handball session. His armpits and the back of his neck were soaked. Who had been grilling whom? he wondered.

He felt that the boy, in spite of his attempt at flippancy, had been trying subconsciously to tell him something. The strange riddles and terms he had used . . . Rapier. Could be a murder weapon, or it could also represent verbal sparring. Matthew sounded a lot like Hillary Reed in that regard, and both of them had very bitter memories of Hacchi. And the albatross line. Do students still study "The Rime of the Ancient Mariner"?

Jason crossed the parking lot and opened up the back of his van. Buried under an old sleeping bag and behind a gunny sack of tools was his dog-eared paperback *Collegiate Dictionary*.

He found no listing for the boy's word "synchronicity." The closest he could come was "Synochronism—concurrence of two or more events in time; simultaneousness."

What two events? Hacchi's death and Peterson's? But they occurred more than three weeks apart.

He found low gear in his rebuilt gear box, peeled back the wrapper of one end of his Almond Joy, and started back toward the University.

Chapter Ten

The Chapel service was already well under way. The back seats on the main floor were occupied by young worshipers, and rather than march up to the front, Jason decided to try the balcony.

The Chapel was yet another addition to the potpourri of building styles on campus. It looked like a stage set for *Goodbye Mr. Chips*, with massive slabs of wood paneling with enough character to have come over on the *Mayflower*, and lots of thick cement pillars shaped like carved stone arching toward heaven. The landing halfway up the balcony stairs featured an elaborate stained glass window depicting a knight in shining armor kneeling, sword in hand, before a clerical figure who was extending a blessing. Hint, hint.

A few other faculty members and stray students were already seated in the small balcony. The main floor was crowded with young bodies with full healthy heads of hair. Jason estimated the place held around eight or nine hundred, so only a fraction of the student body—perhaps all of the faithful—were present. He sat at the railing off to one side and tried to understand what was happening down below.

Soft organ music was playing as a series of youthful

speakers got to their feet and prayed or said something nice about the departed Barry Peterson. There were several robed figures up front, but President Rollins seemed to be operating as master of ceremonies. He would point to the different hands as speakers volunteered, then make some comforting comment after each had finished.

Jason picked up a few details about Barry as he was eulogized. He had been a communications major with plans to go into religious broadcasting. His father was already established with Far-East Broadcasting, beaming the "Good News" into Mainland China, et cetera. Barry had only one semester to go before graduation, and everybody loved him. His good-natured kidding and pranks would be sorely missed.

When one of the speakers mentioned a girlfriend left behind, there was audible sobbing from the front row.

There was a certain sameness to the prayers of the students, most of them imploring the Almighty to make them more spiritual, to give meaning and purpose to the terrible tragedy. Jason had the feeling many of the students regarded God as a friendly waiter or plumber hovering patiently in the wings, waiting to do their bidding.

President Rollins welcomed another speaker. Harold, the round-faced boy from the steps of the fraternity house, came to the front to address the gathering, looking nervous and still showing signs of having been crying. Maybe the pinkish eyelids were a permanent condition for him.

Harold went into a personal confession. He admitted the only reason he had come to Trinity was because it was the only medical school to accept him. He had done the minimum amount of work and had a good time, and his parents had had it up to here with him. But God had been working in his life. The experience of having a good friend die so tragically had shown him how fragile life can be. He learned to make every moment count, for only the things that are done "unto the Lord" were of lasting value.

Harold pledged that Barry's death was not a wasted death; that he as a Doctor of Medicine would give one-fourth of all his earnings to the Lord in a living tribute to his fallen friend. And he, personally, with Christ's help, would show a new attitude of seriousness and dedication in his studies.

His emotional outburst had a snowballing effect on the students, and soon several hands were going up indicating similar promises to keep Barry Peterson's memory alive by personal pledges of time and sacrifice.

Perhaps President Rollins realized the emotion of the moment was carrying the students beyond their practical abilities to follow through. He gently interrupted, explaining that their time together was drawing to a close, that they must now each search their hearts in this troubling time. He added that the University would set up a special memorial fund in Barry's name, to be used for future needy and deserving students in Christian Communications.

He also pledged that the University would make a new commitment to "real Christian higher education." He was convinced that the creeping secularism that had been allowed to penetrate the school might have contributed to this tragedy, and in the future such influences would be discouraged.

Soon the organ was near full volume and the congregation was on its feet, holding hands by rows and singing a heartfelt "Because He lives, I can face tomorrow, because He lives all fear is gone. . ."

Jason checked his watch and started toward the exit before the final benediction. In the foyer he met up with Miss Merkle, ducking out of the main sanctuary.

"Hello, Mr. Bradley," she greeted him. "I like getting out ahead of the crowd, because of my leg, you know."

She shook Jason's hand, then hung on to it so that he ended up helping her down the outside steps.

"Did you know the boy well, Mr. Bradley?"

"I didn't know him at all."

"Oh, really?" she said in sweet surprise. "I understood you were over at the fraternity house to see him this morning."

"Well, I went there with that in mind, but I never had the chance to see him."

"Now, isn't that strange how these rumors get started. I understood you had been to see the boy, but then—oh, well. If it's incorrect, it really doesn't matter, does it? Such sad doings. I tell you, I don't know what this tired old world is coming to, when such things can take place on a Christian campus."

"It is very surprising. . . ."

"I thought Dr. Rollins did a fine job, considering. Didn't you, Mr. Bradley?"

"I noticed there was no mention of Matthew Tye, but I came in late, so perhaps I missed something."

"No, he was not mentioned, as I recall."

"I wonder why not."

"Well, after all, it was a memorial time for the deceased." Miss Merkle caught sight of the president's secretary and waved. "Oh, Elsie, are you going back to your office?"

She hobbled off toward her friend, and the two of them fell in like old conspirators.

The students were pouring out now, and Jason stepped onto the grass, hoping to catch sight of Harold. For some reason, when he thought of Harold, he thought of characters in Shakespeare's plays, but since the connection didn't make sense to him, he forced it out of his mind.

Harold was one of the last students to come out. About five of them came out together arm in arm, as if they had just made a major pledge of undying friendship.

Jason called him a couple of times before Harold caught the sound of his own name and separated from his group.

"Yes, sir?"

"I'm Jason Bradley, the new psychology teacher. Just came on board. Mind if I ask you a couple questions?"

"No, I guess not. What about?"

"I take it you're living at Beta Rho?"

"Yeah, I do. I'm not too proud of it, but I do."

"What can you tell me about your fraternity brother, Matthew Tye?"

Harold looked hard at Jason, suddenly guarded. "Why do you want to know about him?"

"He's in a tight spot. He has friends who are anxious to find out what happened."

"Then why doesn't Matthew tell them what happened?"

Harold was getting a little testy. Jason tried to keep their exchange calm. "You have a minute? Let's sit over here, shall we?" He headed for an ancient live oak tree and sat in its shade. Harold straggled behind and did not sit right away.

"I've been over all this with the police, you know."

"I know, but I'm sure you'd like to help a fraternity brother if you can."

Harold sat down, reluctantly. "How does anybody help Matthew? He's an enigma."

"He doesn't seem to be generating much sympathy

around campus. It's almost as if everybody's convicted him already."

Harold shrugged. "Well, most people who know him could see him doing it."

"That's a rather cruel thing to say—that you think he's capable of murder. What possible motive would he have had to kill Barry?"

"I don't think he had any motive. I think he did it for a thrill, like that old thrill killing in the twenties with Sacco and Vanzetti at the University of Chicago."

"I think you mean Leopold and Loeb."

"Oh, yeah, right." Harold pulled at some tufts of grass and waited.

"You mean he actually talked about a thrill killing?"

"Oh, no, not in so many words. But we have a lot of bull sessions over at Beta Rho, and in the course of an evening we usually get around to things like the basis for morality in the world, and good versus evil. You know, the usual college stuff you put on the back burner after you're out in the world making a living. And Matthew would always be putting in his two cents' worth with the idea that there is no basis for good or morality if there is no God to answer to. He would say that if we just sprang up out of primordial slime, then we were not answerable to anyone, and we could do whatever we want."

"Sounds to me like he was playing the devil's advocate," Jason said.

Harold shook his head. "Maybe, but I don't think so. He was too adamant on the subject, as if he were on a crusade or something. Don't just take my word for it. Ask anybody in the house. It got so we hated to see him coming. He made atheism sound so unappealing, I think he was what got me to rethink Christianity."

It was Jason's turn to shake his head. "It's hard to

believe. I mean, here he's the product of missionary parents—second generation, from what I understand. He was probably raised close to the apron strings."

"I think he's gone to Christian boarding schools since he was in grammar school."

"Okay, but even then, he was no doubt brought up within the faith, so to speak. Where did this big spiritual swing come from, I wonder?"

"Oh, he was straight arrow when he came to Trinity."

"You *sure*?"

"That's what I hear. I've only been here two years myself, but I understand he was the original Goody Two-Shoes."

"So . . . what could have happened to him here?"

"College can be a great awakening, you know," Harold said seriously, totally missing the irony that Jason was ten years his senior. "No supervision. Cars. Beer just down the highway. Girls in the other dorms, a lot of 'em with the same ideas."

"And teachers that challenge traditional thoughts?"

Harold scoffed, "You won't be in danger of much of that on *this* campus."

"How about Dr. Hacchi? Matthew seems to have a particular animosity toward him."

Harold scowled. "Come to think of it, I think I did hear something about him taking Hacchi's classes and having a rugged time. Hacchi was a great one to educate by ridicule."

"Let's see. How does this sound to you? Hacchi the psychology pro zeros in on young Matthew, who is unfortunate enough to verbally defend conservative Christian values in class. Hacchi takes pot shots at him during the lecture." Jason leaned back, pulling on his crossed knees for support. He was enjoying his vision. "Let's see, what topic would it be? Hacchi could argue anything. Take divorce. Matthew would be opposed to it, while Hacchi would cite case studies of psychoses resulting from the refusal to dissolve a bad marriage. Or he could take 'Honor thy Father and Mother.' That's always a popular theme for the psychiatrist's couch. A grown child is driven to a mental breakdown because of the conflicts with his unyielding, wrongheaded mama or papa."

Harold laughed, now comfortable talking with Jason. "You sound like you were there in class with him!"

"I could have been," Jason said. "We had a practicing psychoanalyst teaching at Cal Berkeley who got on a religious kid's case and turned his lectures into one-sided debates. It's a familiar pattern. Listen, can you give me the names of some of Matthew's friends? I'd like to verify my prejudices, so to speak."

Harold searched the grass, as if looking for names. "You know, I can't think of any. He was always a loner."

"But wasn't he a member of Beta Rho?"

"I think he joined Beta because his father had been a member. The fraternity gives preferential treatment to offspring of former members. I know, because my dad was a Beta back in Michigan. That's how I got in."

"It's hard to believe Matthew has no friends at all."

"I think once he split with the straight-arrow crowd he lost all the friends he had. This school is divided up into cliques, you know. Like, the jocks all hang around with other jocks. Then there are straight arrows and the party guys . . . you get the idea. I think Matthew tried to make a place for himself at the house, but the guys didn't know how to take him. And then, on weekends he was usually down in L.A. He's got relatives down there, I hear. He just sort of fell between the cracks."

"It seems rather sad to me."

Harold changed position on the lawn. He was a little plump and evidently grass sitting was not his idea of comfort. Or was it the topic that was making him uncomfortable? In any event, he changed the subject as well.

"You know, this whole thing reminds me of a World War II book I read once about two GIs going into battle. The one that was a Christian came out of the experience a total agnostic, while the other guy ended up becoming a priest. Same battles. Same experiences. They just reacted differently to the situation. Sort of like Matthew and myself, if you can think of college as a battle."

Harold struggled to his feet, ending their conversation.

The campus had grown quiet during their talk. Except for a few joggers treading the sidewalks in the distance, they had the place to themselves. Then suddenly, from their blind side, two young men on bicycles zoomed by close enough to give them both a start. One of the riders turned and called:

"Hey, Pillsbury, watch your step, buddy!"

Jason looked at Harold for an explanation. "Pillsbury?"

"Those nuts." Harold laughed nervously. "That's my old nickname." He pinched the roll of fat above his belt to explain the nickname. "Pillsbury doughboy. Too much high living."

"That's it!" Jason snapped his fingers. "I just figured out who you remind me of."

Harold looked startled.

"Prince Hal. You know, from Shakespeare's Henry plays. Prince Hal was the buddy to Falstaff and a real rabble-rouser during his youth. Then, when he took the throne, he sent Falstaff away and changed his own nature to fit his new responsibilities. It must be that you're Prince Hal in modern dress."

"Hey, I like that." Harold smiled. "Well, nice meeting you, Mr. Bradley. If I can answer anything else for you, let me know."

At least one of them went away happy. Jason watched the new young Christian hurry off toward Animal House; then, with a trace of reluctance, he checked his watch. Almost three. He had been hoping that it was later—that he had talked right past the hour.

Jason trudged off toward the Campus Police office to pick up his tape.

Chapter Eleven

Hillary was in her office, waiting for him. She had changed clothes. Jason had seen her about ten times since he'd arrived, and he had yet to see her twice in the same outfit. Pants again, a shirt with a high collar, a vest made of ribbed something or other, and a loose-fitting jacket with the sleeves tacked up, as if she were going to be doing some manual labor. He could have sworn he'd seen that outfit on a magazine cover recently.

The office looked in keeping with her outfit. Jason envied her space, noting the gleaming white walls, with green plants around the corners up near the ceiling, the woodwork painted in pastels that made the place look like a confectionary store. There was a hooked rug in one corner, making a nice discussion center for small groups, and beanbag and director's chairs about, with little white end tables. Jason felt like going back outside and wiping his feet.

Hillary closed the mini blinds on her large second-story window and uncovered the VCR. "Why don't you start it up? I'm all thumbs when it comes to these machines."

"You mean, just start watching it, cold turkey?"

"Certainly," she said matter-of-factly. "That's why we're here, isn't it?"

Jason put the tape into the player, but hesitated over the play button. Hillary seemed to have no trouble with the situation, but her coolness did little to help his discomfort.

"Tell you what. I've got a lot of things to do. Why don't you have a look, and then I'll check in with you later?" Jason was sliding toward the door. "Make notes if you think you recognize anybody, okay?"

She smiled after him. "Okay, if that's the way you feel about it."

"Look, this isn't exactly my cup of tea."

"Cup of tea," she repeated. "Isn't it funny how we all resort to clichés when we get nervous?"

"Yes, isn't it?" Jason fought the urge to run.

"And here I thought you were a big man of the world."

"Yes, well—surprise, surprise."

"Sit down, you coward. If I can go through this, you can, too. Anytime you want to stop it and run, you can."

She reached across to the machine and pushed the play button. Jason slid into the director's chair nearest the door.

After about five seconds of blank screen the lens cap came off the camera and they could see a hand recede from their view. Hardly a professional job. A bit of tousled hair showed at the bottom of the frame, slightly out of focus. Jason reached forward and hit the pause button.

"That head of hair. Could that belong to Barry Peterson?"

"It could. Let's see it again."

He backed up and replayed the beginning in slow motion, then paused.

The screen held on a good section of forehead as well as a brown head of hair.

"I'm sure that's the Peterson boy," Hillary stated. "If it's not, it's got to be somebody with a cowlick just like his."

"Okay," Jason said. "So now we know who our cameraman is."

He returned the tape to the play mode, and almost immediately a piece of grillwork came up in front of the lens and the picture darkened a little.

"What's that?" she asked.

"I think he's hidden the camera in the heater duct of a house. He returned the grille to the wall so the camera would be totally hidden. Yes, see there? He's resetting the screws, leaving the camera running."

There was a high-angled view of a bed, or rather, a distinctive chenille bedspread covering a bed, plus a little bit of the nearby nightstand and a peach-colored triangle of carpet next to a doorway. They could hear Peterson gathering up his tools, then had a view of the backs of his legs as he exited through the doorway. It gave Jason a slightly eerie feeling to be watching the surreptitious movements of a boy now dead.

Nothing happened on screen, but out of the corner of his eye Jason saw Hillary's hand shifting on the arm of her chair. She gripped it tightly and moved her upper body slightly forward. Her eyes were riveted on the motionless picture of the bedroom on screen. She had seemed so calm before. This sudden tension didn't make sense.

Nothing moved on the screen. A half minute went by, then a full minute. Then finally, a faint chime sounded.

"Were those our campus chimes?" Jason asked.

Hillary nodded her head slowly. "Three o'clock."

Still nothing more happening, but Hillary remained tense.

"Well, this is getting ridiculous," Jason said, and put the VCR on fast forward. After what he estimated was about twenty minutes of tape time had passed, he noticed some shadows playing on the patch of carpet. He backed up a bit and punched play.

There were voices from the other room—a man's and a woman's, but too soft to pick up. He turned up the volume and sat back. Hillary's knuckles were white.

The noises remained muffled, but the gist of what was going on was obvious. The man was groaning and making sounds like stage whispers. The girl was emitting light sighs and falsetto comments in response to what he was doing. They must have been working their way down the hall outside the bedroom because their noises were getting louder.

He: C'mon in here, okay?

She: Are you crazy? S'pose somebody comes in?

He: You want 'em to find us on the couch?

She: (giggling) You devil, you.

He: C'mon. Okay? I can't stand it any longer. If you really loved me, you'd want to, too.

She: Oh, Richard, I do love you, but we shouldn't.

He: I know, but . . . oh, hon, I love you. C'mon.

"Men," Hillary announced in full voice. "Oh, what *lines*!"

Shadows started appearing in the doorway. Then the legs. Then a muscular youth was backing a stunning blonde into the room in the midst of a tight embrace.

She: Are you gonna take all my clothes off?

He: I kinda had that in mind.

She: Are you gonna take all my clothes off and look at me?

He: Oh, baby, yes. And more. Much, much more.

They were into the room and both sitting on the bed as he started the very serious business of taking off her blouse.

Hillary's hand shot out and turned off the VCR. "Ooo-kaaay, I think I've seen all I need to see."

Jason was surprised and more than a little relieved. Hillary busied herself, readjusting the drapes and pushing the cart around and straightening her hair, which didn't seem to need her attention.

"She called him Richard," Jason began. "Does that help us?"

Hillary nodded. "I know him. Richard Clark. He's in our division. A political science major, I believe."

"And the girl?"

She paused. There seemed to be more anger than thoughtfulness in her expression. "I've seen her on campus, but I don't know her name. Thin-faced little snippet, isn't she?"

"I thought she looked . . . quite nice."

"Oh, did you, now?"

"You don't suppose," Jason said tentatively, "that we've just been looking at our murderers?"

"What do you mean?"

"Maybe these two found out about the tape and murdered Barry. It's the best motive I've come across yet."

"The police have arrested Matthew Tye, and that's good enough for me." She didn't seem to be interested in talking. Jason got to his feet and retrieved the tape.

"Well, at least we know something," he said. "The videotape was shot someplace on or near campus, and the . . . copulation took place about twenty after three in the afternoon."

"Is that important?"

"It could be. You never know what little detail is going to help tie something together."

"What are you talking about?" she asked curtly.

"I believe the police should be given this tape. Unfortunately, President Rollins doesn't agree."

"Why not?"

"Too embarrassing for the school, I suppose. What do you think?"

Without hesitation she answered, "I think you should listen to your president."

"I was afraid you were going to say that. Well, thanks for the information."

"What are you going to do now?"

"Oh, I thought I'd try to contact this Richard Clark and see if I can find out who the girl is."

"She used to date Alex Hacchi," Hillary said suddenly.

Jason stood immobile in the doorway for a time. Then he closed his mouth and came back inside.

"Why didn't you tell me that before?"

"Because I just thought of it. I just remembered where I'd seen her before—on Hacchi's arm."

"Hacchi was dating a student? Isn't that against—"

"I'm not so sure she was a student, come to think of it."

"I see," Jason said, not seeing at all. "No matter what I do around here, it always seems to come back to this man Hacchi. Isn't that remarkable?"

"He was remarkable. Infamously remarkable."

He didn't want her to get started on that topic again.

"So long, Hillary. And thanks again."

He closed the door to her office, leaving her still standing expectantly in the middle of the room. Women. How do you figure them? First she teased him for not wanting to view the tape, then she got skittish herself. And that last little tidbit about the girl and Hacchi going together. Jason wondered if Hillary had been dating the infamous Hacchi herself, and then was jilted and replaced by the narrow-faced blonde who seemed so anxious to have her clothes removed. It might help explain some of her bitterness.

He went down to his own little cubicle in the same building and put the videotape in the back of the top drawer of his filing cabinet. Then he sat and rocked and thought.

The smart thing to do now would be to stay out of it. Report to Dean Kitteridge what he and Hillary had found out, and let the matter drop. But the cover-up had him feeling restless. It was against every ethical principle he held, either personally, or professionally as a forensics man. He'd worked in the business only briefly, but a certain kind of plodding logic had been ingrained in him. Once you start making compromises, then your whole investigation gets thrown out of whack.

What investigation? Listen to him. He was a university instructor, not a policeman. Who was he kidding?

He looked around his office. He could have sworn somebody had moved the walls in a couple of feet while he was sitting there.

Well, what the heck. A little trip to the school's records office wasn't going to hurt anything. He grabbed his coat and locked the door behind him.

A very nice chubby lady, with a picture of her four grandchildren on her counter, greeted Jason. Once she had verified that he was indeed an instructor, she was more than happy to retrieve Richard Clark's files for him.

He was a political science major, as Hillary had said.

It appeared to be his fourth declared major, and after nine completed semesters, he was still a year away from graduation.

"He doesn't seem to be in any hurry to wrap up his schooling, does he?" Jason remarked to the clerk.

"No, he doesn't." She chuckled. "But he doesn't have to hurry. You know who his father is, don't you?"

"Clark? No, I don't think I do."

"He's the 'Accountant to the Stars' down in Hollywood. There was an article about him in the *L.A. Times* just recently. It even named some of the actors he works for. Do you follow show business?"

"No, I'm afraid I don't."

This answer took the wind out of her sails and she was silent. Jason was busy glancing over Richard's papers, trying to get a line on the boy. He noticed that hang gliding was one of his hobbies. Might come in handy, if he needed to strike up a conversation with him.

"I'd like to get in touch with Richard," he said. "Where does he live?"

The records clerk turned one of the sheets over and pointed. "I guess he was one of the boys that got to stay."

"Stay? Stay where?" Jason read the address—Beta Rho Fraternity—next to her finger.

"Most of the boys had to leave, you know, after they got in trouble last semester. They let only the seniors and graduate students stay on."

"Yes, I heard something about that. They got in trouble with some of their pranks, didn't they?"

That was all the priming she needed. "Oh, I should say they did! You weren't here then, were you? The one that did them in, though, was really in very bad taste." She lowered her voice. "The Friday before Christmas break in December, they bought an old horse and walked it right into the chemistry lab late in the afternoon when no one was about. They shot the poor animal right in one of the chemical closets, and there it stayed nine days before anyone knew about it. Well, you can imagine the smell—and the trouble the poor maintenance people had getting the thing out of there!''

Jason had to endure two more stories before he could get away, one about the president's BMW being taken apart and reassembled on top of the Faulker Building, and the other, which she wasn't very specific about, concerned loudspeakers in the ladies' restrooms.

Apparently there had been a contest among the fraternity houses to see who could pull off the cleverest prank, and Beta Rho won. They also got caught.

The clerk stopped long enough in her recitation to readjust her picture of her grandchildren and give it a friendly pat, as if to say her darlings would never do things like that.

Jason went back to his office to pick up his briefcase and got his next emotional jolt. The latch for his Yale lock was hanging from the splintered door frame by one loose screw. The door swung open freely.

There was no one inside, but the place had been invaded. Papers were askew, a couple of drawers were open. It took Jason several seconds to think of what the intruder must have been after. Then he mentally kicked himself. It hadn't occurred to him to lock the two-drawer file. He opened the top drawer and felt all over in the back.

The videotape was missing.

Chapter Twelve

In the morning Jason started down his apartment steps as usual, on his way to his eight o'clock class. The tinny sound of a Japanese car horn made him look back up the street, where he saw Dean Kitteridge beckoning to him from within his yellow pickup.

"Good morning," Jason called. "Anything I can do?"

"I thought we might ride together," Kitteridge said.

Since he was only a block and a half away from his classroom, Jason hardly needed a ride, but he stood by the pickup to talk.

"What's up?"

"The board met last night."

"Yes, so your wife told me last night when I tried to call you. I talked with your friend, Matthew."

"How did it go?"

"Not very well. He's very bright, but all he wanted to do was play games. The only thing I know for certain is that he was not very fond of my predecessor and cares little for the practice of psychology in general."

"I see," Kitteridge responded without expression. "We have some other matters to discuss."

Jason took the hint and slid into the passenger's seat

and waited. When Kitteridge didn't start up the engine right away, Jason reminded him, "I have an eight o'clock class."

"Yes, I know."

The dean was looking for a way to say something he didn't want to say. Jason tried to make it easy for him. Jokingly, he said, "Don't tell me—I'm fired. Right?"

"No, nothing quite that serious. They did, however, get into some rather unfortunate resolutions, I'm afraid."

He got the engine turned over and they eased slowly down the street.

"The board has decided to take some actions . . . in an effort to get matters back under control. Unwise actions, I'm afraid, although understandable under the circumstances. They're pretty jittery."

The preamble was making Jason impatient. Finally, the old gentleman cleared his throat and got to the point.

"The board, under President Rollins' direction, has decided that all new and untenured employees should be asked to sign a declaration of faith letter. I'm not sure of the exact wording yet. I imagine they are still working on it. The letter is supposed to assure the Administration of each instructor's Christian commitment." He watched Jason for his reaction. "Anyone who refuses to sign will be asked to leave at the end of the term."

Jason reached for his beard. He suddenly wished it were back in place. "No doubt the letter will include clauses on the Virgin Birth, and I suppose one or two on scriptural infallibility. How about withholding evidence from the police? Will that be covered, too?"

Kitteridge drove in silence, taking the long way around the Quad.

"I'm very sorry about this," the dean said. "I was fairly certain you would not be interested in signing a pledge of any sort."

"What are they trying to do, purify the staff?"

"Something like that. I just wanted to let you know ahead of time."

"What's your position in all this?"

The dean smiled and shook his head. "It's a tough one. A university should be free and open to all ideas. On the other hand, God-fearing parents send their young people to us expecting us to nurture them and strengthen their faith if we can. At the same time, we're supposed to prepare them with the skills that this modern world needs. Unfortunately, when you learn about the things of this world, there is also the danger that some of the philosophy of the prince of this world will rub off on the learner."

"The prince of this world? Who's that?"

Kitteridge smiled. "Never mind. Tell you what I'd like you to do. I'd like you to think about writing a declaration of your own. Get down your thoughts of what you do believe in—what makes you tick. Several of the other deans are not happy with this new ruling. We're going to try to modify it. At least, maybe we can slip in some substitutes. In the meantime, you start getting some of your thoughts on paper."

"You know, it's rather funny, in a way." Jason smiled. "When I was driving down here from Berkeley, I was thinking what a wonderful chance this would be for me. The pay is not all that great, but at least teaching at Trinity would give me a chance to get my own philosophical house in order. I wasn't expecting a baptism by fire."

Kitteridge was so lost in his thoughts he didn't realize he had been speeding up slightly, and in front of Jason's office building they hit a speed bump rather hard. The stiff springs of the empty pickup put them both against the headliner for a nice little jostle. Several students on their way to class saw the incident and started laughing.

"Sorry about that," Kitteridge said. "That's a new bump, and I keep forgetting about it."

"Strange, what makes people laugh, isn't it?" Jason said. "What is it, 'man's inhumanity to man'?"

"Yes, that's part of it."

"I suppose that's why college students pull pranks, too, isn't it?"

"Yes, we've had quite a rash, haven't we? Every class seems to have its own fads. A few years back they were into baby talk and water pistols. That was considerably easier on the furniture."

Jason, remembering yesterday's incident, changed the subject. "That reminds me. My office was broken into late yesterday afternoon."

"Anything taken?"

"I think you can guess."

"The videotape?"

Jason nodded. Kitteridge shook his head slowly.

"Oh, dear. What's this place coming to?"

"I suppose Hillary Reed told you about our viewing the tape."

"Yes, she did—including your reluctance in the matter."

Kitteridge pulled into the faculty lot, parked in an unassigned slot, and turned off the engine.

"This poor school. It seems to be unraveling at the seams."

"Dean, has it occurred to you that some of these would-be pranks are really not pranks at all? Everything is tied together."

"What do you mean?"

"Richard Clark, the boy on the video, and Matthew Tye are both Beta Rhos, as was Barry Peterson, who also most likely was the cameraman for the video and the one who planted the tape in my class. Plus, according to Hillary, the girl in the video used to go with Dr. Hacchi. Hardly just a series of coincidences, do you think?''

''No, no. Hardly coincidences.'' Kitteridge was uneasy.

Jason drummed his fingers nervously on his briefcase, then turned directly to his dean. ''I think the time for fun and games is over. It's time the police knew about it, whether this school gets a public black eye or not. We're playing with dangerous chemicals here, and if we aren't careful, they're going to blow up right in our faces. Your board can pass all the resolutions it wants to pass—'' He didn't know where he was going with that line so he broke it off and shut up.

For a while they sat in silence, watching the happy and carefree students walk by.

''They look younger each year,'' Kitteridge said. ''It's something you'll notice as your years here pass. Younger and wiser.''

''If I'm around that long,'' Jason said dryly. ''Tell me, did Hillary and Alex Hacchi ever have a thing going?''

''Yes. Very briefly. I thought they would have made a very nice couple.''

''Is matchmaking one of your sidelines, Dean?''

Kitteridge only chuckled.

''Is that why you suggested Hillary view that tape with me? Because you thought the two of us might make a 'nice couple'?''

Kitteridge shot him a quick glance without enough expression to decipher. ''I admit I had an ulterior motive. But that wasn't it.'' He let it hang there.

"Just what we need, more questions." Irritated, Jason popped open the passenger door and started to leave.

"I'm going to try to talk to some of Matthew's relatives," the dean said. "He has two uncles living down in Glendale. Apparently he has been spending a lot of his time down that way."

Jason shrugged noncommittally.

"Jason, I was rather hoping you'd stay with me on this thing."

"It sounds to me like I'm being invited out."

"Oh, it's a little early to get so discouraged. You will think about your own version of a declaration of faith, won't you?"

"I doubt I could come up with anything that would satisfy any religious board."

"I'm not asking you to swear to anything you don't believe in. Why not give it a try?"

Jason, ready to get out of the pickup, turned his back to the dean. "That Chapel service yesterday really bugged me. Those kids, praying to their God as if He were some everlovin' sugardaddy, just waiting to do their bidding. I can't buy that kind of faith."

"I see."

"No, I don't think you do see. This whole loving and caring heavenly Father bit doesn't wash. If He's so loving and caring, why are there so many people slipping through His fingers and getting bashed on the hard pavements? Where was He when I was institutionalized for fourteen years? I've had to live by my own wits since I was sixteen. I've never known any TLC or favors in my life. I studied psychology, hoping and praying that I might find some kind of direction, some purpose and meaning in this messed-up world—a reason to go on, a way to find a place and explain away the stupidities.

"Two kids, probably high school seniors out on their

prom night—at least the dates would about match up—stop for a little fling. Just what all the kids are doing. Why not? Isn't it the age of liberation? Have a little instant gratification. Don't worry about the consequences. Only the consequence comes popping into the world nine months later. Born at the wrong time, and with a cleft palate and a harelip, just for good measure. Too bad about that. By the time he'd had the operation, he was no longer young and cuddly enough for the adoption game.

"I often think of that happy little couple and their happy act. I wonder what they're doing today. I wonder, every time I see a picture from a pornographic magazine, or hear a dirty joke, or watch prank tapes made by college kids about other college kids getting their jollies. That's when I think of the night I was conceived, only to be discarded like so much extra baggage.

"Tell me, Dean Kitteridge, do you think there will be room enough in my declaration of faith for all that?"

He looked up at Kitteridge's face for the first time since he'd started his tirade. The old man had tears brimming in his eyes.

Jason didn't know how to handle that. He jumped out, slammed the door of the little pickup, and started for his office. He heard Kitteridge calling after him, but he continued without stopping.

In his office he sat and stared at his green blotter and felt his heart pounding against his ribs. He had never opened up to anyone like that before. For a couple of minutes he thought he was going to throw up. Why had he done it? So whining and self-serving, too!

What was the lesson today? Something clinical, he hoped, with lots of numbers and long words that would have to be memorized.

While he was searching for his notes he heard the

eight o'clock chimes in the distance. He looked up at his wall clock. Eight o'clock. He hurried out, closing his damaged door the best he could, and headed for his classroom in another building.

It was the first time he had been late for any of the classes he had conducted.

Chapter Thirteen

When Jason returned to his office after his morning classes, a maintenance man was applying several C clamps to his freshly glued door frame. The workman scowled at Jason as he edged his way into his office.

"What happened here? You forget your key or somethin'?"

"Yup. I guess I've been watching too many Rocky movies. Thanks for fixing it. I appreciate it."

"Yeah, well, let's not make a habit of this, okay?"

"Okay. My fist is getting a little tender, anyway."

The man eyed Jason's slender right forearm and scowled some more.

"Your telephone's been ringing off the hook," he growled.

Jason dialed the department secretary, who told him that Mrs. Whitehall, an associate librarian, had been trying to reach him. He returned the call.

"Mr. Bradley, thank you ever so much for calling," the librarian said hurriedly. "I'm trying to run down some library materials that Dr. Hacchi checked out, and I understand you now have his office. I was wondering if you might look about for us. You see, there is another request in for the Shaker songbook and two of the records that he had out.''

Jason agreed to look. He tried the top file drawer again, where he had consolidated all of Hacchi's papers. Let's see, his thick file of correspondence . . . Jason opened it up. Evidently the man had had ambitions. Judging from the thirty or so form letters that were ready for mailing, he had a campaign under way to get himself elected vice-president of the California Association of Psychological Educators and Counselors. And, no doubt, the vice-president would be the following year's president. That's the way those things usually worked. And judging from the phrasing in his form letter, he was in no danger of dying from modesty. ''My years of experience on the cutting edge of our professions . . . My papers published in *Psychology Today* have established new directions for test standards. . . .'' My, my, my.

Ah, here we have something. A file labeled ''Shakers.'' Quite a stack of material. Copies of magazine articles. Ideas and comments on yellow paper in Hacchi's hand. Maybe he'd been planning an article on the psychological aspects of the Shakers.

Tucked in the back were two paperbound songbooks. One had a sales sticker indicating it had been purchased from a local music store for $5.98. The other had the University's library mark in it. It was called *Old Shaker Hymns and Chants*. So what were the new ones? Jason wondered.

He couldn't find any trace of the phonograph records, so he took the songbook, eased his way once more past the maintenance man, and headed for the library.

Mrs. Whitehall was overcome with gratitude. ''*Thank* you for returning this book so promptly. We do *so* appreciate it. And the student who wants it will, too, I'm sure.''

''You're entirely welcome.'' Jason tried to get around her and head for the exit, but she continued.

''It's so strange in our business. We never know what is going to be popular from one semester to the next. We haven't had any interest shown in our material on the Shakers for over fifteen years, and then suddenly we receive these two frantic requests for anything we have.''

Jason's interest in the library sciences took a sudden turn.

''Excuse me, but can you give me that student's name?''

''I don't see why not. Just one minute.''

Mrs. Whitehall was delighted to be able to demonstrate one of her services. Behind the checkout counter she thumbed through pink slips stacked in a small cardboard box until she found the right one.

''Here we are, *Shaker Hymns and Chants*. It was requested by . . . oh, dear.'' She paled and became flustered. ''I should have looked at the name before I called.''

''There's no name?'' Jason asked.

''It's . . . it was the Peterson boy. Oh, dear me. Doesn't that make one feel strange?''

''Yes, it does. Can you tell me when he made his request?''

She went to a computer terminal on the counter and punched some keys and waited.

''Well, now, isn't that interesting.''

''What's that?''

She pivoted the screen so he could see. ''This is Barry's record of library usage. He must have put this latest request in last week. But look here . . . back in November. He requested several things on Shakers then, including the Shaker songbook. He must have been doing a major paper or thesis.''

A communications major doing a thesis on the Shakers? Jason didn't think so.

''Mrs. Whitehall, how many students are there at the University?''

''Oh, my. We have over five thousand full-time students. And I really don't know how many part-timers.''

More than five thousand students, and all these coincidences keep happening to a handful of people. A club within a club. Or fraternity. Why would the two dead men share a common interest in the Shakers?

''Mrs. Whitehall, since Barry Peterson obviously has no further need for that songbook, would you mind if I checked it out myself?''

She looked at the book as if Gutenberg had just finished binding it. ''Why, no. No, I suppose not. It is for use, after all.''

Once outside, Jason sat on the lawn and thumbed the little book of hymns. Most of them seemed to him to be repetitious little ditties about working as unto the Lord and dancing with the spirit.

He looked for signs of writing in the margins. Then he held individual pages up to the light, looking for hidden markings. When he found nothing, he felt silly.

He closed his eyes to soak up a few rays of the noonday sun, but through his blood-red eyelids he could see a film rack. And peering out from between the rows of films were the penetrating eyes of . . . Barry Peterson? Matthew Tye? He closed his lids more tightly, trying to wipe the screen clear again, but this time he saw the tear-filled eyes of Kitteridge. What was the dean doing in the film library?

''Well, if it isn't our new young friend with the two first names,'' a voice boomed at him.

When his eyes adjusted to the light, Jason recognized the outline of Orville McCaully peering over his glasses at him. The old philosophy professor took the songbook Jason had been studying.

"You thinking of opening up a local chapter of the old Shaker order? You'll have to go celibate, you know. Not much of a following in that these days."

Jason got to his feet. "No, no. I found this among some of Dr. Hacchi's effects. Just wondering what his interest in the subject was."

"Oh, well, that's an easy one. You headed for lunch?"

"Yes, I guess so."

"Fine. Let's go. I'll walk with you as far as the mailboxes."

They started for the administrative building in lockstep. Jason waited for McCaully to explain about the Shakers and Hacchi, but he took another tack.

McCaully was a broad, expansive man, and he spoke in a loud, pontificating voice, as if he had forgotten to turn down his volume after he had finished his last lecture.

"I hear you got the bombshell dropped on you this morning. You planning to sign the loyalty pledge?"

"Dean Kitteridge seems to think there may be a way around it, but it sounds like a long shot to me."

"I feel for you, young man. When I first landed here, they told me I could talk about any philosophy I wanted to, just so long as the Christian perspective came out on top. That really stuck in my craw. It so happens I am a follower of the Nazarene—up to a point, that is. I have yet to sell all my worldly goods and give them to the poor. Still, the thought of a former lumberman turned board chairman telling me how to teach galled me no end."

"So, what did you do?" Jason asked.

"Do? I'm still here, am I not? I swallowed my pride and took some solace in historical precedence. I took the Galileo dive and bowed to the order of the day. Your predecessor knew how to play the game. He waited until he had tenure before he started his acidic attacks on the rigid moral codes of organized religion."

"So, the moral of the story is, you think I should sign their paper."

McCaully smiled. "Young man, I know all there is to know about driving a car. I could probably pass the test for a driver's license with flying colors. But I don't drive. My wife drives me everyplace I want to go. I only teach philosophy, Mr. Bradley. I leave the application of principles to others. How's that for a cop-out?"

"Pretty good," Jason said, then tapped the songbook. "You were saying something about Hacchi and the Shakers?"

"Oh, yes. I take it you missed his memorial service, when the chaplin talked about Hacchi's background. He lived with an elderly aunt for part of his formative years, up until she died, I believe. She was one of the Missouri Shakers. I was surprised to hear it myself, knowing what a cynical agnostic the man was."

"But I was given to understand that Hacchi was a Christian. Which was he, anyway?"

McCaully snorted. "You must be referring to his phantom conversion. About a month before his . . . demise he had started making noises about a change of heart. I, for one, never put much stock in it."

Jason shook his head in wonderment. "I've never seen a place quite like this—people undergoing conversion experiences at the drop of a hat."

"Easy there, young fella. You'll have our founding

fathers turning over in their graves. This school was founded on the conviction that the heart of man can be changed. Don't forget that. Aren't you in psychology? Why do you people do all that counseling and psychoanalysis, if it isn't intended to change people?"

"A mannerism or two, maybe. But changing one's basic approach to life . . ."

McCaully shrugged. "It happens. Who can really look into another's heart and know all the furies that may have brought those changes about? What may appear to be a spur-of-the-moment thing to an outsider may have been the culmination of years of thought."

"That could apply to Hacchi, too, couldn't it?"

"Please don't start saying nice things about people I dislike. Venomous thoughts are one of my only remaining pleasures."

"Did you know Barry Peterson, Doctor?"

"No, I didn't. Communications major, wasn't he?"

"Yes, I believe so."

"Those modern major types don't have much interest in philosophy, unfortunately. It's their loss. No real roots."

They had gotten as far as their mail slots where McCaully was busy dropping fliers from his mailbox into the wastebasket.

"Why do these people want to sell me insurance? Don't they know philosophy professors all live to be ninety-five?"

"Good-bye, Professor. Thanks for the information."

"So long, Jason. Give my regards to the Argonauts."

Chapter Fourteen

All during lunch Jason kept wondering about the Shakers. What did he know about them? They were a religious order that had made great furniture. What else? They practiced celibacy, and if he was not mistaken, they were like the Quakers in their attitudes about war. What else? The odd connection between Peterson and Hacchi was getting on Jason's nerves. Since neither was available for an interview, he decided to find out what their friends knew.

He went by the records office again and had another gossipy visit with the chubby grandmother. She got out Richard Clark's file again and set it before him. What he was looking for he couldn't say, but he thought looking over the records might give him a direction.

The lovemaking incident had occurred after three, and quite close to the University campus. Richard's schedule of classes, assuming he attended them, showed he had a three o'clock statistics class Monday, Wednesday, and Friday. Otherwise, he was free at that hour.

Jason then asked for Barry Peterson's records. That narrowed it down a bit. Peterson's schedule showed he had a drama class on Saturdays, and his Tuesday afternoon had been taken up with a scuba diving class that met for three hours or longer. That meant the tryst took place on Sunday or Thursday. And since Peterson had anticipated the meeting, maybe it was a regular thing. Was there a possibility that Clark would be meeting the girl again? It was worth a try. This being Thursday, Jason decided he didn't have anything better to do after his one o'clock class than try to follow the boy, just in case.

He went by the Campus Police office again and got the stats on Clark's car, a red 560 SL Mercedes. A nice little runaround, Jason thought, but what did the poor boy do for formal dates?

At two-thirty Jason drove his ancient van over to Beta Rho and turned into the driveway. Half of the building was on pylons, which allowed a long series of open parking places underneath. The last car in the line was a new red Mercedes with a license plate reading RCLARK. He didn't want to hang around it too long. His van seemed to age by the second just being next to it.

On the street again he found an empty slot near the Prayer Tower, where he could watch the frat house. He pulled in and cut his engine.

A coed version of a touch football game was going on on the Quad. Lots of squealing and shouting with each play. Actually, they were pretty good. A little more polish and they'd be ready for a lite beer commercial.

Jason pulled out the papers he'd just gotten back from his one o'clock students and started to grade them with one eye while he tried to watch the street ahead with the other.

After about fifteen minutes of waiting he was startled by a friendly greeting through his passenger window.

"Hi, Mr. Bradley," Harold Horwald called. "What are you doing over here?"

"Oh, Harold. I'm . . . waiting for someone."

"Oh? Who?"

"What about yourself? Off for a run, are you?"

Harold was in a jogging suit that did little to hide his spare tire. "Oh, no. I was just on my way up to the Prayer Tower."

"What goes on up there?"

"Why, prayer, of course. It's open twenty-four hours a day for students' use."

"Is it used much?"

"It gets a bit busy around exam time, I'm told," he joked. "Seriously, I don't know. I just started going, myself. Grading papers, huh?"

"Yes, trying to," Jason said. "Tell me, Harold, were you involved in any of the pranks at Beta Rho?"

"Oh, sure. We all were, I guess. There was a contest, you know, for the whole row. Where'd you hear about that?"

"Contest? What do you mean?"

"All the fraternities were in on it. We tried to get the sororities to go along, but they wouldn't. We had a contest among the houses to see who could come up with the best prank. Each house was to pull one, and then we were to vote on the best. I think everybody got involved to some extent."

"But you guys were the ones who got caught."

"How were we supposed to know that the guy who sold us the horse was Elsie Berkaw's nephew?" Harold laughed. "She's the president's secretary, in case you didn't know."

"Ah, yes." Jason nodded. "And Barry and Richard Clark were in on all this, I imagine."

"Of course. Richard is our best brain. He's got a devious mind by nature. He can think of more weird things," Harold said in an admiring tone.

"But no girls were in on it. That's amazing." That didn't draw any response, so Jason tried another angle. "Richard's girlfriend didn't help out, I take it?"

"Which girl? The guy has so many."

"What about his latest?"

"Oh, you mean the actress? What's-her-name?"

"Yes. That's the one I mean. Being an actress and all, I thought she might have given you a hand. What *is* her name?"

"Darned if I can remember. I think it sounds like another old-time actress, but I can't recall." Harold frowned. "I only met her once."

Fishing was good. He thought he'd try another line. "She's the blonde with the narrow face, right?"

"Yeah, that's her. A real looker, isn't she?"

"A real looker," Jason repeated.

Harold rapped on the roof of the van. "Gotta be off. I got two anatomy chapters to get through before dinner. So long!"

Jason waved after Harold as he headed for the base of the tower.

The papers were graded, but still no sign of the red car. He watched the football game for a while and started favoring one side over the other. The slower and shorter team was behind, he gathered, and just when they were making a good drive for a touchdown, one of the girls turned an ankle. That seemed to put the kibosh on the game. The girl, supported by two teammates, hobbled off in one direction, while the rest scattered in all directions, some of the guys coming toward fraternity row.

Jason checked his watch. Almost three. This cat-and-mouse business wasn't going to work. Now he'd try to talk to the kid directly. He got out of the van and started toward Beta Rho, and when he reached the front steps, the red Mercedes with a modified muffler roared out of the parking area and burned rubber up the street.

Jason went into action as quickly as he could, but by the time he got the van started and turned around, the red car was out of sight. At the first stop sign Jason turned off his engine and got out to listen. The red car was still making noises, and if he wasn't mistaken, it was now north of the campus.

Fortunately quiet little Almaden didn't have too many noisy red Mercedeses. Jason started cruising the long streets running east-west along the hillside, and before long he spotted the red car moving parallel to him one street up. He shifted into second and headed up the first cross street. He'd lost Clark again, so he sped on ahead and at the same time tried to look in the driveways as he went by.

About halfway down the second block he spotted the red Mercedes parked at the rear of a large two-story brick home. He parked at the curb where he could watch, then impulsively got out and started down the driveway without really knowing what he was going to do. He toyed with the idea of knocking on the side door and asking for the McGillicuttys, just to see who would answer. Bad idea. And he would feel rather foolish hiding in the bushes in broad daylight.

Just then he heard a woman's voice coming from behind the house. She was shrieking mad.

Jason eased on down the driveway several yards. The noise was coming from a cottage in the rear. A male voice was trying to placate the shrill female, but without any noticeable success.

"Get out of my sight!" she screamed.

"Okay, okay."

"If I ever see your slimy face around here again, I'll call the police, so help me."

"*Okay.* Can't you see I'm leaving?"

Jason was still trying to get a peek at the participants when he heard the door of the Mercedes slam. What to do? In a second Clark would be backing out of the driveway right over him. There wasn't time to get back to his van. He ended up hiding in the bushes.

He needn't have bothered. Clark went so fast and looked so stunned that Jason doubted the boy would have noticed him if he had remained right next to the car.

Clark hit the street and burned rubber, moving west.

Where would he be going so fast? The University campus was to the south. Jason decided the woman wasn't going anyplace. He could check on her later, after she had calmed down a bit. He trotted to his van and fired it up, but again he was no match for the speedy Mercedes. Clark was going through the Yield signs as if they weren't there, and before Jason could cover three blocks, Clark had vanished beyond the winding streets and the jacaranda trees.

Oh, well, Jason thought. There was nothing to the west except an older section of Almaden and then the ocean. Maybe he was just getting his exercise.

On the way back to the cottage Jason tried out several different reasons for knocking on the woman's door. He couldn't seem to bring himself to try the truth. It was too confrontational. Okay, lady, I saw a videotape of you and your boyfriend doing it. Now which one of you killed Peterson? By the time he got to the front door, he'd decided on the McGillicutty line again.

He rapped the knocker and was surprised to hear children's voices. "Mommy, somebody's at the door," they whined in tandem.

"I heard, I heard," a familiar voice answered.

Jason sucked in his breath, realizing too late he had

made a slight mistake. The door opened and Hillary Reed, dressed in a stained wraparound apron with her hair falling in her face, frowned at him.

''What are *you* doing here?''

''I, ah, I, ah . . .'' Jason stammered.

A toddler with what Jason hoped was peanut butter on his hands came at him like a magnet to steel and latched onto his left trouser leg.

''Memom, memom,'' he chanted.

Hillary snatched at the child. ''Valerie, will you get over here and help with your brother for once,'' she snapped.

''Aw, Mom,'' Valerie whined from the dinette table, where she was busy with a coloring book.

The place held an aroma of something like very old boiled potatoes, Jason guessed, and judging from the look of the small kitchen counter, he might have been accurate. Popcorn was spilled across the newspapers and magazines on the Naugahyde couch, and in the corner, an old fifteen-inch television was running cartoons with the sound off. Jason could hardly believe this was the home of the fashion plate he knew at school.

Hillary pushed the little boy in the general direction of his sister. ''I'll get a towel for your slacks,'' she said curtly.

Hillary found a halfway-clean hand towel, dampened a corner of it in the dirty kitchen sink, and came back to Jason, who had moved into the small entryway. He took the towel and dabbed at his pants—not that water was going to do much to peanut butter.

''I was just wondering if you'd had a chance to think of the girl's name.''

''No, I haven't.''

''Somebody told me her name might be like that of

an old actress, and she may be trying to be an actress herself. Does that help?''

Hillary shook her head without considering the matter. ''No, it doesn't.''

The little boy broke away from his sister and headed for a closed door in the foyer, right across from where the grown-ups were talking.

''I wan Fruffy.''

Hillary tried to hold him so he couldn't get by. ''Not now, Timmy.''

He struggled against her grip. ''I wan Fruffy. I wan my Fruffy!''

He won. He twisted out of her grip and pushed his way into the room. Hillary nimbly swung the door shut, but not before Jason had a chance to look inside. It was a bedroom with a peach-colored rug on the floor and a distinctive white chenille bedspread on the bed.

Jason looked away and tried to act as if he hadn't recognized the video tryst room.

''Was there anything else on your mind?'' she asked.

''You talked to Dean Kitteridge, did you?''

''Yes, I did. We had a nice long talk.'' She made no attempt to explain what that meant.

''I see. Well . . .'' Jason sidestepped toward the exit. ''Quite a family you have here.''

''Yes. Would you like to take them for a couple hours?''

''Baby-sitter problems?''

Hillary nodded. ''Always. My afternoon lady got sick, and I had to bring them home. Come back and see us again sometime when you can stay awhile. We have a wide variety of activities I'm sure you'd find interesting. We have a Donald Duck coloring book and several stuffed animals. You can have your choice.''

''Mom . . .'' Valerie called to get her to stop talking.

She was scarcely old enough for coloring books, but she already resented her mother's sarcasm.

"I'll see you back at the shop," Jason said hurriedly. "Good-bye, young lady," he called to Valerie, who showed no interest. Jason was almost home free, his hand on the door.

Timmy came out of the bedroom holding up a teddy bear with an ear missing.

"See Fruffy," he demanded.

Chapter Fifteen

Billie, the secretary for the Performing Arts Department, was the only person in the theater building when Jason got there just before four. She was in a large wardrobe closet counting and hanging up costumes.

"A local high school borrowed these from us last October," she explained. "They're just now returning 'em."

"Does Tri-U have an extensive theatrical wardrobe?" he asked.

"Oh, we sure do. We can outfit just about any play you can name. If they ever close down the school, I plan to open a costume shop!" She laughed.

"You ever let students use costumes for private parties?" he asked.

"No, that would be a Pandora's box. Where would it end?"

"Yes, I understand. I was just wondering if any had gotten borrowed by the fraternity row students during their pranks."

Billie chuckled. "That has been known to happen."

After she had hung up her last cape and checked it against her tally sheet, she led Jason back to her small office.

"What can I do for you?"

"I was wondering if you could help me locate a certain young lady. I don't know her name, but she is an aspiring actress."

"Oh, brother," Billy groaned. "I think half the girls in the county are aspiring actresses—and I'm not too hot on names."

"This is a very pretty gal, blond, with a narrow face. And I understand her name is similar to that of a well-known old actress."

"You don't mean Barbara Langtree, do you?"

"I don't know, do I?"

"But she's not a student, and she's more a singer than an actress. We used her in *Carmen* a couple of semesters back. She's blond, with a thin face."

"You wouldn't happen to have a picture of her around, would you?"

Billie led Jason to the backstage area where a series of posters of bygone productions had been mounted on the fly wall. "There she is." Billie point at a black-and-red *Carmen* poster with a glossy picture in one corner.

He'd found the girl in the video, he was sure, in spite of the black curly Carmen wig and the heavy makeup. If they cast her for her looks, they were right on. It was the kind of face a Don Jose could kill for. And who knows, maybe a fraternity brother, too.

"This was a Tri-U production?" he asked.

"Yes, but in reality, it's a community operation. Many non-students sign up for basket weaving or something so they can take part. It was the first opera we had attempted in quite a while. We had to take a few liberties with the libretto, but it went quite well, as I recall."

"Was Barbara any good?"

"She was good, all right. Not a real opera singer, but she can put over a song. Lots of sex appeal."

"Yes, I can imagine." After another long look at the temptress, he started down the ladder. "Could you tell me how I might get in touch with her? It's important."

Billie got the girl's address and phone number with no problem. It was in the card index file they kept on local talent.

"This is interesting," she said, reading from the bottom of the card. "She's appearing, or was appearing, in one of our local beaneries. Says here she's singing nightly at Omar's Ocean out by Highway One."

"Thanks, Billie. I appreciate your help."

"Watch your step." She smiled. "She's a pistol."

"Did you know she used to date Alex Hacchi?"

"You're kidding! The poor thing has all my sympathy."

Jason went to his office to call Barbara, stopping to read his mail on the way. One letter informed him that Dr. Rollins would like to see him in his office after Jason's ten o'clock class on Friday. Jason scowled. No doubt it was to be a signing ceremony. Another letter was from Kitteridge. He had been in touch with Matthew Tye's relatives living in Los Angeles, and they didn't know anything about his weekend visits to the area. Please call, he pleaded, as he was running out of ideas.

Jason dialed Barbara's number, then ran his fingers over his repaired door without finding any traces of the damage that had been done. The maintenance man was a grouch, but he did nice work. Too bad he couldn't work his magic on human beings.

A man's voice answered the phone.

"Joneses'."

"Oh, I must have the wrong number," Jason said. "I'm trying to reach Barbara Langtree."

"Yeah, yeah. That's my daughter. That's what she calls herself."

"Oh, I see. May I talk to her?"

"Who are you?"

"She doesn't know me. I'm Jason Bradley, calling from the University."

"What's this, your idea of a pickup?"

"Pickup? No, no. I wanted to talk with her about . . . a part."

"Oh, yeah?" The father's voice brightened. "Well, she's at work right now. She won't be home till late. You want her for a part, you say?"

Jason decided to let the misunderstanding stand. "How about I talk with her at work? It could be important."

"I don't know. . . . She gets sore when we give out her phone."

"Okay, don't give me her phone. Just tell me where she works."

The man coughed. Judging from the deep rattle he made, Jason would bet dollars to doughnuts the man was a heavy smoker and a heavy drinker. "She's cashiering at Terry's. You know where that is?"

"It's on the west side of town, isn't it?"

"Yeah. Down by the old highway."

"Thank you, Mr. Jones."

He got out there by five-fifteen. He wasn't hungry, but he sat on a stool next to the cash register and ordered coffee and a hamburger.

As truck stops go, it wasn't a bad place. The linoleum was starting to curl at a couple of seams, and masking tape was holding one cracked window in place, but the food smelled good. Two bony, middle-aged waitresses were frantically getting ready for heavy dinner traffic.

All the same, it didn't look like the kind of place that could afford a full-time cashier. When his waitress came back with his water and silverware, Jason asked, "Where's Barbara tonight?"

She shot back a look of disapproval that Cotton Mather would have been proud to call his own. "The queen bee's straightening up her face. As usual."

Jason wandered over to the jukebox and fumbled in his pocket for change. He scanned the song titles, looking for anything that wasn't rock.

"Try Twenty-two-B," a feminine voice told him.

He turned in the general direction of the cash register and saw Barbara. She wasn't looking at him, but was puckering at a small compact in her hand.

"Twenty-two-B it is. Twice." He put in his money and punched the buttons, then moved back to the counter. "How are you this evening, Barbara?"

She snapped the compact closed and tucked it somewhere near her hip. "Do I know you?"

"I'm Jason Bradley. I work at the University."

"Doing what?"

"I teach psychology."

He watched her for reaction. She didn't even wrinkle her makeup. The jukebox kicked in with lots of violins and cellos. It turned out to be Barbra Streisand singing "Memory."

"I'm on staff to take Alex Hacchi's place," Jason added.

For the first time, she turned toward him, and he understood why she'd been hired. He had to struggle to keep his eyes off her chest—and everything else, for that matter.

"I understand you knew Dr. Hacchi."

"Oh, yeah? And who gave you to understand that?"

"I thought you used to date him."

Someone in the kitchen called out for something. Barbara opened the register, collected a stack of receipts, and headed for the back.

After watching the last swing of her hips disappear through the double doors, Jason pulled a napkin out of the holder on the counter and wiped his palms. He missed her. He yearned for her quick return.

Then for some reason unknown to him, he started thinking of the first time he had heard Judy Garland sing "Over the Rainbow." It had been on a Saturday morning. All the "A" students in the grade school he'd attended had been rewarded with a trip to a real movie theater to see *The Wizard of Oz*. Jason had been swept away by the longing in little Dorothy's song. The ushers and a school chaperon had had to rip his hands off the seat to get him out of the theater. If only he could hear her sing it one more time.

But now it was Barbra Streisand singing, "If you touch me, you'll understand what happiness is. . . ."

He told himself he was only physically attracted to Barbara. He was a psychologist. He was supposed to tell other people about their emotions. The song stopped playing and the kitchen noises, mixed with the passing truck traffic, helped to stabilize his thinking.

Barbara came back and put something in the bottom of the cash drawer. Then she folded her arms and looked Jason's way.

"Okay, so I dated Alex a few times. What of it?"

"I suppose you heard he took his own life."

"Yeah, I heard," she said flatly. "Too bad."

"Do you know of any reason for him to kill himself?"

"No, why should I? He dumped me three weeks before he did that."

"He dumped you?"

''You don't have to broadcast it, fella.''

''Excuse me. I just find it . . . hard to imagine.''

''Yeah. You and me both. I figure he got to thinking about how I'd look with his intelligent friends. The big jerk.''

''No one seems to have thought very highly of him. In a way, I feel rather sorry for him.''

''Yeah, well . . . my heart bleeds.'' She checked the bodice of her blouse, then her fingernails. ''Why are you asking all these questions?''

''We're trying to find out what happened. You know, there was a murder in one of the fraternity houses on Wednesday.''

''Yeah, I read it in the papers.'' She showed a little more enthusiasm for the murder.

''And there is a possibility that the two events were connected somehow.''

''What's that supposed to mean?''

''Did you know Barry Peterson, Barbara?''

''Say, what is this? Who gives you the right to come in here and start calling me 'Barbara,' like you know me?''

''Sorry. But did you know him?''

She shrugged. ''Why should I know him?''

''Why not? He was a friend of Richard Clark's.''

She looked him in the eye for the first time. ''You sure about that?''

''Very sure.''

''Oh, yeah?'' A little of the truck-stop varnish was starting to wear off. ''How much do you know?''

The hamburger and coffee arrived, along with a couple of more looks from the waitress. ''You got the napkins loaded yet?'' she asked Barbara.

''They'll get loaded. Do you *mind,* Ruthie?'' Barbara said pointedly.

When the waitress had huffed off, Jason went on, "I know you used to meet him at the Reed house."

She laughed. "At the what?"

"The cottage north of the University. The one with the kiddies' toys in the living room. By the way, did he reach you in time today to call off your meeting?"

"Yeah . . . yeah, he did." She measured out her words. "What's this all about? I got business with Richard Clark."

"What kind of business?"

"I'm a performer. A singer. He's helping me."

"What is he, your vocal coach?"

"No. He's helping me get a gig down in Los Angeles. He's got contacts. Anything wrong with that?"

"Is that what he was doing with you on the chenille bedspread around three o'clock the other day?"

Her complexion went pink under her makeup and her eyes narrowed. "Very funny, friend. You want me to call Terry and get your keester thrown out of here?"

Jason ran right through her threat. "You know how I know all this, don't you?"

"Yeah, Richard has a big mouth."

"It wasn't Richard," Jason said softly. "You want to tell me about Barry Peterson?"

"Tell you *what*?" she yelled, then quieted. "What do you want me to tell? Richard said his name once. That's what I know. And that's the God's truth."

"You didn't know Barry Peterson videotaped the two of you? He had a camera hidden in the heater duct in the bedroom."

Barbara froze in disbelief. But then the wheels started turning behind her big hazel eyes. She was a girl used to taking care of herself in a tough world, and her brain went into overdrive. She leaned forward and rested her arms on the top of the register. Jason envied the keys.

''So where's the tape?'' she asked.

''I wouldn't worry about the tape.''

''*You* wouldn't worry, but maybe *I* would. I have my career to think of.''

''Your career? That's what you are worried about?''

''Well, yeah. After I make it big, I won't want something like that bouncing around.''

''When did you meet Richard?''

''You selling the tape? Is that your angle?''

''First my questions. Then I'll tell you what I know about the tape. How'd you meet Richard?''

''I don't remember how I met him. I meet a lot of guys.''

''I don't buy that. How'd you meet him, Barbara? Did he make the contact?''

She looked out at the traffic. ''He said he heard me sing the lead in *Carmen* last year. He said he wanted me to sing . . . something for him.''

''What something?''

She shifted her position. ''I, ah, don't remember. It was just a come-on. He wanted to start seeing me.''

''Were you still dating Hacchi?''

A little man wearing a brown pin-striped suit and a green tie left his place at a corner table, then came up and paid his bill and asked where the toilet was. Barbara gave him directions. Jason didn't like the interruption because it gave the girl a chance to work on her answers.

''Richard was planning to produce a record,'' she said. ''His dad's got contacts in the record industry.''

''Did this happen when you were dating Hacchi?'' he repeated.

''Yeah, I guess so.''

''How long afterward did Hacchi break up with you?''

''I don't know. A month, maybe two.''

''So you were going with both of them at the same time?''

''No. I wasn't going with Rich. I know a lot of guys without going with them, you know.''

''But Hacchi could have found out about Richard. . . .''

''No, he didn't.''

''How can you be so sure?''

''I'm sure.''

''Okay, so he didn't know. When did you and Hacchi break up? Give me a date. Was it before Christmas?''

''Yeah. He gave me a Christmas present and said we were through.''

''Sounds like he tried to be nice about it.''

''Yeah, I suppose you could say that. A pat on the back while he felt around for a soft spot for the knife.''

''Did it hurt all that much?''

She shrugged. ''He was a meal ticket out of this dive. Yeah, I liked him okay.''

''That sounds rather heartless.''

''You know what they say—love is never like it was the first time.''

''I never heard that.''

''There's a lot you're not going to find out if all you do is ask questions.''

''How do you mean?''

''You don't know what makes a woman tick. What makes her do the things she does. The crazy things.''

She had lowered her voice now, giving it all to Jason.

''I think you may be right,'' he said. ''I don't think I'd ever understand why a beautiful, very desirable girl would want to take her clothes off and show off for a kid whose father may or may not know somebody in the record business.''

She shook her head slowly. ''You don't understand.''

She looked off, somewhere far from the truck stop. "Not too long ago I was married, right up the street here, in the Catholic church. Frankie was Catholic and he wanted it that way. We were kids, really, but when it's right it's like . . . oh, God, it's the answer to everything. You don't mind working in a sleazy diner or anything else when you can be with the right person and be in his arms at night. It's like . . . it's what life is all about—what we're here for, like God intended it to be.

"We had only a week together. Frankie was in the Marines, and got stationed in Lebanon. I had everything packed. He had it worked out so I could be at Cyprus and we could be together a lot of the time.

"Then two guys in uniform came in that door. They had this paper, you see, to read to me right in the middle of the lunch-rush hour. Frankie had been in the barracks that got bombed. They stood there and read me that letter. . . . Oh, forget it. You don't understand.

"It isn't the other guy. I'm trying to remember, don't you see. I'm trying to recapture something I . . . Forget it. It isn't worth the trouble."

She straightened and pasted a smile. "Tell you what. Come see me at Omar's Ocean. I sing out there every night but Monday. Monday we're closed. I cry on cue at eight, nine-thirty, and eleven. Why don't you come out and catch my act?"

"I hear you're very good."

"When I sing, you know, they turn out all the lights except for a spot on me. And when I finish I look out into the darkness and I can see tears falling on the checkered tablecloths. Yeah, I'm good.

"What did you say your name was, again?"

"When I came in, it was Jason Bradley."

The waitress came back, plopped an empty napkin

dispenser between the two of them, and marched away again.

"I gotta get to work," Barbara announced. "What's the story about the you-know-what?"

"I think it's already been destroyed. I'll know more about it tomorrow. It's been a pleasure meeting you, Ba—Miss Langtree."

"Let me know, will you? It would break my poor dad's heart if that started circulating."

Jason wasn't going to bet the family farm on that one.

She picked up his dinner tab and said, "That'll be two dollars and thirty-eight cents, please."

At the door he turned and watched her putting refills in the napkin dispensers. He tried to think of her with Alex Hacchi, but had a hard time making the connection. Then he thought of her with himself. That was easier and a lot more fun.

Outside, a cool ocean breeze hit his damp body and made him shiver. As if he needed to be reminded how alone he was in the world.

Parking lot gravel crackled like popcorn as two loaded semis pulled up in tandem. One driver touched his air horn in greeting. Barbara was probably the best part of his trip.

On the way home Jason thought about saving Barbara from the truckers and their wandering eyes.

Chapter Sixteen

Friday morning the telephone woke Jason at six-forty-five.

"Are you up?" Kitteridge asked.

"I'm thinking about it." Jason yawned. "Something the matter?"

"I've prevailed upon the county sheriff to grant me an interview with their investigating team. I'd certainly like to have you along. Lieutenant Newcombe will be in his office at eight-thirty."

"But I have a class. . . ."

"I know, I know. I'll arrange for a substitute for this morning. I think this is more important. Can I come by and pick you up?"

"I'll meet you at the County Government Center. Dean Kitteridge, were you ever in the military?"

"No, I wasn't. I had a ministerial deferment doing social work for the denomination in Detroit. Why do you ask?"

"Nothing important. Just had a question for a military man."

Kitteridge got the details of Jason's subject matter for the day's class and said he would pass them on to the substitute. After he hung up, Jason swung his feet out of bed and sat staring at his Spartan bedroom. Kitteridge must have a very deep commitment to the Tye family to be doing all this for Matthew. No stone unturned. Such devotion didn't ring true from Jason's experiences.

Was there something else? Maybe Kitteridge knew something more he was not telling Jason. Perhaps he was trying to get Matthew off the hook because he knew the boy was not guilty. The old guy could be cagey.

While he shaved, Jason remembered his upcoming meeting with the president and decided to wear his one and only suit.

The investigative offices for the Sheriff's Department were modern and colorful. The place could have passed for the home office of an insurance company, with maybe a few extra phone lines thrown in.

Kitteridge was waiting by the entrance for him. With loping strides he led the way through the labyrinth of partitions and cubicles into a glass-enclosed office. Newcombe was on the phone when they went in. His annoyed glance at his visitors indicated to Jason that he was under orders to be nice to the know-nothing civilians from the University. He pointed at chairs, then wrapped up his call in a hurry and smiled for them.

"What can I do for you, gentlemen?"

Kitteridge bounced back to his feet and shook his hand. "I'm Dean Kitteridge, Lieutenant, and this is Jason Bradley from our staff. I asked Mr. Bradley to come along, since he's had some practical experience with law enforcement."

"Oh, yeah? Where was that?" Newcombe asked.

"I worked up in Oakland for about a year as forensic psychologist."

Newcombe smiled. "Well, I guess you could call that experience if you stretched the point. Was that part of the federal monies program that was going around a couple years ago?"

"Yes, it was."

Newcombe condemned the federal program with a snort. He started lifting up manila folders on his desk and looking under them.

Kitteridge went on: "I suppose the sheriff told you we are interested in the case you have against the Tye boy."

"Yes. So I hear. You're not with the school paper or anything, are you?"

"No, no, nothing like that. The sheriff, as you know, is a good friend of the school's, and he understands that our only interest is in protecting the institution's interest—and the boy's, too, if that is possible."

Newcombe didn't find what he was looking for. He decided to give up and talk. "Our investigation is not complete yet." He stopped to fill his lungs with air, then bellowed, "Fred, get in here, will you?"

A detective outside got up from his humble desk, rolled down his shirtsleeves, and grabbed his coat on the way in to answer the call.

"Yes, Lieutenant?"

"You seen the Tye folder with the glossies?" Newcombe asked his subordinate.

The two of them started going over the desk again. Jason went over to the four-drawer file in the corner and pulled out the bottom one labeled "S–Z."

"What do you think you're doin' there, fella?" Newcombe barked. He was a man used to controlling a situation by volume alone.

"I'm helping you find your photos, Lieutenant."

"I think we'll be able to manage without your help." Newcombe pushed out of his chair, waddled over to the open file, and went down heavily on one knee. After flipping through a few folders, he came up with the right one. He heaved himself upright and spread the pictures on the desk.

"These were taken at the scene by our people Wednesday morning. I hope you are not squeamish." He smiled, showing a trace of glee.

Jason started turning the pictures as he and Kitteridge looked at them. The first were color shots of Barry Peterson, sprawled on his back in the upstairs hallway of the fraternity. The body was in white-and-gray-striped pajamas with the shirt unbuttoned, so that the stab wounds and blood smears showed across the abdomen and chest. Close shots of the torso showed five major entry wounds and three superficial cuts. All the wounds indicated lateral and almost uniform angles. Jason figured they probably had been made with a one-and-a-half or two-inch blade. Little tape arrows with printing on them pointed to each stab wound. Parts of the pajama top and the front of the pants near the drawstring were soaked in blood.

Dean Kitteridge shook his head and made sad noises with each picture.

"This was the position of the body when first discovered?" Jason asked.

Newcombe nodded. "That's right. The next one shows where Tye was positioned when the students in the room just across the hall came out and found them."

The picture showed a full shot of Barry, still on his back. Now a detective was kneeling beside him with a small knife in his right hand. Apparently he was supposed to represent Matthew Tye.

After this came pictures of Peterson's dorm room. There were bunk beds in one corner and a small desk nearby. A blotter and other small articles from the desk were messed up enough to indicate a struggle. The top bunk was made up, but the lower one was disheveled and the top covers were thrown back. In the middle of the sheet was a large dark red blotch. The red marks continued across the beige carpet toward the door.

"What was the murder weapon?" Jason asked.

"It's an oriental-style dagger. Peterson kept it on his desk as a letter opener," Newcombe said. "It was in Tye's hand when the other students found them."

"And you are sure it was the weapon used?"

"The coroner is satisfied. There was blood on the dagger, and the wounds correspond to the size of the dagger. Do you want to take a look at it?"

"No, I don't think that will serve any useful purpose," Jason answered. "I suppose you are assuming he was stabbed first in bed, then he went for help and was stabbed some more in the hall."

"That's about the size of it."

"Of course, I'm sure you've weighed the arguments against that, haven't you?"

"What arguments?"

"First of all, the difference in the boys' sizes. Tye is rather slight, I'd guess around one hundred and forty pounds, while Peterson must have been close to one eighty, judging from these pictures. Wouldn't it be rather difficult for Tye and Peterson to move from the bed all the way out into the hall, about twenty-five or thirty feet, in a state of combat, without the smaller man ending up with a few bruises or cuts on his face? I saw

Matthew on the fraternity house steps right after he was arrested. He was shook-up, and his bathrobe was bloodied, but there were no scars on him.''

Newcombe grunted. ''Remember, Peterson was in a dead sleep when first attacked. He ends up with a mortal wound right off the bat. He staggers into the hall. . . .''

''Were all the wounds on the front of the torso?'' Jason interrupted.

''Yes.''

''But if his assailant was following him out into the hall, why aren't there stab wounds, say, on his back or side?''

''How do you know he was following behind?'' Newcombe yelled. ''Maybe he was running ahead, just out of his reach.''

''Okay,'' Jason granted him. ''Let's say he was ahead. So now what happens in the hall?''

Newcombe frowned at the challenge. ''Well, Peterson falls down, and then Tye comes in and finishes him off.''

Jason shook his head. ''Sorry. You're not thinking straight.''

''Okay, that does it!'' Newcombe slammed his desk with his beefsteak fists and got to his feet. ''Out! I don't have to sit here and listen to this. Out!''

But Fred was pushing him back down. ''Wait a minute, Newk. Let's hear what he's got to say. Better we hear these things here than in open court where we can get egg on our face.

''Okay, young fella.'' Fred smiled and sat on the corner of Newcombe's desk.

Dean Kitteridge, wide-eyed and white-faced, was sitting quietly to one side.

Jason took the floor. ''When a person falls down,

say, from a wound to the stomach, he's already crouched forward to cover the injured area, so he inevitably falls forward onto his face, not onto his back. So what does that leave the assailant for a target?''

''He rolls him over and stabs some more,'' Newcombe growled.

''Why bother?'' Jason asked. ''Why not simply stab him as he lies? Why roll him over and risk being kicked or grabbed?''

Newcombe was turning dark, but stayed silent.

Jason fished out the picture of the empty bed from the folder on the desk and placed it in front of the detectives. ''There's too much blood here. If this whole thing happened in sequence—the first stabbing, the scuffle, the scene in the hall, all in three or four minutes—it doesn't account for that pool of blood in the bed.''

''He hit an artery,'' Newcombe countered. ''Arteries can squirt out a tremendous amount of blood in no time.''

''We're talking here of abdominal stab wounds,'' Jason pointed out. ''He may have hit an artery, true, but around the abdomen the arteries are all quite deep. Peterson may have bled a lot internally but not externally—not like a leg or neck wound.''

Fred looked at the lieutenant. ''You know, he may have a point there.'' Newcombe didn't answer, so Fred asked Jason, ''Okay, so what do you think happened?''

''I think we're talking about two different events here. I think Barry Peterson was stabbed in his sleep and left for dead, with the knife still buried in his chest. After lying there bleeding for a while, he regained consciousness and probably rolled out of bed and crawled out of the room looking for help. Help arrived in the form of Matthew Tye, who found Barry in the hall. He turned

Barry over to see what the problem was, and found the knife. He pulled the knife out and unbuttoned the pajama top to see the damage. Matthew then made enough noise to wake up the whole floor, not the mortally wounded Barry.''

Fred smiled down at his boss. ''Your turn, Newk.''

Newcombe cleared his throat vociferously. ''Okay, fella. Number one: Why did Peterson lie there in bed bleeding until he decided to get up? The coroner assures us there were no blows to the head, if you're thinking maybe he was knocked out first and then stabbed.

''Number two: The stuff on the desk was knocked about and a bottle of after-shave was broken. The place reeked of it. That tells me there was a struggle in the room.

''Number three: What was Tye doing wandering the halls at three in the morning? And don't tell me he was going to the john. College students have very healthy bladders and have no trouble sleeping through the night.

''Number four: If this boy is so all-fired innocent, why doesn't he *say* so, instead of giving us that cutesy little smile of his when we ask him questions?''

Jason raised his shoulders in a long shrug. ''Granted, the room looks like there was a struggle. So why didn't Matthew show signs of having been in a fight? If you are thinking of going for a murder-one conviction, you'll have to start supplying answers and not just more questions.''

''The kid's guilty as sin,'' Newcombe said. ''His conscience is tearing him up. You can look at his face and see it. It's eating him up inside.''

''Oh, really? You can determine guilt by looking at someone?''

''There are manifestations,'' the policeman declared.

''You don't get ulcers without something eating at your insides.''

Dean Kitteridge perked up. ''He has ulcers?''

''They took him to the hospital last night with a bleeding ulcer,'' Fred explained. ''They have it under control now, we understand.''

''I'd like to see him, if I may,'' Kitteridge said.

''Sorry. No visitors,'' Kitteridge said, ''except that brilliant lawyer of his.''

''Isn't that a bit severe?''

''When he starts answering questions, we'll be more than willing to relax a few rules.''

''Okay,'' Jason began again. ''What about motive?''

It was Fred's turn. ''We think it was a grudge thing. Maybe an argument. We understand Tye didn't get on well with the other fraternity members.''

''Can you be more specific?''

The two policemen exchanged looks. ''We're still working on that,'' Fred said.

''I think it was strictly irrational,'' Newcombe decided. ''A senseless killing. It could just as easily have been another victim. That's why he unbuttoned the pajama top. He wanted to get his kicks seeing the open wounds. The kid's unstable, if you ask me.''

''Excuse me, Lieutenant,'' Jason said, ''but I think you're fencing with windmills.''

Newcombe raised his voice a few decibels. ''Say, what is it with you? You trying the case here in my office? What difference does it make to you which student did it? If it wasn't Tye, it was another. You're not going to save them all, you know.''

''I hope my motive is the same as yours, Lieutenant. To determine the truth. What do you mean, if it wasn't Tye, it was another student?''

''The building was closed off for the night. The

fraternity house was on some kind of probation, and part of the agreement was to submit to a curfew. There was a monitor in the downstairs lobby, with orders to report any movement after ten-thirty on school nights. And there were no violations that night. Everybody was accounted for on both floors."

"And you've already interviewed everybody?"

"We have. There were twelve students in the house at the time. We've talked to them all."

"What about Richard Clark? You talk to him?"

Fred pulled a notebook out of his hip pocket and thumbed the pages. He looked sideways at his boss. "No. He hasn't been interviewed yet."

"Why not? I think, gentlemen, you are missing a very logical possibility there. I happen to know Richard Clark had a grudge against Barry Peterson."

Both the detectives paused and watched Jason with a tolerance they hadn't displayed earlier. They knew something.

Newcombe smiled. "And what might that have been about?"

Jason looked to Kitteridge, for a sign that he might tell the police about the videotape. Kitteridge either didn't understand his look or was doing a fine job of acting innocent.

Jason cleared his throat. "I'm not at liberty to say, right now. But I know there were bad feelings."

"Thanks for the hot tip."

"Does that mean you are not going to pursue it?"

"It certainly does."

"Why not?"

"Because Richard Clark wasn't in the fraternity house Wednesday night. He stayed at his parents' beach house in Malibu."

Jason gulped. "Are you sure?"

"Couldn't you see the bed was still made?"

"Bed?" Jason looked at the picture of the bunk beds again. The top bunk was still neatly made up. "You mean he was Peterson's *roommate*?"

"You didn't know that?" Newcombe laughed until his stomach bounced. "You better get your facts straight before you march in here and tell us how to run our business."

"Yes, I guess I had." Jason sat down numbly and watched while the two detectives exchanged superior smiles. Newcombe decided the occasion called for a cigar. He took one out of his top drawer and made a ceremony of lighting it and blowing little patterns of smoke in the general direction of his guests.

Jason tried to get going again with another angle. "That was very convenient, wasn't it, though? Barry is killed on the one night when his roommate is out."

"Yes." Fred smiled. "Convenient for Matthew Tye. He was probably waiting for just such an opportunity, so Clark wouldn't wake up and finger him."

"I have to hand it to you." Jason smiled. "You've made me look the fool here. But I still feel we're only on the surface of this thing. What makes these kids tick? Matthew Tye, for instance. What is he really like? Why did he take off for Los Angeles every weekend? How about putting a tracer on his activities?"

"And how would you propose we do that?" Newcombe asked.

"I don't know. Check with Motor Vehicles. Maybe he got a ticket or ran a red light or something. What was he *doing* down there?"

"Maybe he's a Dodger fan." Newcombe shrugged. "Who knows?"

"Well, why don't you get off that fat rear end of yours and find out?" Jason said, then smiled.

Fred got off the edge of the desk as if expecting a handball shot from behind. Kitteridge was busy clearing his throat and pulling on his lower lip.

Newcombe got slowly to his feet. But instead of bellowing, he calmly suggested, ''If there's nothing else on your mind, gentlemen, I think that will be all.''

Chapter Seventeen

"They didn't give the impression of being very co-operative, did they?" Kitteridge said as they exited the building.

"They're not even scratching the surface of this thing. And neither are we, for that matter." Jason rattled on about psychological profiles and handwriting samples and motives of the boys involved, but Kitteridge's mind seemed to be wandering. When he got to his pickup, he leaned against it for support and rubbed his brow.

"Any more suggestions, Dean?" Jason asked.

"Pray. Wait for the Lord's leading. That's all I can think of. It's in His hands, anyway, in the long run." He managed a limp smile. "When do you see President Rollins?"

"Eleven o'clock this morning. How'd you know?"

"The suit," he said, then straightened Jason's tie for him. "You have any idea what you're going to say to the man?"

"No, I really haven't. To tell you the truth, I don't think I know what being a Christian is. And judging from the events at this so-called Christian institution, I don't think I'm in for any easy answers." He kicked at a pebble and looked off toward the County Building like a lost puppy.

"Did I ever tell you what Matthew's parents are doing out in Thailand?" Kitteridge volunteered. "They work with the hill tribes up in the north. The villagers have had protein-starved diets up there for generations, and the Tyes are teaching them to supplement their usual food sources. They've developed a strain of avocado tree that will grow in that climate, and they've taught the farmers to make ponds that will sustain freshwater fish. Mrs. Tye has done a lot with crafts for the women, trying to get them some cash. They sell the crafts now down in Bangkok—"

"Dean Kitteridge," Jason interrupted. "Why are you telling me all this?"

"You said you didn't know what Christianity was. The followers of John the Baptist came to Jesus and asked Him, 'Are you the One, or should we look for another?' Jesus answered by showing them what He was doing. I never worry too much about the theology business. I think of Christianity as a verb." He paused. "When you go in to see President Rollins, try to keep cool in there, won't you?"

"I'll try."

"He loves Trinity. Lives and breathes the place. It may be his failing. Sometimes I think he loves the place too much."

By the time Jason got back to his apartment, a light rain had started to fall. After the dressing-down he had gotten from the police and the prospect of an unhappy meeting with Dr. Rollins, the weather seemed appropriate. What else could go wrong?

He unlocked his door and, as he pushed it open, a streak of yellow-brown bolted from behind him through the door, across the hardwood floor of the living room, and around the corner into the kitchen. Startled and curious, Jason eased his way into the kitchen and found a cat sitting by the refrigerator door, eyeing Jason and giving out a demanding type of utterance.

If it wasn't the ugliest cat in the world, it was at least in the running. Most of its left ear had been shredded, and the other one was folded back like a water spaniel's. Its wet, matted coat gave the animal a monkeylike appearance. It eyed Jason with a fierce expression, then scratched at a particular spot on the linoleum. Jason decided the cat was well acquainted with his home, probably because of an earlier tenant.

He searched his refrigerator and found an aluminum-wrapped piece of processed cheese that someone had given him about three Christmases ago, which he had been saving for just such an auspicious occasion.

"Here. I hope you like caraway seeds."

Apparently he didn't drop the cheese in exactly the correct spot, because the animal pawed it about until it was right, then began to eat.

Jason took his wounded pride to the table and tried to get interested in one of his textbooks. But about four minutes later his new acquaintance jumped up beside him and proceeded to get comfortable on his latest edition of *Soaring* magazine.

"I think we need some ground rules," he lectured the cat. "First of all, you should understand that I've never cared for cats."

This shook the animal to its very core. Jason could tell, because it lifted one hind leg and began preening itself in the general vicinity of its rear end.

"You wouldn't act that way if you knew the kind of troubles I've got. Don't you know that a one-year stay at a teaching position looks worse on your record than no position at all?''

Right on cue, it stopped its cleaning and stared at him with a haughty and superior look, as if to say, ''So you think you're being persecuted, do you? You think giving me your stale old cheese qualifies you in the nice-person department, do you? Well, are you a Christian, or are you not? Have you ever thought of anybody but yourself in your whole life? I should think not. That, my friend, pure and simple, is the reason you can't make your stand. You don't know who or what you are. So what if you were on your college championship basketball team and won a trophy. Your life has been going downhill every since, because you've been afraid to grow up. In your mind you're still a junior in college. And now you're trying to pass yourself off as a college professor. Just whom do you think you're kidding?''

Right about then Jason remembered why he disliked cats.

''And who,'' he demanded, ''elected you the Grand Inquisitor?''

But it had had enough of charlatans. The animal broke off the staring contest by getting onto all fours and arching its back in one great bored stretch.

''Well, thank you ever so much for the benefit of your years in the alley,'' Jason said with as much sarcasm as he could muster.

Not to be outdone, the cat raised its tail and used it to make an obscene gesture at him, then curled up for a nap with its head resting against the telephone.

But there is justice in the world, after all, for no sooner had the Inquisitor gotten comfortable than the phone rang loudly. The cat went straight into the air, came down, did a classy imitation of Charlie Chaplin running in place on roller skates, then disappeared into the living room.

Jason had to wait for the fourth ring before he had stopped laughing enough to talk. "Hello?"

"Hello, Mr. Bradley. This is Detective Sergeant Weir."

"I'm sorry?"

"Fred Weir. We just met this morning in Lieutenant Newcombe's office."

"Oh, yes. What can I do for you?"

"I thought you'd like to know that I acted on your suggestion and came up with something."

"Which suggestion was that?"

"Remember you wanted us to do a DMV check on Matthew Tye's car? Well, I ran it through our state computer and got a very interesting listing." He paused for effect.

"Yes?"

"Are you sitting down?"

"Yes, I am."

"I'm afraid this is going to shoot some heavy holes in your efforts to exonerate him. He drives an old green Pinto, doesn't he?"

"I don't know."

"Well, that's the car registered to him. On two separate occasions we have it listed as being parked illegally near the eighth hole of the Roosevelt Golf Course up in Griffith Park—twice on Saturdays and once on Sunday. Your man doesn't play golf, does he?"

"I have no idea. What's the significance of this, Sergeant?"

Fred seemed to be in a playful mood, and Jason had no alternative other than to go along. "So what do the parking tickets tell us?"

"That particular area in the hills just opposite the golf course is quite isolated, and a large number of the local queers are in the habit of using it as a meeting place for their casual encounters.'' When Jason didn't react right away, Fred felt more explanation was necessary. ''It's a place where lonely homosexual boys go to make it with other lonely homosexual boys.''

''Yes, I understand what you are saying,'' Jason said. ''Couldn't there be another reason for Matthew's car to be up there?''

''Oh, come now. Be realistic. This puts your guy behind the eight ball. I just thought you'd like to know so you could stop spinning your wheels.''

''How do you figure that?''

''Motive, my friend. Isn't that what you've been harping on? Try this on for size: Either Tye killed Peterson in a homo love snit, or Peterson found out about his kinky ways, and Tye had to kill him to keep it quiet. Mark my words, one of those versions will be the way this thing works out.''

''Yes, I see your point,'' Jason said. ''Thanks for letting me know about this.''

After he had hung up, Jason sat for several minutes, his hand still resting on the phone, thinking of the possibilities. And thinking, too, of the impact this would have on Dean Kitteridge and the boy's family. To say nothing of the University. If they weren't shook-up before, this ought to do it.

But the more he thought about it, the more the pieces started to fit. If Matthew had become a practicing homosexual, this would explain several other events that seemed irrational and isolated up until now.

Now the problem was, what to do about it? And was there time?

He looked up the phone number for the Beta Rho House and dialed it. After several rings an irritated student growled, ''Beta House.''

Jason asked for Harold Horwald. He had to wait while

the student dropped his end of the line on some hard surface and bellowed through the halls for "Pillsbury." After several seconds another voice came on line and asked, "Anybody on this line?"

"Yes, there is," Jason said. "I was waiting for Harold Horwald."

"He's at class," the new voice announced.

"Do you know where I might find him?"

"I think he has a lecture at the hospital this hour."

"Very good," Jason said. "Thank you."

He hung up and checked his watch. Ten-thirty. He might have time.

On his way through the living room he found the Grand Inquisitor sound asleep on his old sweatshirt on the couch. He decided to let it sleep.

Chapter Eighteen

He found Harold in the basement coffee shop of the hospital having coffee with several other eager young doctors-to-be. Jason pulled him away from his classmates for a minute and asked him, "I was wondering if you could help me with another little problem."

"Sure, if I can."

He showed Harold the card he had been issued for entrance to the secured area in the mental health facility.

"As a psych teacher, I can get in and out of the psychiatric ward with this. Can you tell me if it will get me into other secured areas in the hospital, such as the ward where they keep jail inmates under medical treatment?"

Harold scratched his scalp. "Golly, I don't think so."

"How about you? Could you get into the inmates' rooms?"

"No, I'm sure I couldn't. I'm only first year, you know. We don't have the run of the place yet."

"Oh, I see." Jason frowned.

"Somebody over there you'd like to see?"

"Yes, there is."

Harold got a twinkle in his eye. "Well, mind you, I wouldn't do it myself, you understand. Not anymore.

But if I wanted to get into a secured area of the hospital, you know what I'd do?"

"No, what would you do, if you were me?"

"You should go over to Maternity and tell the nurses you want to see your baby. You can pick out a name through the special nursery window—say, Baby Mary Jane. They'll give you a green paper gown and cap to wear so you can go in. Then, after cruising the nursery for a while, you go out. But you don't throw away the paper gown. You keep it on. It looks enough like what the doctors wear in surgery so that nobody would dare challenge you.

"Then on your way by one of the nursing stations, you grab an extra stethoscope to hang about your neck for a little added authenticity, and you can get in anyplace you want to go."

"Thanks. I think I'll try it."

"What happened? Did one of your mental patients commit mayhem?"

"No. Matthew Tye apparently has some ulcer problems."

"Oh, really? Guilty conscience, eh?"

"That seems to be the prevailing diagnosis. Thanks for your help, Harold."

Jason followed Harold's suggestions to the letter, without once being challenged. Everyone working in the hospital seemed to be going about his own specialized business, and the problems of wanderers or interlopers was of concern to no one.

He had to ask at the main desk where the prisoner patients were housed, but the Pink Lady only smiled and answered.

The deputy sheriff on duty at the head of the restricted corridor even opened the hallway door for him. After that courtesy, the deputy sat down and returned his attention to the sports page of the local paper.

Identifying Matthew's room was easy. The second door he came to was posted with a yellow mimeographed sign: "Caution, Infectious Blood Disease. Check at nursing station before entering."

He pushed the door open a crack and saw Matthew lying in bed with his face turned toward the wall.

"Hello, Matthew. Remember me?"

Matthew turned with a surprised start, then glared at his intruder. "You sure you're supposed to be in here?"

"I'm not sure of anything anymore."

He walked to the foot of the bed and started to grip the metal railing, but on second thought decided not to touch it. Matthew's cocky manner was gone now. The eyes had a hollow look to them, as if he had been spending time cruising the River Styx.

Jason tried a smile. "I hear they got your bleeding stopped. Feeling better?"

"Better than what?" Matthew faced the wall again.

"Matthew, I'm afraid I'm going to have to ask you some tough questions. You up to it?"

No response, except a movement of the sheets that could have been a shudder.

Jason took a deep breath and took the plunge. "You have AIDS, don't you, Matthew?"

Matthew shielded himself as if Jason were about to strike him. "You have no right to say that! I'm not listening." He put an arm over his ear and rocked against his pillow.

"I'm sorry, Matthew. It isn't idle curiosity."

"This turkey institution! They said medical histories would be kept secret. God damn 'em all to hell!"

Jason waited for a time while the tormented youth rocked under the sheet.

"Nobody had to tell me, Matt. I. . ."

"Don't call me Matt. A mat is something you wipe your shoes on. I'm not that low yet."

"Okay, Matthew."

"As a matter of fact, don't call me at all. Get out of here."

"Okay, fella, fun-and-game time is over. Life has dealt you a hard one. But that's no reason to make other people suffer."

"Suffer? What do you know about suffering? To hell with other people. I don't care what happens anymore."

"Yes, you do. People care about you, and you care about them. Dean Kitteridge is turning into a basket case worrying about you. They've about convinced him that you killed Barry Peterson. But you and I know differently."

Slowly Matthew's penetrating eyes found Jason's face. "How did you know I'd contracted. . . ?"

"I didn't. But I had a pretty good idea when I found out about your weekends in Los Angeles, plus the sign on the door says you have an infectious disease. But the clincher was when I realized the reason you were in the hallway the night of the murder. You were up with a case of the sweats, weren't you?"

"What do you know about the sweats?"

"I come from the Bay Area, remember. You don't live there long without learning the basic symptoms. That's why you happened to find Barry staggering out of his room. Right?"

For the first time, Matthew indicated the extent of his involvement with the murder by giving a slight nod.

Jason heaved a sigh of relief. "That's what I thought."

Matthew spoke hoarsely. "He was already in the hall,

groaning, on all fours. I . . . I didn't know what to do. I started yelling."

"Never mind about that now. The sign on the door . . . Did you tell the doctors about your condition last night when you were admitted?"

Matthew shook his head. "No."

"Okay. That seems to imply they found out from another source. Tell me, when did you first learn about your . . . condition?"

The question seemed to frighten him and he turned away without answering.

"All right, never mind. Let's see if I can guess. You started having something like a cold you couldn't seem to shake, so you checked in with the University infirmary. They monitored your condition for a time, but you weren't getting better. So they ran some tests and came up with this discovery. What was it, two or three months ago?"

Again, no response.

"How else could the hospital have found out about your"—he searched his mind for another euphemism—"situation so rapidly? Now listen, this may be important. When did you find out about your condition?"

Matthew turned toward him with some of his old viciousness. "I'm not going to help you, if that's what you want. There's enough misery in the world. You should have kept your nose out of things and left me alone. Let me die with a modicum of peace, will you?"

"I wouldn't call playing the central character in a murder trial peaceful."

"Why don't you let me worry about that?"

"Matthew, there's no way you could have gotten through a trial and a conviction without the district attorney finding out about your illness. This country no longer practices speedy trials, in spite of what our founding fathers may have said.''

The door to the room flew open and Lieutenant Newcombe entered with a nurse, followed close behind by Sergeant Weir. They stopped short at the sight of the figure in green.

''Sorry, Doctor.'' The lieutenant started to retreat, but then he recognized Jason. ''Just what the devil are you doing in here?''

''I'm doing your work for you, Lieutenant.''

''Nurse!'' Newcombe boomed. ''This man has no business in here!''

The befuddled nurse stepped forward. ''Pardon me, do I know you?''

''Not unless you are taking a psychology class at the University. I'm leaving quietly. Good-bye, Matthew.''

Jason stepped past the entourage into the hallway, but Newcombe followed and grabbed him by the arm, tearing the paper sleeve.

''Is there something wrong with your hearing? I told you no visitors.''

''Hey, easy on the sleeve. This is my good suit.''

''I could have you arrested, you know that?''

''No, Lieutenant, I don't think so. What would the charge be—getting lost in the hospital?''

''Listen, smart aleck. You're in over your head. Didn't you read the sign on the door?''

Newcombe took Jason by the arm and led him down the corridor away from Matthew's room, then went on in a lower voice. ''It so happens, smart guy, that Tye is a very sick boy. And I don't think you want to be spending time hanging around here.''

''So you know,'' Jason said.

Newcombe blinked at him. ''How did you find out?''

Jason looked at Fred, who stood nearby with crossed

arms. He seemed to be checking to see if his own shoes were shined. Jason guessed he hadn't told his boss about his phone conversation with the upstart psychologist, and he would be just as happy if Newcombe never found out.

''Oh, I put two and two together,'' Jason replied. ''This puts an entirely different light on the murder, doesn't it?''

''Yes, it certainly does. It strengthens Tye's motive. Maybe Peterson found out about his condition and Tye killed him to keep him quiet. Or there was a lover's quar—''

''Oh, Lieutenant, we're not going back to that, are we? Don't you see what the boy was trying to do? He was trying to commit suicide. He was trying to get himself killed by the state.''

''Ridiculous! Why would anyone in his right mind want to do that?''

''I'm not so sure he was in his right mind. He is a terribly tormented kid who feels his life is over. AIDS is a death sentence, Lieutenant. And remember, he was raised in a strict family environment—''

''Oh, brother,'' Newcombe groaned. ''Here comes the psychological mumbo jumbo.''

''Yes, Lieutenant. That's where we all do our living and our scheming. Inside our heads. He was raised in a strict environment that condemned homosexual activity in no uncertain terms. Now he's faced with a double whammy—with two albatrosses about his neck, as it were. And the thought of his parents and friends finding out about all this was more than he could stand. He would rather have his parents think of him as a murderer.

''Then this golden opportunity presented itself. He found Peterson dying in the upstairs hallway of the fraternity. When the other students came out and found them there, naturally they assumed that the troublesome loner, Matthew, had committed the murder. All he had to do to continue the charade was keep his mouth shut."

Newcombe had started shaking his head midway through Jason's explanation, and near the end, the tempo of the shakes picked up. "It won't play. Your psychological contortions won't cut it this time. We've got a very unsympathetic personality that we can place at the murder scene, with the murder weapon in his hand. And with a little more prying, we're going to have motives coming out of our ears. You mark my words."

Jason looked at Fred, but he was still avoiding eye contact with them both. It was hard to tell what he thought.

"Say, don't you ever have classes to teach?" Newcombe said. Then he used his hands to hurry Jason out of the area, as a farmer's wife directs baby chicks. "Get along home now, sonny."

In the outer corridor Jason found a men's room and threw his disguise away. He felt an overwhelming need to wash his hands and face and spent several minutes at the sink.

At the university infirmary Jason waited for the nurse to finish up with a young female student, then introduced himself. The nurse was a motherly woman named Mrs. Towner. Jason was convinced the University would have to close its doors if the Grandmother's Union ever went out on strike. He closed the door to her small office behind him and sat in the interview chair.

"May I ask you a strictly hypothetical question?" he asked.

She laughed. "I get a lot of those kinds of questions.

'I have a friend who is having trouble with . . .' Only there usually is no friend."

He smiled. "Yes, I see what you mean. But this is a little different. Can you tell me if there are any ground rules about notifying the authorities if you should identify a student with AIDS?"

This wiped the warm smile off her face. "Mr. Bradley, I'm sure you understand that confidentiality is vital if we are to have the trust of our patients."

"Yes, certainly." He waited.

"What is your purpose in asking that question?"

Jason thought about that for a while. "I take it you do have a policy?"

"Mr. Bradley, you aren't answering my question."

"Nor you mine."

"Are you concerned about the contagious nature of the disease? Because if you are, it can only be transmitted sexually by the transference of body fluids—"

"I know that. Thank you. But isn't it possible that the University could be held liable if this infirmary identifies a student with AIDS but does nothing? Suppose another student is infected by the student you knew had the disease but did nothing about?"

Her expression had now turned sour. "Are you saying that such a condition now exists?"

"No, I'm not. Please stop reading things into my questions. All I want to know is, what would you do if you discovered a student had come to you for help and you diagnosed AIDS?"

"We would notify the patient, of course."

"Would you notify anyone else?"

"Such as?"

"Such as the Administration."

She fingered the blood pressure gauge on her desk while she thought about that. "Mr. Bradley, if you have a health problem, I'll be glad to help you. Otherwise, I don't think there is anything I can do. Do you understand?''

''Yes, I guess I do.''

Jason thanked Nurse Towner for her time and excused himself. Since he hadn't found out what he wanted to know, he'd have to wing it from here.

It was eleven-fifteen. He was late.

Chapter Nineteen

"You are late, Mr. Bradley," Elsie Berkaw announced, with a trace of pleasure in her voice. She was standing next to her favorite window overlooking her university world, a ruler in her hand.

"I apologize. I had some important business to take care of."

"More important than seeing your university president?"

"I said I was sorry. You aren't going to spank me, are you?"

"What?" She made the connection with the ruler, then snapped it briskly onto her desk and buzzed her boss.

"Mr. Bradley has just come in, sir," she said on the phone, then hung up. "He'll be with you in a moment."

Today she was wearing a white-on-white blouse with a high collar and lots of buttons on the tight sleeves. On her bodice sparkled an ornate pin with a tiny watch dangling from it. She looked like a parody of herself.

Jason sat down near her. "I hear you blew the whistle on the fraternity boys after their horse-in-the-chemistry-lab stunt." He tried to sound admiring.

She looked at him, first over the old-fashioned glasses,

then through them. "I most certainly did. It put a stop to that foolishness in short order."

"How did you manage to do that?"

"It was pure coincidence, really. I happened to find out that they bought the horse from my nephew east of town."

"I'm surprised the culprits were not thrown out of school."

"There's no need to be vindictive, is there? The important thing was to get the nonsense stopped. I think President Rollins followed the right course."

"Did the pranks stop?" Jason asked.

"Why, yes. Of course they did. Why?"

"I'm just curious. There have been so many odd things happening lately, I thought maybe the pranks were continuing."

"I seriously doubt that. After all, the boys gave their word."

"I see," Jason said musingly. "Those Beta boys are really something."

"Actually," she said with a sniff, "it was Robert Ernshaw of the Farley House who bought the horse."

"Farley House? What's that?"

"It's a new fraternity house. They don't have their charter yet, so they don't go by the Greek letters."

"So why did Beta Rho get put on probation?"

"I really don't know. All we know is that the boys came forward and confessed, and that was the end of that."

"But—" Jason was interrupted by two quick buzzes from the president.

"You may go in now, Mr. Bradley."

"Thank you," he said. He straightened his tie in the reflection of the glass in the large clock in the corner, then went on in.

Rollins was in his shirtsleeves working at a paper-strewn desk. He looked up over his reading glasses and gestured at a chair. "Come in, young man. I'm happy to see you finally made it."

While Rollins concluded whatever he was working on, Jason looked at the pictures on the wall behind his desk. Funny, he hadn't noticed them before. Maybe he was too shook-up about the videotape on his last visit to the inner chambers. Lots of hand shaking and plaque giving. Dodger infielders and old Ram quarterbacks were shown with their arms about President Rollins. And there was a shot of Rollins in his playing days, a helmet tucked under his arm, jaw firmly set as he looked off into the distance toward a glorious future. Framed with that shot was the all-American certificate he had won his senior year.

Jason had often wondered what happened to former all-American athletes. Do they gather annually for a banquet in some lofty Elysium setting? Do they grow old and stout, hanging pictures of past triumphs on their office walls while they struggle at jobs unsuited to their mentalities, and spend their evenings wondering why the glory has gone from their lives? It was easy for Jason to imagine all that, for he had experienced the same things on a smaller scale after his triumphs on the basketball court his junior year. The world hadn't been responding to the head fake the way small college guards in his old league did. He was still feeling his way. He wondered if Rollins was, too.

With his desk finally cleared, Rollins turned his attention to his new problem at hand. He smiled at Jason. No doubt it was the same smile he used on opposing quarterbacks as he lined up over center.

"I understand Kitteridge talked with you about our

new policy regarding the University's hiring requirements."

It appeared the videotape thing was a dead issue. Jason cleared his throat. "Yes, sir."

"We want to be assured of the depth of Christian commitment in all our new teachers. We don't want any more surprises."

"I can see your point," Jason said. "But it goes against my grain, somehow. Do you understand what I mean?"

"Yes, I do. If you are not a team player I can certainly respect your feelings. I blame Kitteridge for this, really. He was the one who rushed out and hired you before we had a chance to talk about the kind of person we really would like in this position. He's a dear old codger, but I'm afraid he doesn't use good judgment sometimes.

"Please understand, you have the position until the end of term, and we will not withhold favorable references, should you want them."

"It sounds like you are anxious to be rid of me, Dr. Rollins."

"What? Why, no, no such thing." He moved uneasily in his leather chair.

"Have you drawn up a form you are asking people to sign?"

"Yes, we have." He got a sheet out of his side drawer and pushed it across his desk to Jason, who scanned it quickly.

It looked like an abbreviated version of the Nicene Creed: "I believe in God the Father Almighty and in Jesus Christ His Son our Lord . . ."

Jason moved forward in his chair. "Nothing here a committed Christian wouldn't be willing to sign, I should say."

"Correct."

"I'm just interested in how this came about."

"I thought you understood," Rollins said, with a slight edge to his voice. "It is an attempt to stop all the bad publicity. Er, that is, to get this school back to what it is all about: education in a Christian environment."

"Yes, I see. You mean because of Dr. Hacchi's suicide."

"Yes, in part."

"But I understood Dr. Hacchi had gone through a conversion experience before his suicide."

"Well, yes, some people think that he . . ."

"So that means Hacchi would have been willing to sign a document like this himself."

"Well, yes, I suppose he would have."

"So the document itself would not have prevented the man's suicide. Is that right?"

"Look, you want to argue fine points, you go right ahead. You might also say that the devil himself would be willing to sign such a pledge. But the fact remains: This document will let new people know where we stand."

"I see."

"There are plenty of people, myself included, who think Hacchi was not on the level with his so-called conversion to Christianity."

"Why is that?" Jason asked with genuine interest.

"I think the man was unbalanced."

"But if that were the case, why did you let him go on teaching?"

"I didn't mean the man couldn't function. What I meant was he had a lot on his mind. He was upset."

"About what?"

Rollins got up from his chair and assumed a defensive spread. "Are you or are you not willing to sign this?"

Jason tried to be conciliatory. "I'm merely asking about the man I'm supposed to be replacing. If Hacchi was out of his mind, I think I'm entitled to know why. Had he been given some bad news?"

"What do you mean by that?"

"Dr. Rollins, you said the man was unbalanced. You must have some reason for thinking that." Jason looked as innocent as he could.

"I told you, he was distraught."

"So you naturally inquired what he was distraught about."

"Say, what is this, a third degree?"

"Was he upset about a student's illness, perchance?"

Rollins nervously rolled his tongue over his lips; then he pushed his white hair back over his ears. "What makes you say that?"

Jason knew he had hit pay dirt. Now the question was, how to draw the information out of him. "You knew he was disturbed, and you knew what he was disturbed about, didn't you, Dr. Rollins?" Jason sat as quietly as he could and watched the president starting to perspire. "About Matthew Tye's condition . . ."

The old linebacker had just figured out he'd been blindsided. His eyes narrowed and his jowls turned crimson. "All right, what's this all about? You have something you want to get off your chest?"

"Yes, I do." Jason tried to keep his voice smooth and conversational. "The way I see it, the doctor from the clinic told you about Matthew Tye's condition, didn't he? It's not too difficult to figure out what happened next. Knowing your penchant for directness, I think you tried to find out how such a thing could have happened on this special campus—how the son of your old football teammate could contract such a disease. And it wouldn't have taken you long to find out about Hacchi's influence over Matthew Tye. Everyone on campus seemed to know that story. Elsie Berkaw knew, and I doubt seriously if she would have withheld such information from you. I hear Hacchi ridiculed Christian morality because it inhibits healthy mental adjustment. No sin means no psychosis, et cetera. And all this led our missionary's son, who probably had latent homosexual interests, to start experimenting, to start pursuing rather than inhibiting some of his secret desires.

"Again, I think you followed your natural tendencies. You called Hacchi here and confronted him with what you knew about Matthew Tye."

Rollins sat down heavily. "My, my, such a vivid imagination."

"And I think you probably did a little vindictive leaning on him, with plenty of righteous indignation thrown in. Something like: 'You see what your hedonistic humanism has cost this poor boy? Are you proud of yourself, Dr. Hacchi? Proud of destroying this boy's life with your sexual revolution?' "

"That's enough!" Rollins roared.

"You were right to say Hacchi had things on his mind, because you put them there, didn't you, Dr. Rollins? You laid a guilt trip on that man that wouldn't quit. You'd probably been waiting for years to get him. He was a tenured professor who could speak his mind right in the midst of the faithful, and he'd been festering there in the classroom where you couldn't touch him, like a burr under your shoulder pads, undermining your moral principles."

Rollins eyed Jason narrowly. "All right, young man. Yes, I showed him the fruits of his labor. And why shouldn't I? He was so eager to condemn the moral standards of our community, I wanted him to see what the world is like without those standards. What are you getting so high and mighty about?''

''Dr. Rollins, the man went over to the Faulker Building and took his own life. Don't you feel just a little bit of remorse?''

''And you think I'm responsible for that?''

''I don't know. Are you?''

Rollins snorted. ''Why did he wait until three weeks after our talk to do the job?''

Jason blinked.

''You didn't know about that, did you? You thought you knew everything. Well, you're not going to hang that at my feet. I wash my hands of it.'' He literally wrung his hands before him. ''I have an obligation to this institution, to the principles of this institution, and to the board. That's where my loyalties lie.''

''So for three weeks,'' Jason pondered, ''Hacchi lived with that knowledge, and it preyed on his mind. Then he tried to show his remorse by seeking forgiveness in Christ.''

''By hiding behind Christianity,'' Rollins corrected.

''Oh, so it wasn't a genuine conversion, is that it? You're the judge and jury on that account?''

''You weren't here, Mr. Bradley, to see how he acted afterward. The man was illogical. He started singing in the middle of a staff meeting, trying to disrupt it.''

''Singing what?''

''Who knows? It was in a monotone. He was only baiting me. The man had already used up all his sympathy points with me and with the whole staff. I couldn't manage him. And I didn't want any part of him.''

''I see. . . .''

''No, you don't see. You don't know the kind of abuse I've taken, the fears I've had to live with. Is Tye an isolated case, or is he the tip of an iceberg? He assured me he got the disease off campus, but how can I be sure? And what do I do? Kick him out of school, only to have him throw a lawsuit at us and publicize the whole thing? I could end up the president of a ghost town, not a university! I've been in a living hell."

The two men sat quietly for the first time. Jason again became aware of the clocks ticking.

Dr. Rollins' armpits had been perspiring freely against his shirt and vest. He found a Kleenex in a drawer and wiped his neck until the tissue rolled up and tore apart. He wadded it the rest of the way and fired it into the wastebasket with finality.

"I have no trouble living with my conscience," he announced. "I'm sorry Hacchi couldn't manage to do the same. I love this school, and nothing, *nothing* is going to damage it while I . . ." Without finishing the thought he reached for another tissue and continued the wiping. "Now, are you going to sign that document or not?"

Jason got to his feet. "I have one more question, Dr. Rollins. Did you destroy that videotape?"

Rollins cleared his throat, which didn't need clearing, then casually pushed his hair back over his ears. His cheeks had gone ashen. "What videotape would that be?"

"The one you and I talked about on my last visit here. The one you took out of my office."

"What makes you—"

"Oh, please. Don't sit there and try to deny it. There weren't that many people who knew about it, and you are the only one with enough beef in your shoulder to punch in my office door. And you are the one with the clock fetish. I always operate with my office clock set ten minutes fast. But while you were visiting my office, you couldn't resist turning it back to the right time, and you made me late for class for the first time in my brief and fading career as a university professor. Did you destroy the tape, Doctor? The girl wants to know.''

Rollins pinched his eyes shut and held his head in his hands. ''I knew this was going to happen. I knew it. The minute Kitteridge started talking about bringing you here. Why didn't you stay away? Damn you, Bradley.''

''And a hearty thank-you for that warm welcome.''

''Don't you care at all what happens to Trinity? Yes, I took your tape and I erased it. Don't you realize what such publicity could do to us? The effect it could have on denominational giving?''

''Does that excuse breaking and entering? And stealing? And withholding evidence in a murder investigation? That's why you had to steal it, instead of just asking me to hand it over to you. You didn't want it to look like you were destroying evidence.'' Jason turned the pledge paper around and pushed it back toward the president. ''Here. Maybe you are the one who needs to sign this.''

Rollins got to his feet and crumpled the pledge in the same motion. ''Listen, fella, I don't have to take your crap. Everything I've done has been for the good of this school. All my adult life has been tied to this institution. Do you know anything about such loyalty? No, I should think not. I've given my life's blood. I played three games my senior year with a broken bone in my right foot. Don't talk to me about what's right. I love this place!'' He suddenly ran out of steam, but kept on gesturing at Jason as if more words were on the way. But it was because he was fighting tears that the words stopped coming. He sat down in the large desk chair and stared at his adversary.

''Yes, I believe you do love this place,'' Jason said quietly. ''Kitteridge said that about you. It was really what got me to thinking about you. He said you loved the school too much."

When Jason closed the door to the president's office behind him, he heaved a sigh of relief. But things weren't quieting down inside him. His heart was pounding, and he felt as if he had a chicken bone stuck halfway down his esophagus.

He had just faced his nemesis and had left him on the verge of tears. His brilliant wordplay and deductive logic had won the day. Victory was his. So why did he feel like a piece of garbage?

Outside, the world was going on its merry way. The weather had cleared, and classes would be letting out any minute. The Chapel carillon had already started ringing its noontime selection of old hymn favorites.

Amazing grace, how sweet the sound,
That saved a wretch like me . . .

The brilliant California sun played on the pink blossoms of the bougainvillea branches that arched over the Administration Building's breezeway. The colors were so vibrant they were hard to look at. For a minute Jason thought they were causing the sick feeling in his stomach.

As he walked by the Science and Technology Building, the two large lecture halls emptied a horde of happy students out onto the campus. They ignored the tired young teacher in his poorly fitted suit. Jason found them to be like creatures from another planet. They were jubilant to be out of class for the day—and it was Friday. That meant kickback time. Maybe hit the beach for a while. Maybe touch football on the Quad. The agonies of life would have to wait for them for another day.

"Watch it!" a familiar female voice yelled.

Jason went up on his toes in order to stop in his tracks. From a connecting crosswalk, Annie from Audiovisual came barreling by on her electric cart, on her way to deliver a sixteen-millimeter projector someplace. Her "Are you lost? Ask me" sign brushed against Jason's pants, and she was gone again as silently as she had appeared. Somebody ought to put a bell on that woman.

Chapter Twenty

Jason headed for the records office once again and looked up the schedule of Robert Ernshaw, the mysterious horse buyer. As he did so, he had the distinct feeling he was floundering about without any real direction, pursuing one more question that was bound to be answered by three more questions in what seemed to be an endless cycle. He thought of all the loose strings that had been left dangling: Hacchi's unexplained activities before his suicide, Hillary Reed and her bedroom, the girlfriend that Hacchi and Clark unknowingly shared, the strange interest in Shaker music . . . Well, at least it would keep him off the streets at night.

Robert Ernshaw turned out to be a freckle-faced kid that Jason had already seen several times busing dishes in the cafeteria. Jason caught up with the boy as lunchtime traffic in the main dining room started to thin down.

"Hi, Bob. Do they call you Bob?" Jason asked.

The boy eyed him innocently and put a load of trays into his cleanup cart. "Yeah. Who are you?"

"I'm Jason Bradley, the new psychology teacher, picking up for Dr. Hacchi. Mind if I ask you a couple of questions?" Jason sat down at one of the empty tables and pulled a chair out for the boy.

Bob looked off toward his supervisor, working the cash register, and hesitated.

"It's okay. I talked with your boss," Jason assured him.

Bob slid uneasily into the chair and smiled nervously. "What's up?"

"I understand you bought a horse last semester. Could you tell me about it?"

Bob's face flushed, and he wiped his hands on his cleaning rag. "Why? That's an old story now."

"Okay, so bore me with the details. How come you bought the horse?"

"I . . . uh . . . bought it for somebody else."

"For the members of the Beta Rho Fraternity?"

"That's right. I even gave them a bill of sale when I resold it to them."

"Very formal about it, weren't you?"

"I guess so. Look, I got tables to clean and a one-thirty appointment."

"Whose idea was the bill of sale?"

"I forget."

"A lot of extra work, just for a glue factory horse that they were going to shoot in the chemistry closet anyway. Was it Richard Clark's idea?"

"Come to think of it, I guess it was."

"I thought so. He seems to be the one with all the ideas over there."

Bob snickered. "You're right. He's rich, too."

"So he just asked you out of the blue to go out and buy a horse for him? Why didn't he have one of his own fraternity brothers buy it? Why did he pick you?"

Bob shrugged. "Why don't you ask him?"

"I'm asking you. Didn't it seem a bit strange to you at the time?"

"No, not really."

"Do you have a car?"

"Yeah, I got my grandmother's old Dodge. It gets me around."

"Did you have a horse trailer and a hitch for your car?"

The boy looked increasingly uncomfortable. "I rented them."

"Did Clark reimburse you for that, too?"

"Ah . . ." He paused much too long.

"Oh, come now, Bob." Jason was in a bad mood, and he felt a certain blunt necessity to lean on the boy. Bob started to get up, but Jason put a hand on his shoulder. "I've been doing a little reading over at the records office. You're a science major, aren't you, Bob?"

"Yeah, chemical engineering. I'm just a sophomore. I might change."

"All the guys in the Farley House are science and engineering guys, aren't they?"

"Yeah. We want a frat house of our own."

"You know what I think? I think the horse prank sounds like a Farley House idea more than a Beta Rho scheme. What do you think?"

Bob only shrugged and twisted his towel.

"I'm sorry, Bob, but I think your story stinks."

"Okay, so it stinks. So what?"

"So why don't we go down and see how the police like it?"

"Police?" He squirmed.

"There was a murder in the Beta House Wednesday morning."

"I had nothing to do with that! I didn't even know the guy. Hardly."

"Are you sure, Bob? Are you certain there's no connection?"

"What is that supposed to mean? What's all this to you, anyway?"

Jason gave him his best steely-eyed stare. "We're going to get to the bottom of this one way or another. Now, do you want to tell me what really happened, or do you want me to go to the police with my information?"

"What information? What are you trying to do here?"

"The horse prank was supposed to be the Farley House prank, wasn't it, Bob? Tell me the truth. I'm not going to go tattling to the Administration, if that's what you're worried about."

"Oh, crime-in-itly," Bob moaned, throwing his rag at the cleanup cart. For a moment his eyes darted around the room, as if he were looking for moral support from some fellow students. But when help didn't materialize, he slumped back in his chair and gave a nervous sneer. "If this gets out, we're gonna lose our fraternity charter. Yeah, you're right. It was our prank. There was this stupid contest, see, among the fraternities, and we got invited to participate, even though we aren't really a frat house yet."

"Your group put the horse in the chem lab, right?"

"Right. But then I got tagged. The guy I bought the horse from identified my picture in the yearbook. With all my freckles I stood out like a neon light. President Rollins was going to start a formal hearing about it, and we heard we would lose our charter."

"So, why didn't you?"

"Rich came over to the house and offered to bail us out. He said Beta House would say it was their prank and they would take all the flak."

"Why would he offer to do a thing like that?"

"He said he didn't want to see us get bounced. If the Beta guys admitted they did it, the administration probably wouldn't hit them so hard. And they didn't. They only got probation and the juniors and lower classmen had to room somewhere else.''

Jason was perplexed. This didn't fit in with the mental image he was building of the infamous Mr. Clark. The aroma of this story was almost as bad as that of the first version. He looked Bob Ernshaw over, freckle by freckle, but couldn't see why the boy would come up with this tale unless he thought it was the truth.

''Clark doesn't impress me as the kind that goes around doing favors.''

''Oh, I don't know,'' Bob said. ''After Dr. Hacchi's death a lot of people on campus became kind of softhearted, you know. Kind of reflective about life . . .''

''You say this offer of help came after Dr. Hacchi's death?''

''Yeah, right after. Why?''

Jason got to his feet. ''Thanks, Bob. You've been a big help.''

''Does all this have to come out? The other guys will skin me alive if they find out I've been talking.''

''Maybe not. I'll see what I can do.''

The advanced tennis class for girls was just finishing up for the hour. Jason asked the instructor if Tracy Rice was about. She pointed to a stately blonde in the far court still volleying with a fellow student. Jason walked closer and watched. Tracy showed a very good backhand for a casual player. When her practicing partner cried for relief, they finally decided to call it a day.

Jason waited by the gate and introduced himself when she came by. ''Do you mind if I ask you some questions? I understand you used to date Barry Peterson.''

She stopped in her tracks. ''What kind of questions?''

''Dean Kitteridge and I are trying to gain some understanding of what happened. I'd like to know more about Barry."

She picked up her towel and dried her face, then looked right at Jason. "I'm not sure I can talk about it yet. But then, maybe I should. It seems like nobody talks about him now—as if everything there was to say came out in the Chapel service, and now nobody talks about him. I think the other kids have started avoiding me just so they won't have to talk about him."

She got very busy putting her racket in its protective cover and canning some of her tennis balls. Jason picked up a sweater that appeared to belong to her and held it for her.

"I'm a psychologist, Tracy, if that helps any. I'm supposed to be able to help people in times of crisis."

She took the sweater from him and tossed it around her neck. "I gotta shower pretty soon or my calves cramp up. What do you want to know?"

They started a slow stroll in the direction of the women's locker room.

"Were you and Barry thinking of getting married?"

Tracy inhaled sharply and let the breath out slowly. "We talked about it. That was all. He had his heart set on doing work like his father's—Christian broadcasting in foreign countries—but I wasn't wild about foreign living. That was our hang-up."

"But I take it you liked each other well enough."

"He wanted to give me a ring at Christmas, but I said we should . . . wait." In an effort to keep things light, she tossed her racket into the air. The handle came around faster than she was expecting and Jason ended up retrieving her racket off the asphalt. Tracy had buried her face in her towel again and was a little while coming out of it.

"Now, you know, I think of all the things I should

have said. It really gets to you. I should have said I'd go overseas with him. It seems like such a little thing now. It probably wouldn't have been so bad, living in Singapore or someplace. I wish I hadn't been so difficult. His folks are flying in for the funeral. They'll be here tonight."

"Would you say that Barry was a tidy person?"

"Yeah, he was. What a strange thing to ask."

"There were signs of a struggle in his room. I was just wondering if the struggle could have happened earlier and he simply hadn't bothered to clean things up before going to bed."

"Oh, no. There was a broken bottle, wasn't there? I read about it in the paper. Barry would never go to bed without cleaning up a mess like that. He would even go home and change his slacks if they got a spot on them."

They had reached the locker room, and Jason had to get to the point.

"Tracy, I've got to ask you a difficult question. I hope you'll understand I'm not doing it to pry into your personal life. It may have a bearing on the murder. Do you know for a fact that Barry was strictly heterosexual?"

"Why, what a cruel, stupid thing to say! Of course he was. The poor guy is dead, and you start rumors like that? What on earth—"

"Okay, okay! That's good enough for me. I just had to be sure. If you say he was, that's all the assurance I need."

"Well, now, wait a minute. What do you mean by that? We didn't ever, you know, go all the way or anything like that. But I could tell. We always talked about having children and how we'd, you know, be together. We're both Christian and believe in the sanctity of the marriage bed."

"That's fine. I understand."

She had started using the racket to gesture with, and Jason was as concerned about his safety as he was about calming her down.

"Hey, wait a minute." She stopped in midstroke. "Is that guy who killed him gay? You think he killed him over some sort of lovers' quarrel? Oh, no. Oh, gad, no. Barry couldn't stand queers."

"How do you know that? Did you talk about it for some specific reason?"

"No, no specific reason. But he said they gave him the willies. He hated them."

"Not a very Christian attitude, I should say."

"Christian," she cried. "Why, of course it's Christian. Moses spoke against homosexuals, and the prophets did, whenever they talked about them. Jesus did, and so did St. Paul. What do you mean, not Christian?"

"Okay, okay." Jason stepped back, out of range of the reactivated tennis racket. "I guess I have a lot to learn about your theology. I was under the impression that forgiveness and compassion fit in there someplace."

"Oh, they do, but a person has to recant his sins first. How can you forgive someone something if he's still doing it?"

"Is that the way Barry felt, too?"

"Of course it is. What other way is there? I mean, if you go by the rules. That's what the Bible is, mostly—rules about how we should live. Well, isn't it?"

"I see your point. Yes, thank you, Tracy. A set of rules."

"You oughta read the Book of James if you don't believe me."

"Okay, I'll put that on my reading list," Jason assured her. ''I imagine Barry got into a few arguments about topics like that, didn't he?''

''They were always arguing about something at the house. Why?''

''I was just wondering if maybe he'd had a run-in with, say, Richard Clark about anything.''

''Yeah. How'd you know? Barry had a mouse under his right eye last week, and when I asked him about it, he said he got it in a shoving match with Richard.''

''What about? Religion?''

''I don't know. Maybe.''

She reached down and rubbed her right calf. ''I gotta go. I'm tightening up.''

''Yes, okay. Thanks for talking to me.''

''Glad to. I think talking helps. I don't think we should forget our loved ones, ever. Do you?''

''No, I don't think so, either.''

She smiled and pushed some wet hair away from her cheek. ''Sorry about yelling at you. You understand, don't you?''

''All is forgiven.''

Jason watched as she trotted down the hallway in her white tennis outfit. Innocence incarnate. Or ignorance. He wasn't sure which.

Chapter Twenty-One

Jason climbed the circular stairway to the Prayer Tower, all one hundred and sixty-two steps. There was a small elevator in service, but he held to a theory that physical exercise stimulated his thinking process, and he had decided this would be a dandy time for a little help.

By the time he reached the top, he had barely broken a sweat and had had no revelations. He sat on one of the long cement benches that looped around the main floor and looked about as he waited for Dean Kitteridge. He was surprised at how small the circular room was, scarcely thirty-five feet in diameter. It looked so monstrous from the ground. And how sparse. Cold benches, a few small tables, kneeling pedestals for those who wanted to kneel for prayer, and a plentiful assortment of paperback Bibles on the one small bookshelf.

The large glass windows were closed on the west and southwest sides of the room, no doubt against the prevailing breeze from the ocean. The other windows were tilted out, open to the great outdoors. Jason stood on a bench and tried to look down onto campus. The place was obviously not designed for sight-seeing. It took a real neck-craning effort to see below.

He watched the people moving about on the walkways, like markers on a game board, and he couldn't help but think what a logical place it would be for a suicide leap. He wondered why Hacchi had not used it in place of the rope. Was it the spiritual connotations of the place that had turned him away?

The elevator door opened and Dean Kitteridge waved.

"Thank you for coming," Kitteridge said as he slid onto the bench next to Jason. "I wanted to find out how things had gone with President Rollins."

"It was a standoff. We got on to another topic that seemed a bit more pressing."

"What topic was that?" the dean asked.

Jason heaved a sigh and launched into his explanation, including Matthew's illness and his attempt to get himself executed. He tried to keep his report as dry as possible, but halfway through he found his voice doing strange warbly things that undermined the cool image he tried to portray. Matthew's illness had gotten to him, even more than the murder had. Or was it the accumulation of events? Death all around them. Past, present, and future.

Outwardly Kitteridge took it better than Jason was expecting. After he'd heard the full story, Kitteridge slid over to one of the prayer benches, knelt down, and prayed silently for what seemed several minutes. Jason, embarrassed, sat nervously by, not knowing exactly what was expected of him. He wondered if Kitteridge had selected the Tower as their meeting place because he'd been expecting something like this.

When Kitteridge finally recovered from his prayer time, Jason dealt him another blow. He explained that Rollins had taken the videotape in an attempt to cover up the whole thing.

"I'm afraid I made something of an ass of myself,"

Jason admitted. "I was so upset with the man, and with that pledge, that I read him the riot act. Now that I've thought about it, I can see that in a way I was doing the same things to him that he did to Dr. Hacchi—forcing my opinions on him and browbeating him. I don't know that my perspective on the whole thing is any better than his. At least he has the University's interests at heart, however he tries to protect them. In the long run, is serving empirical truth always best? We've all been standing on soapboxes—me, Rollins, Dr. Hacchi, Matthew. Where do we get these all-important convictions? Maybe we're all a bunch of self-righteous prigs."

"That is a very intelligent observation." Kitteridge smiled. "You have wisdom beyond your years."

"I don't know what you mean by that," Jason grumbled. "I don't feel very wise."

"Judgment belongs to God. That's a lesson most people never learn, I'm afraid."

Jason got up and paced. "You remember the prank that got the Beta House on probation?"

"Yes, the horse in the chemistry lab. What about it?"

"It turns out that Farley House actually committed that prank, but the Betas took the rap for them."

Kitteridge was slow in assimilating that new idea. "Why would they do a thing like that?"

"My question, precisely. They're not exactly a selfless bunch, and it's totally out of keeping with the ringleader over there. So I asked myself, what possible *selfish* reason could there be for them to take the blame publicly?" Jason was almost thinking out loud. "There must have been another prank that the Betas either had committed or were in the process of committing, a prank we don't even know about yet. Something involving Dr. Hacchi in some way. You see, it was immediately *after*

Hacchi's death that they made the offer to plead guilty about the horse thing. They needed a cover."

"But they *did* commit another prank," Kitteridge said. "The videotape thing was certainly a prank, wasn't it?"

"I thought the same thing at first. It was a prank, yes, but it doesn't qualify for the contest among the fraternities. You see, the butt of that joke was one of their own members. The other pranks are all at the expense of other parties. The horse one was against the Chemistry Department, and it was pulled by a group of students who have to take chemistry. The president's car on the roof speaks for itself. The loudspeakers in the ladies' bathrooms was against women, I presume. And I think Beta House was working on a prank that was supposed to be at Dr. Hacchi's expense. What could it have been? I'd give anything to know what was going through the man's mind last November and December. Did you notice any change in him?"

Kitteridge shook his head.

"What about illness? Did he meet all his classes? He'd have to report to you if he were ill, wouldn't he?"

"He did have an emergency appendectomy during that time, but it happened on a Friday and he only missed two days of classes. I told him to take off the following week, but he didn't. I'd say he enjoyed very good health. I'm sorry, Jason, but I don't see what all this had to do with the Peterson murder."

Jason slumped down next to the older man and rubbed his forehead. "I don't know, either. That's what's driving me batty."

"What about Matthew Tye? Maybe when they learned about his condition, they wanted to hush the matter up."

Jason shook his head. "Only the medical staff and President Rollins knew about that. At this point I think that Matthew Tye's appearance in the hallway was just an unexpected occurrence that happened to get in the way."

Kitteridge pulled on his lower lip. "He's still the number-one suspect as far as the police are concerned."

"Well, the police are all wet," Jason declared.

Kitteridge looked at him and smiled his sad smile, but didn't say anything.

"We've got to know more about the people involved. What do we really know about Peterson? According to his girlfriend, he was a very conservative moralist. What's a guy like that doing in the midst of a prank contest? And there were a total of twelve students in the Beta House on the night of the murder, according to the police. We've got to get to know . . ."

But the dean was slowly shaking his head. "I'm rather sorry now that I got you involved in all this. I'm no longer so certain we should be pursuing this."

"What do you mean?"

"Perhaps the police are right. Perhaps Matthew did kill Peterson. And then, again, if he didn't, that means someone else did. From what you are saying, it was probably another student, or even a group of students. Is that really what we want to discover?" He sighed dejectedly. "I have no enthusiasm for the hunt simply for the hunt's sake."

"You seem to be saying that since Matthew is probably going to die anyway, we may as well let him die with a murder on his head. Is that what you think?"

"No, no. Of course not."

"We have to keep after this: The most compelling reason for pursuing this is that we have a murderer in our midst. And if the murder was committed in order to keep Peterson quiet about something, then there is the strong possibility that there is someone else who will have to be kept quiet. We may not have seen the end of our problems."

"Oh, Lord, don't say that."

"Well, I'm sorry, but I'm telling you what I think."

"Isn't it all the more reason why we should just leave the whole thing in the hands of the police?"

"You met Lieutenant Newcombe. You have a great deal of confidence in him, do you?"

"He is probably a very competent man."

"I see," Jason said coldly.

"We are educators, Jason. Not policemen."

"And what is education if it isn't the seeking after truth?"

"I guess you and I have different ideas of what the truth is."

Jason snorted. "The truth is what is."

"Are you sure, Jason? Are you so very sure?"

"Why? What's your definition?"

"I always thought of the truth as . . . what ought to be."

"I guess that's where we differ, you and I. Faith and all is nice. But it's doubt that'll get you an education."

Kitteridge turned his sad eyes on Jason. "Yes, but will it give you a reason for living?"

Jason had no answer. He turned on his heel and started down the stairs, leaving the dean to his prayers.

Chapter Twenty-Two

Jason drove east of town, along the river drive until he passed the entrance to Almaden's only private golf course. Giant old eucalyptus trees ringed the course, like antique Mongol warriors in need of new winter coats. He turned in at the sign that read "River View Estates." It was a new residential development, making a valiant attempt at graceful elegance. The residences were a bit too similar and too close together to stake much of a claim as the second Beverly Hills, but they did have a nice view of the river—February being one of the two months of the year when it held running water.

He pulled his van into the driveway of a model house where all the flags were flying. The garage door had been removed and replaced by French windows, and the garage itself now served as a temporary real estate office for the complex.

Inside, Jason looked over the three tables containing relief maps of the grounds. Sold signs adorned almost all of the boxes that represented houses.

"We only have a few left," a lady's voice cooed.

Jason looked up and saw a plump woman in a shiny

blue dress and lots of shiny jewelry. Every part of her seemed to be smiling brightly at him.

"You looking for something for a growing family?" she asked.

"I am interested in something that is probably on your resale list. I believe Alex Hacchi lived out here."

"Yes indeed. He had one of our first town houses in the Marblehead Village complex. I showed it to him myself. You knew he died rather suddenly?"

"Yes. I'm from the University."

"Oh, I see. Well, if you are thinking of a rebuy, I think you'll find it will take some time. He died intestate, I understand, and who knows how long it will take before his estate clears probate."

"What do you mean?"

"Well, they will have to do a search for heirs and so forth."

" 'Intestate' means he died without a will?"

"That's right. And from what we've gathered, he had absolutely no relatives. You're not a relative, are you?"

"No, I'm not."

"Too bad!" she joked. "We'd like to see his estate settled so we can resell the unit."

"What happens to the . . . to his estate if he has no relatives or heirs?"

"If nobody comes forward, I understand all his property reverts to the State of California. A rather sad end, isn't it?"

"Yes it is. The Lord giveth, and the state taketh away."

She laughed heartily, then extended her right hand. "Melody Herron is my name."

"I'm Jason Bradley."

"Would you be interested in seeing his place?"

"Yes, I would. But I feel I must tell you, I'm primarily interested in finding out things about Alex Hacchi. I'm not really in the market for a town house."

"Well, who knows, maybe I can turn you into a buyer. Let's check out his place. I don't have a lot to do around here anyway."

She found some keys in a desk drawer, hung a Be Back in Fifteen Minutes sign on the handle of the French doors, and climbed into Jason's van for the ride over to the property.

"I've been dying to see his place anyway, after all the hullabaloo," she shouted over the sound of his engine.

"You mean because of the way he died?"

"Well, yes, and because of the excitement we had around here. We thought we'd found a relative."

"Oh, really? Who was that?"

"We're not sure. She probably didn't give us her real name. A woman appeared in our office a day or two after his death and said she was his sister. She wanted to get into his unit and get some clothes for his burial. We have passkeys, of course, and we let her in and thought nothing more about it until the funeral director showed up and asked for the same thing. Oh, turn left here."

They moved out of the section of Mediterranean villas and courtyards into the Southern California version of a quaint New England fishing village.

"What did the woman look like?" Jason asked.

"She was an attractive brunette. I'd say around early thirties."

"Sharp dresser? With a high collar on her blouse?"

Melody was thrilled. "You know her, then?"

"I think I do. I think it's a lady that used to date Hacchi."

"Aha, just as I thought! She was here to pick up a few old love letters, I'll bet."

"Or to destroy the evidence," Jason suggested.

They pulled into the driveway of a clapboard-and-plaster unit that looked indistinguishable from all the others, except for the house numbers and the gas lantern post that was slightly listing riverward. Pale blue trim against beige stucco. In the entranceway three large clay pots held the remains of geranium plants, now dried and shriveled from neglect.

Melody opened the front door and led the way into the living room, and then pulled open the drapes.

"There are two bedrooms up, along with a full bath. . . ." She went on listing the selling points of the place, while Jason looked around. A wall of hi-fi and video equipment. Five-foot-high speakers bracketing equalizers and tuners and disk players, and on and on. Modern furniture of steel and glass with lots of cold sharp edges showing. Just like their owner, Jason thought. Stuffed leather chairs and a sofa that looked as if they should never be sat in.

Jason tried to imagine people living in the room. He thought of Hillary Reed. She had the style to go with a place like this. But then he thought of the peanut-butter fingers of her little tyrant. No, no, no. That would never do. Had that been the bottleneck in their suggested romance?

The bookshelves were mostly for show, too. The familiar names of Kierkegaard, Kafka, and Camus seemed to jump off the dust jackets of their twenty-five-dollar volumes.

It wasn't until he got to the kitchen that Jason found any inconsistency. On the tile sink, next to the counter where Hacchi had no doubt eaten most of his solo meals, stood a small black-and-white photograph in an ancient, very ornate frame. The scene showed two people on the porch of a farmhouse. An elderly woman in a thin white bonnet was working at something in her lap. It could have been knitting or sock darning. The other figure was a small boy, eight or nine years old, bareheaded, in shapeless dark pants, with broad suspenders looping over a white shirt. He was squinting in the sunlight with a hard expression on his young face.

Jason took the picture over by the light and studied it. He knew the boy. Not by name, but by type. He had seen him in a hundred faces while growing up. The raw, hungry yearnings for something out there beyond the farm and its dreary labors. He wanted to be where everybody looked the way they did in the magazines and talked the way they did in the movies. Someplace where he would be loved. And girls would come when he was working hard on something important and run their fingers through his hair, just because they liked him and trusted him and wanted to touch him. And rich men would come to him and offer him money for his opinions. What would be the best car to buy? Is there a God, or not? And which fork *should* you use for the salad?

The old woman, on the other hand, was content with her lot. Although her face was not turned toward the camera, the bonnet told of her spiritual commitment, the round shoulders told of her humbleness, and the large gnarled hands of a lifetime of work. She was too humble to look up, but still eager to work and continue to be what life had given her to be.

The contrast of the two people within the same frame gave the picture power and balance. Repose and tension. It was the only picture on the ground floor even remotely associated with the human form. Jason could fill in the blanks with imagination and a few scenes from his own life. He could see the trip made by the scowling youngster up to the time he harbored Camus on his bookshelves. The youth had found part of his dream, all the way to the steel-and-glass coffee table.

But it was the other trip that now puzzled Jason, the trip from the confident, cynical university professor, on the verge of recognition in his chosen field, to the defeated candidate for suicide. Would one case of AIDS be enough to turn the tide of the man's life about? If he felt personally responsible for Matthew Tye's plight, it possibly could. Jason hoped he would never know how that felt.

The Camus Club certainly looked with sympathy on suicide as an honorable ending to life. But if Rollins was right, three weeks elapsed between the time Hacchi learned of Matthew's illness to the time he hung himself. Did it take that long for the impact to register? Or for his guilt-ridden conscience to torment him to the point of desperation?

The bubbly lady who lived by commissions was recommending the view from the master bedroom upstairs, so Jason followed her up.

The view from the bedroom window was indeed nice, but Jason was more interested in the interior, which was decorated very simply, like something out of a Quaker farmhouse. Or a Shaker house? Jason's limited knowledge of the different religious groups was rather hazy, but he couldn't help noticing that the room stood in stark contrast to the modern trappings downstairs. There was a double bed with a simple wooden headboard, and one antique-looking nightstand with a crack in the wood. On the stand was an old paperback copy of the Bible, like the copies Jason had seen in the Prayer Tower. By the window there was a single rocking chair, a high-backed affair with narrow spindles and a low, broad seat. Very severe, but somehow quite complete in itself. And that was it.

"Were there two people living here?" he asked, only half kidding.

Melody Herron laughed. "You'd think so, wouldn't you? No, just Dr. Hacchi, as far as I know." She looked about, with a trace of curiosity showing. "I wonder what our mysterious Lady X was after."

They opened the door to the second bedroom and saw that Hacchi had used it for catchall storage. Ski boots and gear, a weight-lifting set, an old tank from a scuba diving unit, along with half a wet suit, suitcases, and boxes of old college materials. And in one corner, an aging set of beginners' golf clubs. It looked as if he had tried most of the standard recreations.

"Hello, anybody home?" someone called from below.

"We're up here," Melody answered.

Downstairs in the hallway stood a man of about sixty in his gardening clothes. He removed his cap and put his clipping shears in his pocket as Melody and Jason came down.

"Hello, Mr. Crumpacker, how are you today?"

"Just fine, Melody. I heard voices over here and wondered if I had new neighbors."

She did the introductions and tried to get an endorsement for the tract out of Mr. Crumpacker, but Jason was more interested in what the gentleman might know about Hacchi.

"You live right next door?"

"Yes," Crumpacker said. "As a matter of fact, we share the common wall there." He pointed at the entertainment equipment. "That's a very powerful set of speakers there, I can tell you."

"Did he disturb you?"

"Oh, he was very good about it. All I had to do was knock on the wall and he would turn it down."

"But I assure you," Melody was quick to point out, "the place is totally insulated, walls and ceilings."

"Did you ever hear anything else over here?"

"He was a pretty private kind of fella. Not real friendly, if you know what I mean. I gave him some geranium cuttings to fix up his front entranceway, but you see what he did with them. We didn't have a lot in common."

"Did you see or hear anything unusual going on over here before he died?"

Mr. Crumpacker scratched at the gray stubble on his chin. "No, I don't think so. Just the singing, once in a while. He took to singing, sometimes at two or three in the morning. I could hear him through the wall. Sorry, Melody, but I could. Not loud, mind you, but when everything else is still in the middle of the night . . ."

"What kind of singing?" Jason asked.

"I think they were hymns, but I didn't recognize them. They're not in the Methodist Hymnal, I can tell you that."

"Could they have been Shaker hymns? I understand he was raised by an aunt of Shaker persuasions."

Crumpacker shrugged his sloping shoulders. "Could be. What do they sound like?"

Jason pulled the Shaker hymnbook out of his coat pocket and handed it over to the man. "Would any of these be what you heard?"

"I might be able to spot some words, but the guy couldn't carry a tune in a bucket if you put a lid on it." He thumbed the little book. "Here, I remember this one. 'Trust in me, trust in me,' and, 'I'll sustain you with my right hand, when you pass the desert land.' "

He thumbed through more of the songs, but Melody had grown impatient. She got them out the door and back down the driveway. Crumpacker stopped long enough to pull a couple of dried weeds from the planters.

"Hope you buy the place, young man. Nice talkin' to you."

Jason returned Melody Herron to her office with only a little sales talk on the way. Then he tucked her business card in his overhead visor and headed back toward town.

He tried to imagine Hacchi lying in bed, singing the hymns he had learned, no doubt, at the old lady's knee. Were there two people inside everybody? he wondered. The skeptic and the would-be saint? He wondered about Tracy Rice, with her white tennis dress and her book of absolute rules. Did she ever waiver or doubt?

Through the dark grove of ancient eucalyptus trees Jason could see the sky to the west. It had turned pink as the sun found its way under the few deep blue rain clouds out over the ocean. He put on some old sunglasses from the glove compartment, but the color was still brilliant. Yellow shafts of light hit the ocean and set it afire. Another blast of light was hiding behind the thin clouds, teasing the edges with its yellow-and-orange fireworks. Louis the Fourteenth, eat your heart out.

He pulled over to the side of the road and watched the road show. He found his bootleg copy of Larry Adler mouthing his way through "Jesu, Joy of Man's Desiring" and slipped it into his portable cassette player.

The flaming sun went red as it neared the horizon. Then it flattened out and lingered there, like a three-year-old who didn't want to go to bed. Finally it slashed into the waiting sea, taking all its outlandish color with it and darkening the clouds over the water. It was perfect. Once in a while the scar tissue under his mustache didn't seem so important after all.

Chapter Twenty-Three

Jason had hoped to be at Omar's Ocean in time to talk to Barbara before her second performance, but it was going on ten-forty by the time he located the right strand of beach south of Almaden.

He had to park his van about four blocks away. Omar's little parking lot was crammed, and so were the few slots behind the run-down old waterfront shacks along the strip that led to it. Sand had drifted across several stretches of the old road. Most of the houses were on stilts. Jason noticed a street sign that read "Caution, streets flooded in high tides." And judging from the aroma that hung in the damp air, there had to be some part of a fishing industry in the neighborhood. Still, the stars twinkling over the quiet, shimmering ocean made up for a barrelful of atmospheric shortcomings, and—smell or not—Omar's didn't seem to be hurting for business.

"Omar's Ocean" was spelled out in ancient pink neon lights over the entrance, and palm trees outlined in neon yellow on either side kept tipping toward the letters in a three-step animation breeze. They don't make signs like that anymore.

At the guest entrance Jason stamped the sand off his

feet. An Oriental woman in a skintight sailor suit looked up from her booking form and flashed him a big smile. He asked her where could he find Barbara Langtree. A four-piece combo was playing jazz in the noisy bar right next to them, and he had to cup his ear to hear her say that Barbara was getting ready for her performance and couldn't be disturbed. He went in and, undaunted, looked for a way to get backstage.

It was a small place, built to maximize its ocean view. Bright outdoor floodlights were aimed at the water about a hundred yards distant so the paying customers could watch the surf playing on the rocky beach. There were a few people seated around the small tables, but most of the crowd was jammed into the bar. It was a mixed crowd. A few ties and coats, but mostly blue work shirts and a smattering of cowboy hats.

Jason had just made it to the curtain covering the raised stage and was poking his nose behind it when he felt a friendly tap on his shoulder.

"Can I help you, buddy?" asked a fireplug of a man in a bow tie and an apron. The scar tissue in the eyebrows indicated what his favorite sport used to be.

"Yes, I want to talk to Miss Langtree."

"She don't see guys before her act."

"Why don't we let Barbara decide?"

The fireplug gently took his right arm. "Look, be nice, okay? Every guy wants to see Barbara. You wait awhile; then we can all see her."

"I think she'll want to see me. Go tell her the man with the videotape is here."

"Do I look like a messenger boy to you?"

"Look, Omar, she'll want to see me."

They were beginning to have a disagreement regarding the space Jason's right elbow should occupy.

"I ain't Omar. I'm Omar's good friend, though. You wanna see Omar?"

"Why don't we leave Omar to his prayers. Hey, didn't I see you go against Willie Pastrano once?"

"Nope. I was middleweight. Come on, now."

"Okay, okay, but Richard Clark isn't going to like this."

The elbow dancing stopped abruptly. "You a friend of his?"

"Do you think I'd say I was if I wasn't?"

The old boxer thought about it. "You wait here."

He disappeared behind the curtain for a minute, then came back. "Okay, but don't be long." He held the curtain aside for Jason, as nice as pie.

Jason headed down a dark hallway behind the stage and pushed open the door where there was light. Barbara was stretched out on a wicker sofa, with an old afghan over her legs. Her top half wore an evening gown with lots of sequins and stars. Even up close it was hard to tell where the costume stopped and the white skin started. When Jason came in, she pointed at the chair in front of her small makeup table.

"You got a lot of nerve, you know that?"

"How so?"

"Billy likes to throw guys out. He thinks he gets points for it. How come you used Rick's name?"

"You told me to come and hear you, so here I am. Are you okay?"

"Yeah, I like to rest between shows. What's on your mind?"

"I thought you were going to ask me about the tape."

"Okay. What about the tape?" she said without feeling.

"Oh, good. I thought you'd never ask. Now I'll ask one. What were the songs you recorded for Richard?"

"You already asked me that."

"Yes, I know, but you didn't answer. How about it?"

"I tell you, and then you tell me about the tape, is that it?"

"Something like that. An even exchange."

"Sounds like blackmail to me."

"Barbara . . . May I call you Barbara? I feel funny calling you Miss Langtree."

She shrugged.

"Barbara, why don't you want to tell me about the songs? Did Richard tell you not to tell me?"

"I don't live in his pocket, you know."

"Oh, don't you? His name seems to pull a lot of weight around here. Are you sure you're not getting in over your head? Think how sad it would make your poor father if he should lose you."

She sneered. "My poor father . . . You got a good memory, don't you?"

"You are a very easy person to remember." Jason didn't know where he was going, but he decided to keep on jabbering in hopes that something would loosen her tongue. "I wonder what memories you gave to Hacchi? I don't imagine they were musical memories, were they? What with his tin ear."

"Tin ear? What are you talking about?" she asked.

"The man couldn't carry a tune."

"You're crazy. Of course he could. He could even harmonize to my melody line. He knew a lot about music. He's the one who introduced me to my French stuff."

"French stuff?"

"Yeah. I'll sing one for you tonight. Just for you. Now what's the story on that videotape?"

"We seem to be at an impasse here. You must have

a powerful reason for keeping this music a deep dark secret. You got a long-term contract with this Omar fellow—whoever he is?''

''He's got nothing to do with it.''

''Who does, then? Richard Clark?''

She sat up and tossed her covering to the side. ''Let me sit there, will you?''

They exchanged places in the small room, and Jason sat watching her run a comb through her hair. In the mirror she watched him watching her.

''You're not going to find anything written on the back of my neck, you know.''

''Just window shopping.''

''Why don't you take off now? I gotta fix my face.''

''You mean you're not going to exchange notes with me?''

''That's right. I'm not.''

Jason sighed. ''Too bad. It would make things so much easier for all of us.''

''Yeah, easier for you.'' She got out her lipstick and screwed it up, ready to apply. ''And don't think about doing anything cute with the tape. You could be in big trouble. Just a friendly little hint.''

''I wouldn't think of it.''

Back in the main room, Jason found a corner spot where he could watch both the show and the audience, then sat down and waited. A waiter came over and explained the ground rules during the entertainment, including the cover charge prices. Jason tried to get by as a special guest of Barbara's, but it didn't work. He ended up having the first seven-dollar-and-fifty-cent Diet Coke he had ever had in his life.

It wasn't hard to figure out what most of the crowd had come for. As show time neared, the bar activity waned and the tables started filling up. The combo men got to their places behind the curtain. After a drum roll and a taped intro by someone who claimed to be Omar himself, the curtains opened and Barbara made her entrance under a spotlight. Most of the audience seemed to be familiar with her, for the applause was friendly and loaded with anticipation.

Her first number, she announced, was a request from a special party in the audience. She gave the name of a French street singer who had made the number famous. Piaf, or something. Jason didn't catch it. And she went into a sentimental ditty in French, singing in a thin, reedy style and translating occasionally as she went along. Her voice was disappointing to Jason, but the emotional impact was strong. The song was about a girl who'd been abused by her father and everybody else she had ever met, but she still liked to smell the flowers in Madame DuFay's window box. Very sad. It got a polite response.

Then Barbara slid into a song with dirty lyrics about the bronc-riding circuit and the girls who followed the men. This was the number the cowboy hats in the place had come to hear. Lots of boot stompin' and doggie yells. She did it in a full, loose West Texas twang and a totally different vocal manner from the first.

The next two numbers were love ballads of World War II vintage that held the audience very well—including Jason. As he applauded he was surprised to look around and find that Billy the boxer had materialized in the chair next to him.

"Too bad about her husband, isn't it?" Jason said, trying to make light conversation, as well as show he knew Barbara.

"What husband?"

"Frankie. The one who got wiped out over in Lebanon."

Billy shook his head. "Man, that's part of her act. She ain't never been married. You sure you're a friend of Rick's?"

"Of course I am. Didn't Barbara tell you?"

Just then, Barbara started in with the intro to her next song. It was the same tale she'd told Jason back in the diner, about poor Frankie and the wedding in the Catholic church just down the street, because Frankie wanted it that way. It was word-for-word.

In the darkened room Jason tried to sneak a glance at Billy, but found he had already left the table. He was over behind the bar making a telephone call. Jason watched him in animated conversation, using his left index finger like a jab. Billy turned and looked back at Jason with a scowl on his mashed-potato face.

Barbara was moving into the first verse of "Can't Help Lovin' Dat Man." Judging from the way the combo players were working themselves up, this was the biggie for the show. This time Barbara's voice filled the room without benefit of the mike, and it seemed to carry with it all the longings and sadnesses of mankind in general, and not just those of a woman for her man. She was out there beyond the words of the song, beyond the sex and sequins, somewhere everyone lives at one time or another when the reality of his brief existence hits home. No wonder she had to rest between shows. She was singing from her soul and without a safety net. Why are we here? Why the beginnings and endings with all the pain in the middles? Even the cowboy hats were still.

Then, much too soon, the moment was broken and the crowd was clapping and whistling. Barbara left, then came back out, just like a ballerina after *Swan Lake*. They wouldn't let her go without another number, so she asked the audience to pick a favorite and she would sing it.

Billy had slid back in next to Jason. His elbow fetish was acting up again and he was trying to say something, but Jason was busy shouting a title. He pulled his arm free from Billy and went up by the stage. "Trust in Me, Trust in Me," he shouted persistently. Barbara looked over at him and frowned. Jason yelled it again.

Barbara smiled sweetly and beckoned to him with her finger, acting as if she couldn't hear him over the crowd. She pointed at her own ear, as if she wanted him to whisper to her. He obliged by getting onto the small stage and calling the title into her ear.

She drew back in mock horror, as if he had made an improper suggestion; then she slapped his face, much to the delight of the audience. Then Barbara got a glass of ice water from a nearby table and poured it over Jason's head.

Billy the bouncer got an armlock on Jason and hurried him toward the back exit, once again setting off the boisterous crowd.

Once outside, Billy let him go. Jason turned to face him. "Hey, that wasn't very—"

Halfway through he got caught by Billy's firm right fist as it struck squarely his solar plexus. Fortunately, Jason had seen just enough of it coming so he could set a grunt, and that probably kept his lungs from collapsing. Then, while Jason was searching the gravel driveway for his next breath, Billy hit him again in approximately the same spot. Jason's quick basketball player's legs had deserted him, and in their place were two heavy tree stumps. He used them to back up a few feet, but Billy was still coming at him. He seemed to enjoy his work.

Jason tried to hold Billy's hands, just in case he

wanted to dance this time. There was plenty of music for dancing, somewhere behind Jason's left eye socket.

"Lay off the girl. You got that?" the former champion of the whole world said.

Jason wanted to agree, but he had forgotten how to breathe out. He nodded his head and sucked in.

"And don't show up around here again. You understand me?"

Jason finally got himself upright and sucked in a little air. "What's with you, Billy? Can't take . . . joke?"

"You like another joke? I'll give you another joke."

As he lunged forward Jason found he could move again. He sidestepped out of Billy's punching area by about half a boxing ring. It gave him a little more confidence.

"What's the matter, Billy Boy, the footwork gone?"

"I just want you out of here, that's all."

"How come? Who did you call up? Richard Clark?"

"You want a punch in the face?"

"What's he to you, anyway? His old man wouldn't happen to be Omar, would he?"

"Whadda you care?"

"Come on, Billy, answer me. Try real hard and nod your head up and down for yes, or shake it this way for no."

Billy didn't take a ribbing well. He started after Jason again. Jason moved in what he thought would be the direction of his van, but in the darkness he ended up sidestepping into a weedy gutter filled with deep and brackish water. The hillside increased his momentum as he stumbled forward, and he quickly found himself treading water.

Billy was on the road above laughing like a hyena. "You leave those fish heads alone, down there, you hear me? Nod your head like this if you are being a good boy, and shake it like this if you aren't.''

Jason could see Billy silhouetted against the light which hung over the back door of the club. He was going through the motions of head shaking in the darkness and enjoying every minute of it.

Jason sidestroked away from him and finally found some solid footing, so he could fumble his way through the weeds and back up onto the road. It wasn't until he'd started for his van that the smell of his clothes started to nauseate him. He smelled more like bad crude oil than fish parts, but he wasn't in a position to argue the point.

When he got to the van, he stripped to his shorts in the darkness, then found an old blanket to wrap around himself on the ride home. At least the Grand Inquisitor should like him better this way. As he tried to wring the water from his one and only suit, he thought about taking it back to Sears and telling them he wanted his money refunded because it was losing its shape. He laughed aloud. Then he kicked himself for laughing when he should be thinking of other things. A clear case of misery denial.

Chapter Twenty-Four

When Jason got back to his apartment, the Grand Inquisitor was still sleeping on his old sweatshirt, but it looked like a different cat. Its matted fur had been licked dry now and had fluffed up so much, its ears were almost invisible. It had gone from looking like a monkey to something of a cross between an otter and a tomcat. Jason shooed it out the back door.

Should he buy some real cat food or not? If he bought it, he'd probably never see the animal again.

He got himself into the shower as quickly as he could and got set for a long session with plenty of soap. Billy the bouncer had done an expert job on his midsection. Not a mark to be seen. Apparently he knew his business.

He was tired, but he made an effort to run the events of the long day through his head. Was there anything that he was misreading? Or that he had forgotten?

It was all those lovely ends that were dangling out there with no answers. He had heard from two sources that Hacchi was virtually tone-deaf, yet Barbara, who certainly ought to know, insisted he had excellent pitch. Good enough to sing harmony. Somebody made a mistake. Okay, so what?

But there was also that unlikely matter of Richard Clark offering to take the rap for the horse-in-the-chemistry-closet stunt. What in the world did that all mean? Jason felt a certain prejudicial twinge against the boy in the Mercedes.

Then there was Barry Peterson, and the mouse under his eye, supposedly administered by his good friend and fraternity brother Richard Clark. Things always seemed to get back to Clark. Richard Clark, who took Dr. Hacchi's girlfriend. Richard Clark, who was using Hillary Reed's little house for his love nest. Could Barry have been upset about that?

Before he started his second lather, Jason reached up to turn on the small pocket radio he kept on the top of the shower door frame. The soap bar slipped out of his hand. He retrieved it from the bottom of the tub, but as he straightened he became momentarily dizzy. It was only from the fatigue of the day, he told himself. He held on to the walls for a moment, listening to something from Tchaikovsky and waiting for his blood to get back up to his head, and as he did so, it seemed as if all the pieces of the jigsaw puzzle had gotten tossed into the air as well. And as he watched in his mind's eye, they all came to rest in different spots. Suddenly, they all fit. Yes, they *all* fit. The strange quirks about Hacchi, the fraternity cover-up, the songs by Barbara Langtree, the tie-in with Matthew Tye, and the fraternity pranks as well. Jason got so excited he found himself suddenly clearheaded and wide-awake. He turned off the shower and the classical station on his little radio, and stepped out.

Now the problem was how to unravel this mess to the maximum advantage. He had things to do. He made a glancing pass at drying off, then got into some clothes as quickly as he could. It was going on twelve-fifteen, but there was still time to do what he had in mind.

There was an all-night market about three blocks in the wrong direction, but he decided to take the time. He got four cans of assorted cat food. That darned cat better show up again after this outlay. The sleepy gal at the cash register gave him his change and told him his collar was inside out.

Next, he drove over to Beta Rho and parked in the first available slot under the building. The area was quiet. The campus was dim now except for some grassy spots illuminated by the city streetlights, and for the crosses on the top of the Chapel and the underbelly of the Prayer Tower.

Jason walked all the way around the fraternity building, looking for the master switches for the electrical system. The overhead power line in the alley linked up with the building at one back corner. The master switch must be inside, he decided.

He mounted the front steps quietly and found the front door still open. The lobby was lit by dim bulbs on the wall sconces in the shape of flames. Jason's eyes had adjusted to the semidarkness, and he could see quite well. The lobby was empty, except for the stately old sofas and a television in one corner that looked as if it hadn't worked since Ed Sullivan's last show. One sofa showed stuffing coming through the armrests and another was missing its legs. Fraternity house traditional.

Before Jason could take two steps across the lobby, he heard an intermittent beeping coming from the first closed door beyond the lobby. Then he heard feet hit the floor and someone called out: "You, hold it right there."

In the next moment, the apartment door was opened and campus police officer Ryan came out, still fastening his belt over his ample middle. His gray hair was tousled, and his uniform was quite wrinkled.

"Oh, it's you." He blinked. "You set off our alarm system." He momentarily disappeared back into his room and turned off the beeping, then returned. "What brings you around here at—" He checked his watch. "What's the matter? Something wrong?"

"I wanted to see if I could get in without being noticed. Apparently I can't."

"Well, thanks loads. I'll do the same for you sometime."

"Sorry about that, Officer," Jason apologized, "but there *is* a reason behind my visit. How come you are drawing duty here tonight?"

"It's a long story. You sure you want to hear it?"

"The night is young."

"Like heck it is." He pushed at his hair to get it back behind his ears and yawned. "No students to do night duty. You know how weekends are. I talked to President Rollins about dropping this guard-duty stuff for this weekend, but he wouldn't hear of it. He was very . . . well, he was very loud about it. So here I am. The three of us on staff are taking turns. This is my night. It isn't so bad. With the house just about empty, and with this alarm system we've rigged up, it more or less takes care of itself and you can get some shut-eye." He frowned. "Under normal circumstances."

"What kind of alarm system is this?"

"Say, what is this? You a one-man police investigation or something?"

"More of a 'something,' I think."

"Whatever happened with the information I got you about the fingerprint? You never did get back to me on that."

"What do you want to know about it?" Jason asked.

"Well, what did the police say about it?"

"The police don't know about it yet."

Ryan stared at Jason, then hitched up his pants and stared some more. "That could be crucial to the murder case, you know."

"My sentiments, exactly."

"That's the same as withholding evidence. You know that, tiger? We could both be put in the hoosegow for that."

"Talk to our president. He's the one who didn't want it released. You want to call him?"

Ryan smiled and scratched at his ample midsection. "No, thanks. He's already uptight about something or other."

"That is one reason I'm here," Jason said. "As I understand, Richard Clark was signed out of the fraternity house all night Tuesday. The police say he spent the night at his parents' house in Malibu. But I was wondering if he might have gotten back into the house sometime during the night."

Ryan nodded his head slowly and raised his eyebrows. A big gesture for him. "You're thinking he's the only one with the motive, right? Because of the video."

"I'm thinking the video may not have been the only motive he had to wish Barry Peterson ill."

"Oh, really? What's the other?"

"First, let's find out if he could get into the place. If he didn't, the rest is academic, isn't it?"

"You're a real bundle of information, aren't you? I tell you what I know, and then you run off somewhere and hide."

"Come on, Officer Ryan, we're both working toward the same goal, aren't we?"

"I don't know. Are we?"

"Wouldn't it be interesting if you showed up these local police by finding out who really did kill the Peterson boy?"

Ryan smiled. "Oh, I'm too old for this nonsense. The locals have their man." But he started to perk up anyway. "What you want to know?"

"That's the spirit." Jason slapped him on the shoulder. Somewhere in his training he had been told that people are more apt to do a favor if there is some physical contact between the one asking the favor and the one who is asked. "Tell me about your alarm system. How does it work?"

"It's the standard heat-sensor system that just about everybody uses now. The little sensors detect any movement or quick temperature variation in the area, and they in turn trigger the beeper in the other room with a radio signal." He walked over to one of the sensors in the room, a small gray box that had been attached to the wall just under a fading print of a van Gogh. "Very simple, you see." He tapped it and shrugged. "We got three of 'em here in the big room, and another for the hallway back yonder where the back door is."

"I see." Jason paced and looked toward the back door. "No possibility that somebody could know the patterns so they could sneak around them?"

Ryan shook his head. "Very unlikely."

"What about power? Suppose somebody knew where the power to the building was and threw the switch?"

Ryan was shaking his head again. "Battery backup system."

"What about the fellow who was on duty Tuesday night? Could he have slept through the beeps?"

"Not likely. He's worked for us for three years. A very reliable fellow by the name of Tim Regan."

"I see."

"And he's the nephew of Miss Merkle."

"Why do you mention that?"

"I don't know. I just think of her as being one of the stalwarts around this place."

Jason sighed and looked at the ceiling, trying to come up with more possibilities.

Ryan excused himself for a moment. "I gotta log your presence in our logbook." He returned in a second, flipping pages. "How shall I list your visit?"

"How about as an electronic aberration?"

Ryan was in no mood for frivolity. "I'll just say you came by to see me," he decided, and made a brief entry.

"Any entries for Tuesday night?"

"Not a one after ten-thirty." Ryan turned to the page and showed how blank it looked.

Jason took the book from him and flipped back a few pages. Ten-thirty curfew on schoolnights and eleven-thirty on weekends. He wondered if the students up at Cal Berkeley would have stood for it. They probably would have been tearing down the Sather Gate in protest.

"Rather curious, isn't it? The president of a university getting so involved in a fraternity's probation?"

"What's so funny about it?" Ryan wanted to know.

"I didn't say it was funny. I said it was curious."

Jason kept on reading the entries in the book, hoping something would spark a fire for him. Most of the notes were about so-and-so's being five minutes tardy for curfew, et cetera. Ryan was getting restless.

"You're not planning on memorizing that, are you?"

Jason put a finger on the page for the previous Monday. "Here's something: 'Had to separate Clark and Peterson. Heard them fighting in bathroom. Clark's nose was bleeding. They both clammed up about it when I came in. Tim R.' Do you know anything about that, Officer?"

He took the book from Jason. "No. First I've seen of it."

"Did the police see that book?"

"Yes. You'd think they'd have picked up on that, wouldn't you?"

"Maybe they know more about this than they're letting on. Do you mind if I pop upstairs to Clark's room and see if he's asleep?"

"No, I don't mind a bit. He moved out of the murder room, you know."

"What's his new room number?"

Ryan went over to a list posted over the lobby phone. "Oh, no, you won't go up and see him, after all. He's checked out for the weekend."

"Back to Mama and Papa down in Malibu?"

"No. It says here he's at a hang glider event up in the Topa-Topa foothills."

"Oh, really?" Jason's eyes widened, and a smile forced its way on his face. "How very interesting."

"Why?"

"I hang glide, too."

"You do? That's a pretty dangerous sport, isn't it?"

"Not if you know what you're doing."

"I don't know, hanging up there by a bed sheet isn't my idea of a way to spend a Saturday. I hope you'll be careful."

"Why do you say that?"

"I imagine that's where you'll be spending your time."

Jason smiled. "Thanks again. It seems that I'm always in your debt. Hope you can get back to sleep."

Jason headed toward the exit with a spring in his stride.

Chapter Twenty-Five

There was little chance to sleep now. He found himself driving around campus thinking about how providence had dropped the hang gliding event into his lap. What a perfect way for him to get acquainted with the elusive Mr. Clark.

As he drove past the dark old Faulker Building, he wondered if the suicide stigma would ever be lifted from its gloomy gables. He swung behind the massive structure and turned west, passing the football practice field with its winter coat of gray-brown grass. No doubt the site of some of President Rollins' fondest memories. How still the whole place seemed now, in the middle of a California night, as if human activity were not really that important, after all. The night would cool and the dew would form and the stars would twinkle through the ocean mist just as if a prank had never been committed or a lustful eye winked. Nature's indifference seemed to throw the whole scene out of balance, somehow. Was it because it was too shameful to admit that man's only real enemy was himself?

He looked up at the homes facing the campus on the west and noticed there was a light on in a second-story room in Dean Kitteridge's house. Perhaps, without realizing it, that was where he had intended to go all the time. He swung his van into the Kitteridge driveway and revved the engine a bit more than necessary before turning it off. The dean came to the door in his heavy woolen bathrobe. Jason apologized for the intrusion.

"Quite all right, son. I was up reading, anyway. Come upstairs, why don't you?"

The old man graciously led the way up to the second story of his old frame house and into the solarium that must have been added in recent years.

"I think I probably already told you that this is my favorite place in the entire house," the dean was saying, probably to make light conversation. "It gives me a chance to look out over the campus, and I'm at an age now where the extra warmth of the sun feels pretty good on the old bones."

He sat in what was obviously his personal rocker. Jason sat on the edge of a chair and rubbed his hands.

"I've been driving around, trying to think things through, and I've got to try this on somebody. It'll either make sense or it'll sound too hokey to be true."

"This is about the murder?"

"Well, it's leading up to it. It's about the secret prank that the fraternity boys performed. I think I've figured out what it is they pulled."

"Oh, have you?"

Jason thought he detected a slight tone of artificiality in Kitteridge's rhetorical question, but he was too excited to stop and play with that.

"Imagine yourself, now, as a member of Beta Rho. Your house has already agreed to take part in this prank contest. But your prank can't be just any prank. This is the Animal House, and you have a certain reputation to maintain. It has to be a beaut. And as you are looking around for possible things to do, what do you see in your midst? You have one fraternity brother whose mind has been poisoned by the evils of secular psychology. At least, if you were Barry Peterson, that's how you'd view Hacchi's effect on Matthew Tye. So you start to think of ways to make Hacchi, the acid-tongued agnostic in your midst, the butt of the joke.

"Now, how to do it? What kind of joke would be the most fitting for someone who doesn't seem to believe in any religious influences at all? Why, naturally, you create a situation that makes him into a religious man, a situation that convinces him of a world beyond his scientific measurements and psychological humanism. You give him a connection with the world beyond."

Kitteridge grunted. "That's a rather tall order, isn't it? I've often wished there were an easy way to bring the reality of a Supreme Being into people's minds. But, so far, any such foolproof method has escaped me."

"Ah, but this isn't your standard conversion experience. This is to be God by machine."

"Why, hello, Jason," a friendly female voice called from the doorway. It was Mrs. Kitteridge with a tray of refreshments. "I thought I heard your energetic voice in here. I hope you like lemon meringue pie."

Jason got up and helped her slide the tray onto the small coffee table. Without asking, she gave him a fork, a napkin, and a plate containing a wedge about the size of a quarter pie.

"Oh, this is much more than I can manage."

"Well, do what you can with it. It'll just go to waste if you don't eat it. Lemon pies don't agree with the dean anymore, but I'm still in the habit of baking them." She walked over and kissed her husband on the top of his head. "Good night, dear. I'll be turning in now."

"Good night, Angie. Thank you."

"So nice to see you again, Jason. Don't be a stranger, now," she said on her way out of the room.

Jason eyed the pie and wondered what to do with it. It wasn't his favorite, but it did smell homemade and looked so yellow and white. While Kitteridge was fixing himself a cup of Sanka, Jason cut a small piece with the fork and popped it in his mouth, then went on.

"Now remember the kind of people we have working on this problem. There's Peterson, the communications student; Horwald, the first year medical student; and Clark, the professional student with money to burn—a jack-of-all-trades and master of none. But a man with a yen for a certain young lady. Remember that, because it'll be important.

"Now, let's take a few things we do know about Hacchi and see how they tie into this scenario. We know that Hacchi had an emergency appendectomy about three months ago. We know that he visited the dentist on the same day he took his life. Suppose that while he was in the recovery room after his surgery, these three students visited him while he was still under the anesthetic? I've been over to the hospital, and Harold Horwald showed me how easily people in the right kind of uniform can move about with no questions asked. So the three students visit the sleeping Hacchi. They proceed to remove one of the fillings in a back molar and replace it with a miniature crystal set that can pick up a certain radio frequency. They imbed the crystal with super epoxy into the tooth in place of the filling."

"Is such a thing possible?"

"Indeed it is. I've even heard of normal fillings being sensitive to certain strong radio signals. But with Peterson and his skills in communications, I'm sure it would have been easy to rig something to do the job. And if the device was expensive, he had Richard Clark right handy to pay for it."

Jason went on. "I think they arranged to broadcast songs of a particular interest to Hacchi who, the students had found out—probably during a lecture—had been raised by an aunt who was part of the old Shaker sect. You see, Shaker songbooks had been checked out of the University library by one of the students.

"Clark had Barbara—who, incidentally, was seeing both Clark and Hacchi—record some old Shaker hymns the way an old lady would sing them."

"You mean these songs were broadcast into Hacchi's head through the crystal thing in his tooth?"

"Exactly."

"Where on earth did you ever come up with an idea like that?"

"When I was taking a shower earlier this evening, I happened to bend over to pick up the soap I had dropped. And as I came back up, the blood was a little slow coming back up to my head, the way it does sometimes when you are a little tired. As I stood waiting for my head to clear, the music on my little radio right near my head seemed to be inside me, somehow."

"Excuse me," Kitteridge interrupted. "But I don't see how that made you think of Hacchi and the idea of a radio-activated tooth."

"I'm coming to that. On two separate occasions I was told that Hacchi couldn't carry a tune, yet the girl, Barbara, said he not only could sing but could harmonize with her. Now what would account for that? Then it came to me. Have you ever heard a person try to sing along with a song he is listening to through earphones? It sounds terrible, because the person wearing the earphones can't hear the sound of his own voice. Don't you see? That was Hacchi's problem. While he could hear the sound emanating from his own tooth, he couldn't hear his own voice, and therefore he couldn't keep his pitch. It's as simple as that."

"I'm not sure I follow all that." The dean frowned. "Why wouldn't Hacchi recognize the singer as being his own girlfriend?"

"I've heard the girl sing. She can do marvelous tricks with her voice, and if she were imitating an old woman, I don't think it would occur to Hacchi to think of Barbara. And if he *did* think the voice sounded familiar, he would associate it with his deceased aunt rather than his current girlfriend."

Kitteridge shook his head. "I don't understand the purpose of the songs. Why not simply pipe in a resonant voice saying something like 'This is your Maker speaking,' or words to that effect?"

"I'm not sure. Probably too far out to be believed. But the small, quiet reminder of hymns from his past could have a powerful effect on a person.

"What the boys at the fraternity didn't know was the emotional trauma Hacchi was facing from another source. President Rollins had read him the riot act about Matthew Tye. He practically accused him of being responsible for the boy's encounter with his deadly disease, AIDS. On top of that, he starts hearing these sounds from his past. No wonder the guy started singing along with the hymns.

"I think Matthew Tye knew about this double impact on Hacchi. When I talked to him in the jail, he alluded to synchronicity. He couldn't come right out and explain because he was still trying to keep his condition a secret."

Jason stopped for a reaction from Kitteridge. He looked down at the pie and noticed it was half-eaten.

He wondered who had done that while he wasn't looking.

Kitteridge had risen to his feet and was walking around the room, checking some of the hanging ferns for brown shoots. He came back to his rocker and sat.

"Your theory certainly satisfies so many of the odd things that have happened. If it wasn't exactly the way you describe it, it must have been very close. You are to be congratulated, Jason. That was quite a piece of work."

"Thank you. It also explains, I think, why the Beta Rho guys were willing to take credit for the horse prank that they didn't commit. They wanted to throw suspicion off themselves."

"But what could have indicted them at that point?" the dean asked. "It seems to me they were home scot-free."

"I think they were afraid the radio device would be discovered. Perhaps in an autopsy. Remember, they came forward about the dead horse directly after Hacchi's death. They no doubt thought their prank led to Hacchi's suicide. They probably decided that Hacchi thought he had become schizophrenic because of the music, and that he decided to end it all rather than go into treatment."

Kitteridge rocked slowly and shook his head. "Those poor kids," he said with characteristic forgiveness. "Living with that over their heads."

"Only one of them isn't living anymore, is he?"

Kitteridge blinked. "You think all this—"

"I think we now have more room for a motive."

"What motive? Silence?"

"That's the most logical one, isn't it? They found themselves in a conspiracy to silence, whether they liked it or not," Jason mused. "Barry Peterson may have gotten a bit restless. I found out that he and Clark had a little shoving contest in the bathroom at the fraternity house last Monday. Clark had a bloody nose and Barry ended up with a bruise under one eye."

"Why would they be fighting? It seems to me they would want to stay the best of friends."

"The answer to that probably lies in the personality differences between the two boys. Clark probably performed the prank merely as a lark. But Barry, with his rigid fundamentalist background, looked at the prank as something of a just retribution kind of thing. However, when Hacchi ended up killing himself—and Clark ended up with Hacchi's girl—Barry didn't like it. Maybe his conscience started bothering him. I can see Barry accusing Clark of deliberately planning the whole thing so that he could have Barbara free and clear."

Jason sat back in his chair and watched the older man's face. When the dean didn't respond, he continued. "I'm doing a lot of guessing, I know, but it's the only solution I can think of that makes sense. Why else would the two boys be fighting? And why else would Barry take it upon himself to embarrass his fraternity brother, along with Clark's new girlfriend? He did the secret videotaping in order to hurt them both. He didn't want to see anybody benefiting from what he had come to feel was a very bad act on their part. Guilt complexes can work that way. It's one thing to take part in a bad or sinful event, but it's altogether different to take part *and gain* from it."

The dean got up and started his tour of the plants again. Then he suddenly turned and faced Jason. "Quite a commentary on human beings, isn't it? I almost wish you hadn't come here tonight."

"Dean Kitteridge, you are the one who got me started in all this! We can't run away from it and act like it never happened. And a murder was committed to keep a secret. There is always the possibility that someone else will need silencing."

Kitteridge didn't want to hear that. He sat down and rubbed his forehead.

"And poor Alex Hacchi. I'm afraid I misjudged the man. The trauma he must have gone through!"

Jason was getting a bit peeved at the dean's attitude of passive handwringing, but he tried not to let it show.

"Think of the heartache and loneliness he must have suffered when the dentist identified the source of the music. That very evening he took his own life."

"What's your point, Dean?"

"I mean that for three weeks he lived with the knowledge of Matthew Tye's illness, and probably he accepted some of the responsibility for that. And then he learned the truth about his voices. I wonder if it was not the music and the old hymns that *sustained* him for three weeks, not driven him mad—kept him going with some little comfort and hope of forgiveness. I don't think the music contributed to his death."

"You may be right. That's something we'll never know, I'm afraid."

"No. Not on this side of the veil, at least."

"Veil? What veil?"

"The one that Barry Peterson crossed last Wednesday morning. The one that we all must cross someday."

"Oh, yes, that one. Sometimes I wonder, Dean, if we are speaking the same language."

Kitteridge smiled his sad smile. "We do seem to be coming at this from different ends, don't we? Tell me, Jason, in your headlong dash to gain all this knowledge, have you gained any salvation for yourself?"

"Salvation for myself?" Jason stared down at the empty plate he was holding in his hands. This was the last thing he was expecting to hear from the older man. He had come over to explain his ideas and maybe to get a little pat on the back. What was he driving at, anyway?

"I'm like most people, I suppose," Jason began tentatively. "I have a strong sense of right and wrong, and I want to see things set right again. I hold little hope of keeping my position here at Trinity, but at least this will help clear the air and help me make a clean start somewhere else."

"I thought you got into the study of psychology in the first place in order to seek your own salvation."

"I think we have a problem in semantics. I've always wanted knowledge and an education so I could find my way in the world. Find out more about myself and where I belong."

"Okay." Kitteridge nodded. "Has all this expanded your knowledge and insight into the human condition?"

With his fork Jason chased a few remaining crumbs around his plate while he looked for the right words. "I've been surprised at the events, primarily because of the reputation of the school."

"Yes. Amen to that."

"But I think everyone has a capacity for doing good or evil, given the right set of circumstances."

Kitteridge let out a groan. For a moment Jason thought he was in pain. "I have spent my life teaching that faith in Christ can make the difference—that when people who have accepted Christ as Lord of their lives come to the hard places, He will help them choose the good in life rather than the other road." The dean shook his head slowly. "This has been a shattering experience for me. Shattering."

He got to his feet and turned off the overhead lights,

then walked to the window and looked out at the midnight campus spread below them.

Jason put down his empty plate and stood beside his dean. For a while they didn't talk, only stared at the outline of the trees and buildings, and the ever present Prayer Tower before them.

"Isn't there a story somewhere in the Bible," Jason began, "about a farmer with two sons? He asked his two boys to go out and work in the fields. The first boy said he would go and do his father's bidding, but the second one said it sounded too much like work. But when it came time to get down to business, the first one took off without really doing what he said he was going to do, and the second boy had a change of heart and actually ended up doing what his father wanted in the first place. Did I get that right?"

Kitteridge nodded. "Matthew 21:28. One of Jesus' parables. What's your point?"

"Aren't you the one who said I should think of Christianity as a verb? Talking 'Christian' and doing 'Christian' really aren't the same things, are they?"

"No, you're right. They're not."

Kitteridge took a handkerchief out of his bathrobe pocket and blew his nose. That seemed to perk him up a bit.

"I must be on my way," Jason said. "Thank you for letting me bend your ear on this."

"You know, of course," Kitteridge said, trying to get his voice into a cheerier tone, "that in spite of all this talk, you really aren't any closer to knowing what happened in the upstairs hallway at the Beta House last Wednesday. It may have been something altogether different from what you expect."

"You may be right. But I still have a couple of surprises up my sleeve."

"So, what are you planning to do?"

"I'm hoping for a nice sunny day tomorrow. I thought I'd do a little hang gliding."

Jason said he could find his own way out, but the dean insisted on going downstairs with him and seeing him out the front door. On the porch Kitteridge shook Jason's hand and gripped it an extra long time, as if to convey something he couldn't put into words.

Chapter Twenty-Six

The diminutive dentist opened his front door and squinted into the bright sunlight, trying to see who had disturbed his Saturday morning breakfast.

"Dr. Collins?"

"Yes. Who are you?" he asked, eyeing the young man in cutoff jeans and a T-shirt delivering a warning from Smokey the Bear.

"I'm Jason Bradley. I need to talk to you about a patient of yours."

"I'm sorry, but it's out of the question, young man. This is my day off, and I don't discuss my patients . . ."

Jason put a hand on the door that seemed to be edging closed on his face. "Dr. Collins, this is an emergency. I'm with the University, and I need to know about your treatment of Alex Hacchi."

"What about Alex Hacchi?"

"He visited you last month with a tooth problem. I need to know what that problem was. He took his own life, as you're probably aware."

The dentist looked wary. "Yes, I know. What seems to be the problem?"

"We are trying to find out what he did just before he

died. Did he have something strange put in place of one of his back fillings?"

"No, he did not. All his fillings were intact."

"Oh, really?" Jason wondered where to go from there.

"Who did you say you were?"

Jason got out his billfold and showed his faculty library card and the pass he had been given for easy access to the county's psychiatric facility. "Please excuse the appearance, but I'm just on my way to a hang glider rally. I know my question seems a bit odd, but it is important. Would you tell me what Dr. Hacchi came to see you about?"

"He had a bad infection behind his second molar, upper left. If it hadn't been treated, it could have been serious. He could have lost the tooth."

Jason fought off his tendency to smile at the irony of worrying about one of Hacchi's teeth. "What caused the infection?"

"He had wedged something up under the gumline and had glued it against the back of the tooth with some sort of epoxy so that it couldn't work itself out. The body will try to force out foreign objects like that, you know."

"No, I didn't know. What kind of object was it?"

"It was a little lump of a metallic thing." He held up his index finger and thumb with the slightest bit of space showing between them. "And there was a small wire attached."

"Something like an antenna?"

"Yes, I suppose you could say that. When I did a full examination of the mouth, I found an identical obstruction behind the upper molar on the other side, except it hadn't become infected as yet. I don't mean to disparage the dead, but I was not surprised in the least when I heard he had killed himself. Any person who would do anything like that to his mouth . . . The mouth, you know, is a good indicator of the general health of the body. And it works both ways. If the mouth is traumatized, it isn't long before the rest of the body is, too. It's not something you should take for granted."

"Didn't the implants make you curious?"

"They certainly did."

"What did he say about them?"

Dr. Collins folded his arms in front of him and reflected. "I remember asking him what they were. He looked at them in the palm of his hand for a while, then threw them into the wastebasket and said, 'Only my salvation.' "

"He said 'salvation'?"

"Yes, I'm quite sure he did. It's the kind of phrase that sticks in your mind, you know. I remember he had tears in his eyes at the time. Poking around in the mouth can activate the tear ducts, so I didn't think much about it. But now, of course . . . I don't know. What were they?"

"We think they were some sort of radio reception devices—something like the old crystal sets kids used to play with."

"No kidding? Sort of a poor man's radio, huh?"

"Yes, something like that."

"He was a weird duck, if you don't mind my saying so. Never liked to talk much when he was in the chair. Kind of a superior attitude, if you know what I mean. Did you know him?"

"No. Not firsthand. Although I'm getting to know him, now."

"Taught psychology, as I understand." Dr. Collins leaned on the word "psychology" to let Jason understand what he thought of the subject, then shook his head. "I think most of those people go into psychology because they've got something wrong with their heads in the first place. Know what I mean?"

"Yes, I've heard that," Jason agreed. Evidently Dr. Collins hadn't read the hospital pass Jason had just shown him. "Did you mention this to the police or anybody?"

"Why should I mention it to the police? It isn't a crime to mistreat your gum tissue. Maybe it should be, but it isn't."

"Didn't his irrational behavior bother you?"

"Look, young man. I'm a dentist. If you think there was something I could have said or done to persuade Dr. Hacchi from his chosen . . . destiny, then you're sadly mistaken."

"Yes, you're probably right. Well, thank you, Dr. Collins."

"Is that a hang glider you've got strapped on the roof of your van?"

"Yes, it is."

"Aren't those things dangerous?"

"Not if you know what you're doing."

"By the way, what do you teach at Trinity?"

Jason looked him in the eye. "Me? I'm the new chaplain. It's a new technique we're working on in higher education today. The blind leading the blind."

Jason got his van onto the interstate that ran through the Topa-Topas and tried to think of ways to get what he needed out of Richard Clark. But his mind kept slipping back to Hacchi sitting in the dentist's chair. He had never met the man and had only seen very poor pictures of him, but by now he felt he knew him quite well. Jason was acutely aware of the lifetime of knowledge Hacchi had accumulated to get himself positioned in life. He recognized the philosophical posture Hacchi had taken as a result of his training. And he saw now that this posture had come back on him and bit him in the mind and conscience, leaving him with no bit of reserve philosophy to fall back on except some Shaker hymns generated by the boys of Beta Rho. And when that went into the wastebasket, there was nothing left to cling to. *Only my salvation. Only my salvation.*

Jason came to the first good incline in the road to the mountains and downshifted.

The cat had not shown up that morning. He felt like an idiot putting food out on the back porch for a cat that was never coming back. No doubt it had been playing him for a sucker all along. Not a pleasant way to start the day.

Good thing he wasn't superstitious.

Chapter Twenty-Seven

It was still early in the day for gliders, but there were quite a few already up. Jason hadn't needed directions to the rally location. He could pick out the landing spot from five miles away just from their circling patterns. In fact he had to force himself not to watch them too much while driving, for fear of ending up in a ditch.

As he got closer, he saw that the people aloft now were mostly hotdoggers playing follow-the-leader with a series of daring stunts. Every rally seemed to attract its share, and they gave the sport a bad name because more than likely one of them would end up being hauled away in an ambulance before the day was over. But, oh, how they loved to be at rallies. It wasn't enough to risk their necks with silly maneuvers in unsafe kites; somebody had to be watching.

Jason paid the two-dollar parking fee to a smiling farmer standing at the makeshift gate leading out into his pasture. He asked him where the primary takeoff point was and was told that all he had to do was follow the pickup trucks running delivery services up and down the hill and he'd find the spot. He thanked the happy man and started his van across the open field, following the beaten path toward the action.

Major targets had been laid out on a plateau of flat pastureland about the size of three football fields. Encircling the field on three sides was a grove of ancient California oak trees, and in the shade of most of the trees were vendors in their panel trucks and trailers, ready to service the faithful with their magazines and body suits and altimeters—an array of gadgets that one simply had to have.

Jason drove some distance, then got out and climbed onto the roof of his van, looking for the red Mercedes or anything else that might lead him to the elusive Mr. Clark. No Mercedes in the parking area that he could see. Out near the center target Jason saw a couple of event officials he recognized. He was about to go over and chat with them, but then he noticed a pickup truck that was all set to make the trip back up to the takeoff area at the top of the hill. He decided to tag along behind.

Takeoff areas were normally fairly close to the targets as the crow flies, but the roads leading up to them were often meandering. A good steep embankment is favorable for updrafts, but not too good for road building. Today's route was no exception. The pickup led Jason over a good four miles of cow paths and dusty dirt roads, around to the north side of the hills, before they reached the spot.

The last five hundred yards up to the top was a single-lane fire road along the bare spine of a brush-covered hill. The two vehicles had to wait at the foot of the climb for three other empty pickups to wind their way down the steep road. His VW was the only vehicle without four-wheel drive and he wondered how his gear box was going hold up.

At the top of the crest Jason found a very long area that was cleared of brush, and relatively flat, but it wasn't very wide. Hardly wide enough to turn his van around in, and there were steep drops on both sides. This was not an ideal takeoff area. Definitely not a place for the novice or the faint of heart. Twenty feet above them the air could be quite unstable.

There were a few paneled vans parked on the right side, away from the kites on the left, where several fliers were working at their gear, getting ready to fly.

Jason got out and walked back toward one fellow with an ancient Rogallo who seemed to be having trouble getting his last guy wire stretched onto its eyelet. Jason held the nose and the triangle bar for him, which made the stretch much easier. The young man thanked Jason for the hand, then slipped into his harness and, with barely a two-stride takeoff, was airborne. The kite dipped slightly, building up air speed, then banked right and crabbed along the crest of the hill, taking full advantage of the updrafts coming off the sunbaked cliffs below. A few seconds later it had climbed so sharply Jason had to crane his neck to follow the flight. It had been three months since he had been up, and the sight of this smooth, effortless glide activated his salivary glands.

As he walked back along the hillcrest, watching the fliers and their equipment, his attention was drawn to a big GMC van with a custom paint job and lots of camper-conversion paraphernalia. Right behind it someone was readying an Icarus-style kite for flight. It was a new fixed-wing variety, and very expensive. Jason had read about it but had never seen one before. It consisted of two angled wings that reminded him of the old biplanes they flew in World War I, except there was no tail or fuselage, just a sling below the wings where the pilot could stretch out on his back.

"Hello. Can I give you a hand?" Jason asked.

Richard Clark looked up from his work. ''Just double-checking my stress points, thank you,'' he said and pointed to the manual in his hand. He was dressed in a blue-and-white slick suit which was color coordinated with the designs on the wings of his glider.

Jason, trying to maintain a cool front, eased forward. ''This is the new McMillan, isn't it?'' he asked.

''Yeah. You familiar with them?''

''I've flown Icaruses before, but nothing this slippery. I understand it has a better than thirteen-to-one glide ratio.''

Richard held up his manual. ''Somewhere in here they claim it's even better. Did you notice the vertical fins?'' He pointed at the two small fins on either end of the top wings. ''They really cut down on the altitude loss on the turns.''

''As if you had to worry about that. On a day like this, you could stay up till sunset.''

Clark laughed and made an easy response. What a nice friendly chap. Not at all what Jason was expecting. With his sun-kissed wavy hair and athletic good looks, he looked as though he had just stepped out of a cigarette ad.

''Clark's my name, Richard Clark.'' He held out his hand.

''I've heard of you. I'm Jason Bradley. You're at Trinity, aren't you?''

''Yeah. How'd you know?''

''I teach there. I'm taking Dr. Hacchi's place.''

Clark's easy smile froze for just an instant. Then he wiped his hands and started putting tools away.

''What are you flying?'' Clark asked.

''Oh, I brought along my UP Comet with the modified foils,'' Jason said, his eyes still wandering over the McMillan.

"That's a great old bird. What's your rating?"

"Advanced, I guess you could say. Last fall I pulled a perfect six from Glacier Point to the floor of Yosemite Valley," he said.

"No kidding? With your UP?"

Jason nodded.

"Then you're ready for a step up. Maybe you'd like to give this a try." The boy seemed truly generous by nature.

"I'd love it—if you're sure you don't mind."

"We've got plenty of time before the trials start. It's brand new, and I'd like to see what a real pro thinks of it."

"Quite a van you have here," Jason marveled. "Did you get that to go with the glider?"

"Yeah. It was my dad's idea. I think he's still got a guilty conscience for divorcing Mother. So what can I do?" He shrugged. "I had to take it in order to make him feel good." He laughed at his own joke. "So you're taking Dr. Hacchi's old job, eh?"

"Yes. You wouldn't happen to be a psychology major, would you?"

"No, I sure wouldn't. I tried it for a semester or two, but it was too dry for me. Sorry."

"Did you know Alex Hacchi well?"

He frowned at the thought. "No. Nobody knew him well, I took two classes from him, if that's what you mean. You got a helmet?"

"No, I . . . uh . . . sold mine for gas money a couple of weeks ago."

"Here." Clark reached into the front passenger's seat and got an extra helmet. "I think you can make this one fit."

"Thanks. Where do you want me to bring it down when I finish? Up the ridge there okay?"

Clark smiled with a trace of wonder. "You can do that?"

"If the wind stays down, I think I can. That way we won't have to pack it for traveling again."

"Well, I don't want you to take any chances on my account. We can pick you up below in the pasture with no problem."

They were just in the motion of picking the kite up when the back door of the GMC van slid open. Barbara Langtree, wearing shorts and a halter, squinted out at the world with sleepy hazel eyes.

"Well, well. If it isn't the music lover. I thought I heard your voice. I'm getting so I know it quite well."

Jason smiled at her, which seemed to be the cue for the two men to put the kite back down.

"Hello, Barbara. Fancy meeting you here. You hang-glide, too?"

"Not me. He only brought me along to drive the truck."

Morning was not Barbara's best time of day. The shapely face seemed flat now, except for a little extra puffiness in the eyelids. The bloom surrounding Jason's mental image of the girl dimmed a bit.

"You two know each other?" Richard asked.

"Oh, you bet we do." Barbara smiled. "In fact, he knows both of us quite well. Don't you, Mr. Bailey?"

"Bradley," Jason corrected. "You'd think after all we've meant to each other, you'd at least get my name right."

"Did you get all the fish oil out of your hair last night?" Barbara laughed, then made herself comfortable in one of the folding chairs at the side of the truck, crossed her legs, and started whipping an emery board across her nails.

This was spoiling everything. Jason felt he had just

started building a bridge to Richard when Miss Songbird had to show up. How much did the two of them know? Or how much would she tell Richard while Jason was up floating around in the sky out of earshot? He decided to break the ice.

"I suppose the three of us could stand around here teasing each other all day if we had a mind to."

"Yes, I suppose we could," she cooed.

All he was getting out of her was dance routines. Jason decided to ignore her, but as he moved closer to Richard, he did it in a way that would allow him to watch Barbara out of the corner of his eye.

"Richard, I'm looking into the Beta House problem. I know about your prank. The real prank. I visited Hacchi's dentist this morning."

"What are you talking about?" he said cautiously.

"The morning of the day he died, Alex Hacchi visited the dentist with an infection caused by one of the implants you put behind his molars."

Richard started stepping backward. He bumped against his kite and had trouble recovering his balance. When he finally did, he seemed to be a bit paler and younger than before. Barbara had stopped with the nails and was watching very carefully.

"Very clever of you fellows," Jason went on, "putting in *two* implants. What did you do, broadcast in stereo so he would think the sound was coming from inside his head?"

Richard sat down with a smile on his face, then pulled at a nearby weed. "Yeah, we did. I really didn't think the thing would work so well. We were shocked when it did." He tried a nervous little laugh.

"What was it you were planning to do?" Jason asked.

"We really didn't know. We thought about broadcasting a voice, but we couldn't come up with one that didn't sound like the old Shadow radio voice. So we just kept piping in the Shaker music until—"

Barbara was on her feet. "*My* music?"

Was it possible she didn't know? Jason hadn't considered that angle.

"The old Shaker hymns Richard had you record." Jason smiled at her. "Don't tell me you didn't know about that?"

"No, I didn't know." She was staring hard at Richard. "You piped them into Alex Hacchi's head? What for?"

"It was just a joke, don't you see?"

"The man's dead! What kind of a joke is that?" she shouted.

Richard tried to quiet her down, but without success.

"You have me going around keeping your crummy secrets. 'Don't say anything to anybody,' he says, 'and I'll get you into the L.A. clubs.' You got a big dark secret, and all the time it's because of a crummy *joke*?"

"Barbara, honey, let me explain—"

"And what about my gigs in L.A.? Was that all so much hot air to keep me quiet?"

"No, of course it wasn't, honey. I talked to Dad last night."

"Oh, yeah? Funny you didn't mention it this morning when we was driving up to this cow pasture."

"I was waiting to surprise you."

"I bet." She reached into the van and got out her purse. "It so happens I was very fond of Alex Hacchi."

"No, you weren't, babe. Don't give me that."

"Oh, yeah? Well, it also happens I like to pick my own friends. And I don't like messing around with jokes that kill people."

With that pronouncement she started to head down the path in her high-heeled pumps.

"Where do you think you're going?" Richard called.

"Home—if it's any of your concern."

"Who do you think is going to take you home?"

"Transportation has never been one of my problems," she fired back at him.

Richard scowled at Jason with burning eyes. "Thanks a lot. You could have waited with your news flash, you know." Then he ran down the road after Barbara.

Jason, who had been taking all this in with a trace of pleasure, watched them disappear down the road. He now knew what he had come to learn, and he was feeling a sense of relief as well as amusement at the sight of their squabble. They were a couple who richly deserved each other.

But then he got to thinking about Barbara and her capacity for deception. She was an excellent actress. Was she acting now? Were the two of them just down the hill with their heads together, plotting?

There was one way to find out. If he gained a little altitude he could do a bit of spying on the two of them. Jason hoisted the McMillan glider clear of the ground and started edging sideways toward the takeoff side of the hill. After all, he was all set to fly anyway. And he had already been given permission.

He got into the harness and secured the straps, then checked the controls for the rudders and was ready to push off. He waited for two other kites to go, watching what the air currents did for them, then pushed off, too. The kite was heavier than his own, but considerably more stable. After the initial dip it was like sitting in an easy chair in his living room. If he didn't look down, he wouldn't even know he was flying. He found the stirrups for his feet ahead of him and leaned back to enjoy the flight.

First Jason banked right, away from the retreating

couple, in order to gain altitude. The updraft pushed him up nice and smooth. When he reached a thousand feet, he started a gentle bank away from the hillside. Instead of losing altitude, as he would have in his own kit, he ended up gaining. He watched below for the lovebirds.

He spotted them about halfway down the road. Judging by the gesturing that was going on, they were still not on friendly terms.

So much for Jason's suspicious mind. Time for a little fun. He told himself he deserved it. To the northwest, past the target pasture, he spotted a plowed field and what looked like the beginnings of a thermal lift. At least two hawks thought so, for they were circling clockwise without benefit of a single flap of their wings and holding their own very nicely. Jason decided if he got another thousand feet off the hillside, he could make it over to the plowed field safely.

He got the lift he needed with just one pass. In his own kite he would have ended up doing figure eights along there for two or three passes to get up this high. That convinced him. He would definitely have to have one of these. Someday.

The hawks were still floating over the field, so he decided to join them. There was very little risk involved. He would lose altitude getting over there, and if the thermal wasn't what it seemed, he would lose even more getting back to the hillside. But experience told him he could make it with room to spare.

The hawks squawked their displeasure at his intrusion. Jason found the thermal. By watching his wind ribbon and listening to the sound of the wind hitting his helmet, he very quickly nursed the kite back up to altitude and then some. Three thousand. Then four and five. His bare knees and arms told him that was high enough. Besides, he could see about as far as he was going to see that day anyway. To the west, the coast was still socked in with low clouds, and he couldn't make out the ocean at all, but the Topa-Topas to the north and east looked as if they wanted to shake hands with him. Every crest popped out at him, like wind-carved sand in a child's sandbox, and in the distance the coarse geological layers just below the peaks stood out sharply. He could count the eons.

It was exhilaration time, hanging in space like a free spirit while the cares of the world vanished from his mind. Only the sound of the wind whispering over his helmet and the wire braces of the McMillan.

He could stay up all day, but since it was a borrowed kite and Richard might be getting antsy, he decided to cut it short. He'd have no trouble getting back to the ridge from where he was. He banked left out of his clockwise circling of the thermal and headed for the ridge.

At the top of his bank, he heard something wooden crack. There was no turbulence, no unusual stress to the craft that he could detect, but something definitely was wrong. Jason eased the kite into a slow descent, which would give it the least stressful ride, and then started looking things over. The only wood he could see was a small decorative piece around the yoke that held the two wings together and at the correct angle. He put his hands along it and felt for a break. He found a splintered end but could do nothing about it. The problem must be underneath in the metal tubing.

The kite hit a small air pocket that dropped it, then jerked it suddenly. Normally, nothing to worry about, but the McMillan couldn't take it. This time it broke at the yoke piece. The two wing sets folded up, and Jason found himself in sudden free-fall.

A woman screamed below. In the next instant a chorus of voices started screaming and yelling. For some stupid reason Jason found himself wondering what was going to happen to all the cat food he just bought. Would the state take ownership of that, too?

He wanted to live. Oh, God, he wanted to live! He didn't care if he did get the short end of life. He wanted it, wanted whatever part of it he could have, whether it made sense or not. He'd take it. Oh, it was so sweet. To wake up and breathe, to see light and to hear somebody laughing.

He fumbled for the buckle on the harness that was keeping him pinned to the leading edge of the broken mess. The strap finally gave way and he swung free, holding on to the pile of junk by one hand. Then he worked his way up the bottom of the left wing, hand over hand, kicking his legs free from the stirrups as he wiggled up. Halfway up the wing he tore at the underbelly of thin fiber until he got one hand into the wing. Then he searched for a wire or pipe or anything that would hold his body weight. He found a bracing tube with his left hand, then tried to force his body weight out away from the wing.

What he was striving for finally started to take effect. His body was falling faster than the junk pile because of the difference in wind resistance. His weight started tipping the wing from a vertical free-fall angle to a slight incline. Soon the other wing set started to help, acting like a wind foil, and the angle of the left wing moved closer to horizontal. He was out of free-fall but only slightly. The ground was still coming up at him at a frightful pace.

Still hanging on by his left hand, Jason edged his right hand to the leading edge of the wing he was under in order to get it tipped down. This he hoped would get the wind foil lift it was designed to give. Judging from the noise level, it was working some, but it was hard for him to tell, for he could no longer see the ground. He was spinning clockwise and totally out of control. His only hope of survival was landing in some nice soft chaparral brush.

The women were screaming right in his ears now. He put his feet ahead of him and turned his face away from the impact. He didn't want his mouth ripped up again.

Then the screaming stopped and everything was a fluffy white.

Chapter Twenty-Eight

He found himself floating through the top part of a giant lemon meringue pie. Now and then he would stop in midflight, push away the meringue for a little breathing room, then continue on his way. Mostly he used the breast stroke, although the Australian crawl seemed to work just as well.

When he came to a large air bubble in the frothy stuff, he looked down at a garden tea party that was in progress on a large circular yellow rug. There was Miss Merkle driving the Audiovisual cart, her friend Elsie Berkaw by her side. Miss Merkle was very irate about something. As he got closer, by sliding down the inside of the bubble, Jason realized her walking stick was missing.

"How can I teach home economics without my walking stick? Where is that Alex Hacchi?" she kept demanding. But no one paid the slightest attention to her.

President Rollins was there, too, trying to get all his white hair tucked under the earflaps on his 1920s style football helmet. His major concern was The Game.

"It's time to play," he kept telling the others. "That's

enough eating now. It's time to play. Are we or are we not a team?"

The answer was in doubt, as each guest seemed to be wrapped up in his or her own concerns.

Kitteridge's role was unclear. Part of the time he wore the Mad Hatter's hat and went about serving sassafras tea to everybody, yet at other times he was in a rabbit's suit crying over the great loss of time. Time had been lost for very mysterious reasons, first because they were using the wrong china, and then again because the meringue had settled so low and blotted out the sunshine.

This confusion went on for what seemed like a couple of hours, until a large contingent of Norsemen arrived, marching in to the accompaniment of the overture to *Tannhäuser* and singing the praises of their queen, who arrived riding on the back of a dead horse.

At this point the party picked up considerably. The queen turned out to be Barbara Langtree, dressed in her peasant blouse from *Carmen* and wearing a Norseman's crown, complete with horns and jewels on her head, with smaller crowns on the nipples of each of her four breasts. Her entourage was made up mostly of the members of Beta Rho, who were dressed in costumes that kept changing from football uniforms to playing cards to shaggy Viking battle suits.

Whatever they were, they seemed to be expected, for the games were now started in earnest. Unfortunately, it was hard for Jason to see, for about this time he started slipping further down the side of the bubble. The game had started, but all he could see now was the backs of several players dressed in Bicycle playing cards, along the sidelines cheering for the participants.

Then suddenly a whistle blew and Elsie Berkaw's

shrill voice pierced the air, calling, "Foul, oh, cursed foul! You are out of the game."

All action stopped as the offending player was led away. Most of the crowd was chanting "You, you, you," at him. Jason was straining to see who it was, but the crowd was too great. "If you can't follow the rules, you can't stay in the game," Elsie chanted.

What rules? What game? Jason wondered. Then, for the first time since he had arrived, the people seemed to recognize him. Another player was called for and all eyes fell on Jason. A young woman, not Barbara, took him by his right hand to lead him into the game, but he held back. He was afraid of getting out on the yellow field and not knowing what to do, or of losing his footing on the shaky playing surface and embarrassing himself. But they needed him. Finally, he decided to go. But then he found that he was still strapped into the harness of his hang glider. His left arm was caught in the loose steel wires, and he couldn't get it free to undo the straps.

"Jason, don't struggle. Jason," somebody was calling.

He opened his eyes and found himself out of the tea party. Hillary Reed had him by the hand and was smiling at him.

"You're going to hurt your shoulder if you keep that up," she said.

When he first looked about, he decided he was in the AIDS room at the hospital. He was convinced if he stayed there, he would catch it. He tried to get up, but discovered constraints on his movement. He had a splitting headache that pounded harder when he raised his head.

"Where am I?" he asked.

"You're in the county hospital," Hillary said. "Will you lie still now?"

"Yes."

"Good. I'll be right back." She left his side and went into the hall to talk to somebody, then came back after a minute. "I was to tell them as soon as you woke up. The police want to talk to you."

"How'd I get here? What's wrong with me?"

"You mean you don't know? You had a terrible fall."

"Fall?" He wondered how anyone could hurt himself falling out of such a nice soft lemon pie. Then Hillary's face came back into focus.

"That ridiculous hang glider you were flying had been tampered with. You don't remember falling?"

It was starting to come back to him now. He started checking over the basic equipment under the covers. The toes wiggled, and both knees seemed to flex all right. But the left arm wasn't working. He reached for it with his right arm.

"You have a broken collar bone," she said. "And you had a concussion, but, otherwise, they think you're going to be okay."

"What's this on my right arm? Looks like a burn wrapping."

"It is. You spilled hot grease on yourself when you came down."

"Hot grease?"

"You came crashing through the awning of a taco stand and knocked the whole thing over. I understand the rally people told the ambulance driver that if you lived, they were putting your name in for the award for the most spectacular landing of the year."

He groaned.

"That's a wonderful sport you have there," she marveled. "Ever thought of doing the running of the bulls in Pamplona next summer?"

"Very funny. What time is it?"

She looked at her watch. "Just about two-thirty, Sunday afternoon."

"I've been out all this time?"

"Oh, no. You started mumbling and moving about around noon. That's when the nurse called the police. They wanted to be here when you woke up. They're on their way up from the coffee shop right now."

"What are you doing here?"

"The dean thought it would be nice if you saw a friendly face when you woke up. He couldn't get one, so he sent me instead."

"Who's minding the kids?"

"It's their dear daddy's weekend to have them, bless his little heart. No baby-sitter problems this weekend."

"Was that how Richard Clark got the key to your place?"

She blinked at him in surprise. "Yes. How'd you know? I started questioning all my old sitters until I found one who used to date Richard. He used to come over to the house while she was sitting. One day she lost the key to the front door. She said it turned up later in Richard's car. He must have had it copied. Shortly after that she said they broke up."

It made sense. Richard dropped the girl, but kept the house key for his next go-around with Barbara Langtree.

A heavyset nurse came in, took a look at his eyes, and held him by his wrist to check his pulse rate.

"You with us for keeps this time?" she asked.

"I hope so."

"How are you feeling?"

"If I said I had a headache, what would you do?"

"Give you a shot. The doctor wants you to keep that shoulder immobile."

"I feel great."

She smiled. "Okay. Let me know if you stop feeling great. The police are here and want to ask you some questions. Are you up to it?"

"Yeah, as long as they don't knock me around too much."

She laughed, then put his hand on the buzzer by his pillow. "Your buzzer is right here. If they start the third degree on you, you just let me know."

She held the door open for three men. As they got closer, Jason recognized Lieutenant Newcombe and his little sidekick, Sergeant Weir. Behind them stood Dean Kitteridge. Hillary got out of the way and moved over to Kitteridge's side.

"Hello there, tiger," Newcombe grunted. "You had yourself quite a time, I hear."

"I try to keep my weekends busy."

"Yeah, well, you sure did that. I have to ask you a couple of questions, here." He sat down and got out a notebook.

"About this hang glider. The one you crashed in belonged to Richard Clark, didn't it?"

"He said it was his."

"How did you happen to be up in it?"

"It was a new design I hadn't flown, and I wanted to see—"

"Yeah, I know. But whose idea was it that you go up? Did he offer it to you, or what?"

Jason thought a bit. "I think he saw me looking it over and offered me the use of it before the competition started. Why?"

"That's what I thought," Newcombe announced. "He was the one who suggested you take it up? You'll swear to that in court?"

Jason frowned. "Yes, I guess I'd have to. Why? What's up?"

"That kite had been rigged to fall apart under the first sign of stress. We've had experts look at it. The metal tubing under the little decorative wood handles had been sawed partway through. We've already arrested Clark for murder."

"Murder?" Jason asked. "Isn't that a bit premature? I'm still alive."

"I mean murder. Clark killed Barry Peterson. I guess we have to tip our hat to the amateur on that one. You were a bit ahead of us regarding the Tye boy's innocence. You were on the right track when you went up there after Clark. I just wish you hadn't tried a stunt like that on your own."

"Aren't you forgetting something, Lieutenant?"

"What's that?"

"Clark wasn't at the fraternity house that Tuesday night."

"Oh, yes, he was," Newcombe singsonged. "I'm surprised you haven't figured that out on your own."

Jason shook his tender head, then wished he hadn't. "Okay, so how did he get past the alarm system?"

Newcombe cocked a superior eye and looked around, probably making sure everybody in the room was listening. "He went *over* the system. He didn't bother with the first floor at all. He flew to the roof in a hang glider." Newcombe laughed and snapped his notebook closed. "I'm amazed that you, a glider man yourself, didn't think of it. He flew from the Prayer Tower, which is right across the street, onto the roof of the fraternity house, then went down through the roof door that he had made sure would be unlocked before he left for Malibu. Then, after he had killed his roommate, he went back up to the roof and glided down onto the darkened campus lawn across the street, folded up his glider, and headed back to Malibu.'' He held up his hands to show how simple it all was.

"And the motive?'' Jason asked.

"Again, we have you to thank for that. Dean Kitteridge here got in touch with us after your fall from the skies and explained what you had been working on. Clark had to keep his roommate quiet. And he decided you were getting too close for comfort, and that you had to be silenced as well.

"We got a search warrant and have already gone over his parents' garage down in Malibu. We found a small hang glider down there. A . . .'' He looked to his Sergeant for a word.

Weir said, "A Rogallo wing glider.''

"Yeah, one of those that fold up and open up real easy. And it's light enough to haul up the steps of the Prayer Tower in the dark of night, assemble up there, and glide right down to the roof across the street. It was even a dark blue. Virtually invisible in the middle of the night.'' He clapped his hands together. "You see, it all fits.''

"Yes. Almost perfect,'' Jason admitted. "You are to be congratulated.''

Newcombe chuckled modestly as he got to his feet. "I thought you might appreciate it. And your news about his offering the kite to you is just so much frosting on the cake. An airtight case.''

"Yes. Airtight. Almost.''

"Oh, come now, my young friend. You're not going to be a sore loser, are you? You should be proud of having a part in a real live criminal case. We thank you for your help. We really do. Don't we, Sergeant?"

"Yes, thanks." Weir nodded, with a bored expression.

"You get better real soon now," Newcombe ordered on his way toward the door. "We'll let you know about trial dates and so on."

Jason watched them go out the door. "Remarkable," he muttered under his breath.

Kitteridge came closer. "Is there anything we can do for you, Jason? Anyone we should notify?"

"Yes. I may or may not have a cat that needs feeding. Would you . . ."

"I'll take care of it."

The stocky nurse came in and told them the patient had better be quiet for a while, so Hillary and the dean dutifully filed out of the room. Jason didn't put up a fuss. All the talking had made him surprisingly tired, and he was asleep before their footsteps had faded down the hall.

When he awoke again, it was dark outside as well as in the room, although the door to the hallway was open. He could see someone in a pink blouse serving evening snacks to patients from a large push-cart. It must have been the noise of the dishes that woke him.

This was his first stay in a hospital since he was young, and it made him uneasy. Too much like all institutions. Doing things by the numbers and eating food that had been prepared by the yard and by the bushel was not his idea of living. Then he decided if he felt well enough to start complaining, he must be feeling better. He let out a sigh.

"Are you awake?" Kitteridge's voice came from the darkness.

"Yes, I am. I didn't know you were there."

"I just came by with your mail and thought I would sit with you for a bit."

"That really isn't necessary, you know."

"It's no problem. I didn't find your cat, but the food was gone out of the bowl on the back porch. I put out some more."

"Thank you." Jason reached for the light over his head. When he couldn't make contact with it, Kitteridge turned it on for him. "Did you say something about mail?" he asked.

"Yes. Here it is." He handed it to Jason. "I couldn't help noticing you have a letter from the placement department up at Berkeley. I guess I can't really blame you."

Jason found the letter, the only important-looking piece he had. He fumbled with the envelope one-handed.

"Can I do that for you?"

Kitteridge opened the letter and handed it back to Jason. "Good news?"

Jason read it. "Sort of. The lady says she has a couple of other possibilities for me. The county sheriff's office where I worked before has gotten another federal grant. They want me back on their staff. And she has another teaching lead for me. She thinks I might be happier in a state school."

"I see." Kitteridge leaned against the window and crossed his arms.

The light was beginning to hurt Jason's eyes, so he reached up and clicked it off again.

The dean cleared his throat. "Did you know that

President Rollins has asked the board to grant him an emergency medical leave?"

"No, I didn't."

"It just happened yesterday. The stresses of the job have been a bit much for him, I imagine."

"Will wonders never cease?"

Kitteridge chuckled. "Yes, I thought you might be interested. Another point, too: The Council of Division Chairmen has temporarily been directed to manage the academic affairs of the University until an interim president can be appointed. We haven't had a chance to meet yet, but I'm sure one of the first things we'll do is have another look at that pledge business. You won't need to worry about that, I'm sure."

"I see."

They sat in darkness for a time. Then Kitteridge got to his feet. "I'd like you to stay on, Jason."

"Thank you. I have some things to think about before I can answer that."

Kitteridge edged toward the door. "I won't disturb you any longer. Have the nurse call me if you need anything."

"Dean Kitteridge?"

"Yes?"

"The police aren't holding Matthew Tye any longer, are they?"

"No, he's out of custody."

"What's going to happen to him?"

"My wife and I have talked it over. He's still hospitalized right now, but as soon as he's well enough, we'll be taking him into the house with us. At least for as long as we can manage him."

"I see. Good night, Dean."

"Good night."

Jason rolled up onto his right side and listened to the

night sounds coming from the hospital hallway. He didn't really have much more to think about. He already knew what he was going to do.

Chapter Twenty-Nine

On Tuesday they released him from the hospital on good behavior. The doctor had told him his concussion had not proven as serious as they had feared and there should be no lingering ill effects from it. He was going to have an extra large bump on the top of his left shoulder blade from now on—which could have certain advantages, the nurse told him, if he should start wearing suspenders. And he was to keep his burned right arm out of the sunshine for the next year.

At two-thirty, he walked over to the campus and made his way to the bench under the flagpole on the Quad. He somehow felt it appropriate. Dean Kitteridge was a little late for their appointment, so Jason sat down and waited.

Not much had changed in his absence. Seagulls were still hovering in place overhead in the cloudless sky, patiently waiting for the coed Frisbee exercises on the expanse of grass to finish up so they could get on with their foraging of scraps that had fallen during the noontime pep rally. The Booster Club had stretched a large purple-and-white banner across the front of the third floor windows of the Faulker Building. It read "We're #1," in honor of the Trinity basketball team. It was good to see the important things on campus were still being taken care of.

The dean's yellow pickup pulled into one of the parking slots reserved for visitors, and he ambled with long strides over to Jason.

"Say, you're looking pretty good. I think that stay in the hospital was good for you."

"Thanks. When I get the use of my left arm back, I'll feel even better."

Kitteridge gave a courteous laugh and sat next to Jason. "You had something on your mind?"

"Yes, it's about my staying on here at Trinity. I know the pledge is no longer mandatory, but I'd like to tell you my feelings and let you be the judge of whether or not I belong here. And there's something else that has to be done."

"Sounds very ominous. Okay, Jason, let's hear what you have to say."

He cleared his throat and got his one good arm ready for lots of gesturing. "There is a good deal of Alex Hacchi in me, Dean. Probably more than you realize. It's very easy for me to understand his bitterness and his ultimate rejection of life. I've felt that way more than once in my own life.

"There is nothing in all the world I would like better than to have the overwhelming conviction that there is an omnipotent God in heaven who would like nothing better than to care for my every need. Unfortunately, I don't have that conviction, and I don't know if I ever could.

"Okay, all that is on one side. On the other side: I want my life to count for something. When I was falling toward my death last Saturday, I knew for certain I wasn't ready to cash it in—that there had to be some meaning or purpose to all this that I hadn't found yet. I was willing to claw and scratch and dig until I was exhausted trying to find some hope to grasp. Does that make sense?"

Kitteridge was already nodding and smiling. He just did a little more of it by way of reply.

"I suppose a large part of that feeling is my own selfish sense of wanting to belong someplace, to be a part of, well, a family. You've made me feel that way, although I can't say the same for everyone here at Trinity.

"I'd like to stay at Trinity. I'd like to be a part of a community like this. I know my motivations may not be as pure and noble as yours or others who are dedicated Christians. But I'd like to live my life as though it were true. Does that sound artificial? Maybe so, but it's the best I can offer right now. I suppose what I'm saying is, if I'm going to err with my life, I want the errors to be on the side of the angels. If you want me here on those terms, I'd like to stay."

Kitteridge instantly held out his hand. When Jason took it, the dean said, "Welcome to Trinity. All I would ask is that you be open and truthful with the students."

"I will. I will."

Kitteridge's eyes were watering, and Jason was afraid he was about to be hugged. He couldn't handle that. He got to his feet quickly and looked at his watch.

"Would you like to take a little stroll with me?"

"Where to?"

"To the Prayer Tower. I was going to meet Sergeant Weir over there."

The dean frowned, but got to his feet. "Okay, let's go."

The walked a few yards in silence, watching a Frisbee game on the Quad.

"Funny how those things float so effortlessly, isn't it?" the dean said.

"Yes," Jason agreed. "If you know how to toss them."

"Have you ever thought how similar hang gliding and Christianity are, Jason?"

He frowned. "No, I can't say I have."

"But they are. When you hang glide, you have all the right equipment with you and you push off from a hill into the air. You can't see the air. A person who has never done it might even say it could be disastrous to jump off such a high cliff into nothing. But the experienced flier has faith. He's been there before, and he knows he can trust himself to the wind, even though he can't see it. He knows it's there, and he knows how to lean on it."

Jason laughed. "Always in there pitching, aren't you, Dean?"

He laughed, too. "It comes with the territory, Jason. I do hope you realize I'm not through with you yet."

Jason only smiled and pointed their way toward the Tower. "Shall we?"

Chapter Thirty

At the base of the Prayer Tower Jason reintroduced his dean to the young detective who was waiting for them. Sergeant Weir shook Kitteridge's hand without commitment, then turned his troubled face back to Jason. "Okay, here I am. What is it I can do for you?"

Jason checked his watch and then pushed the button for the elevator. "I thought you'd like to see the spot from which Richard Clark is reported to have jumped with his hang glider."

The elevator door opened, and Jason stepped aside to let Kitteridge and the sergeant proceed him. There was room enough for the three of them, and they rode in an uncomfortable silence all the way to the top.

When the door opened, the three men stepped out onto the landing overlooking the large circular room. There were only two students there, each praying individually at the little kneeling benches.

Kitteridge frowned at Jason and said in a stage whisper, "Okay, here we are. Now, what's this all about?"

"Good, he's still here." Jason pointed at one of the students and looked at Sergeant Weir. "Do you remember him?"

"Yes. We interviewed him about the murder. Why?"

The campus chimes started their familiar three o'clock tolling of hymns, and the other student took this as a cue, got up from his place, and left the room. But not the one Jason was keying in on. He walked over and touched the boy's shoulder.

"Excuse the interruption, but . . . I think you know Sergeant Weir. Sergeant Weir, this is Harold Horwald. He's the one you've been looking for, Sergeant. Aren't you, Harold?"

Harold sucked in his breath, then held it with pursed lips. His eyes turned pink first, and then the rest of his face, but nothing else was happening.

"Are you out of your mind?" Weir asked Jason.

"No, I'm not," Jason said, then looked back at the young man still on the prayer bench. "Am I, Harold? I think it would be better for you if you did the talking. It's time, Harold."

But it was only time for Harold to stare and try to exhale. His breath came out in jerks at first. Then in sobs. And finally in outright tears as he buried his head in the armrest and broke down like a two-year-old.

"I tried. I tried so hard. But I couldn't, couldn't. . . . I would pray my life away if it could only make a difference, but I couldn't make it work."

Jason sat down next to him. "I knew you reminded me of someone from Shakespeare, but I couldn't for the life of me think who. It was your name that kept getting in the way, Harold. It wasn't Prince Hal that you reminded me of. It was Claudius, Hamlet's stepfather, who had trouble with his prayers because of his guilty conscience.

> My words fly up, my thoughts remain below:
> Words without thoughts never to heaven go.

"What the devil is going on here?" the sergeant demanded with confusion.

"Harold is your murderer, Sergeant. Not Richard Clark."

Weir moved forward, still not totally grasping the situation. "I thought you were the one who was convinced Clark had done it. What did you go up to the rally for, anyway?"

"I went up there to make sure Clark *wasn't* guilty. Not to prove he was."

"That he wasn't guilty . . ."

"That's right. When I confronted Richard with what I knew about the dental implant, his only reaction was to try to make amends with his latest girlfriend. Don't you see? He had very little to lose from exposure.

"But now with Harold here, that would be a different story. Harold is in his first year of medical school. And putting implants in patients' mouths while they are in the surgical recovery room is just the kind of stunt that would get him bounced out of the training program in no time. Especially when the patient ends up killing himself because of that little prank of theirs.

"Barry and Harold, you see, thought their prank was actually the cause of Hacchi's suicide. Like being guilty of murder, only in the one-hundred-and-eightieth degree."

"But what about the kite?" Weir demanded. "Clark very nearly killed you with that rigged booby trap."

Jason shook his head. "There was no way Richard could have known that I would show up at the rally. And once I was there, he had neither time nor opportunity to rig it. No, it was booby-trapped all right, but it was probably done the night before by Harold. It was Richard who was supposed to be in it when it crashed."

"And his motive for that—" Weir started.

"Was the same as his motive for killing Barry. Silence. He knew about the videotape stunt that Barry had pulled on Richard, and he probably knew Barry and Richard had been fighting. Their secret collusion was beginning to fall apart, and it was only a matter of time before Barry went to the authorities with the truth about the implants. He had to kill him."

Jason bent over and twisted his head lower so he would make eye contact with Harold. "How'm I doing, Harold? You want to take it from here, or should I go on?"

Harold had started to recover his wits. His red eyes glared out at Jason. "You have no proof. Didn't you hear? Rich was already arrested. It was Rich who killed Barry."

Jason shook his head. "It won't work, Harold. No one who knows anything about hang gliders would go out one of these windows with an old-fashioned Rogallo. There is no way you could get a running start. And the chances of getting the entire kite free of the ledge with one jump is very slim. I'm an expert, and I know I wouldn't try it unless there was something like a burning building behind me.

"But even without that knowledge I had you pegged, Harold. May I tell you why?"

"No. This whole scene is beginning to bore me."

Chubby Harold struggled to his feet and was about to leave. But it was Sergeant Weir who stepped up and put a hand on his chest.

"Not so fast, son. Let's hear what the man has to say." He was listening, but he kept his eyes on Harold and his body between Harold and the exit.

"Thank you, Sergeant," Jason said. "I won't keep you long. The thing that has always troubled me about Peterson's death was the condition of his room and the way he was found bleeding in the hallway outside. All the stab wounds were administered from the same angle and in the front of the torso, and yet the room looked like it had been the scene of a struggle. It didn't seem to fit.

"That leaves us with three possibilities. One, the struggle had nothing to do with the murder, and it happened before the murderer entered the room. In that case, I think the neat and conservative nature of Barry Peterson would have forced him to straighten up the room. Most assuredly he would want to clean up the broken bottle of after-shave. No, that version doesn't seem to work. So, let's consider the second. The struggle and the murder happened simultanously. But that doesn't seem to work, either, because of the nature of the stab wounds, all administered from the same angle and in front of the torso. Hardly the way wounds would be made during a fight. But they are consistent with the way wounds would appear if someone stood over a prone body in the lower bunk and stabbed repeatedly. Yet no one in his right mind lies down on his back and lets someone stab him to death. And the coroner said there were no signs of head wounds or any indication Barry could have been knocked out."

"Okay, friend, get on with it." Weir was getting antsy keeping an eye on the nervous Harold.

"The third possibility strikes me as being the most likely. Suppose the murder was committed and then the room was messed up afterward."

"That makes even less sense," Weir said.

"Not if you consider the reason for it. Suppose there was a smell in the room that the murderer had to cover up. What better way to cover up a smell than with another, stronger smell. He broke the after-shave in order to cover up the other smell, but then he had to mess up the rest of the room in order to cover up his reason—to make it look like the broken bottle was an accident."

"Okay, what smell are you talking about?"

"The smell of chloroform. Or whatever they use in hospitals these days to put people to sleep. Barry Peterson was drugged while he slept and then stabbed. Very sound medical procedure—putting the patient to sleep before you cut."

"Ridiculous!" Harold barked. But Weir was still listening.

Jason moved closer to Harold and continued his story. "Only Barry wasn't killed instantly. He lay there and bled in his drugged state, until he woke up enough to crawl into the hallway where he was found by Matthew Tye, another student with plenty of troubles of his own."

"You can't prove it," Harold whispered through his teeth. "You can't prove a thing."

"Ah, but there is where you are wrong, my friend. Traces of chloroform can be found in the body long after death. I ought to know. In my sophomore year I flunked a biology quiz because I put too much chloroform in the rag I used to kill my lab frog. It totally loused up the rest of my experiment and—"

In a sudden desperate move Harold slammed his left shoulder into Weir's midsection, knocking the startled policeman onto his back. Then, on all fours, he climbed up onto the ledge of one of the open windows. Fortunately he wasn't too swift about getting his legs up. Kitteridge stood about, grunting and yelling, "Stop, stay down. Oh, stay away," and other things which Harold was ignoring, for he had crawled over the window ledge and was in the process of swinging his feet up over the guard railing so he could jump from the Tower.

Jason, with his one good arm, reached up and yanked at the overhead lever that controlled the window. The window came swinging inward hard onto Harold's head, momentarily stunning him and pinning him against the sill and the bottom of the ledge.

By then Sergeant Weir was on his feet and was pulling on Harold's shirttail to get the whole body back into the room.

"I want to die. Let me die. Oh, God, let me die." Harold sobbed.

Weir wrestled him down onto the floor and leaned a knee against his chest. He started reading him his rights. Harold had all the fight out of him and he submitted like a mute zombie.

Weir got his handcuffs on Harold, and in the next few minutes the three men got him safely down from the Prayer Tower to ground level. Dean Kitteridge directed the sergeant to a telephone in the maintenance room in the Tower base, where he called for help.

In the small room filled with supplies and cleaning compounds Weir found a folding chair, snapped it open and sat his prisoner down. The other three found sitting spaces for themselves on the boxes of toilet paper and hand towels and waited quietly. There had been enough talk for a while, and each of them sat lost in his own thoughts. The only sound that could be heard was the closing chorus of "Rescue the Perishing" that floated out from the Chapel tower across campus. Dean Kitteridge finally broke the silence:

"I don't see how you could do such a thing, son," he moaned. "What must you have been thinking of?"

"It started out so simply." Harold smiled. "It sounded like so much fun at the time. Then it just got out of hand. It was Barry's idea. He really started it. He didn't like Dr. Hacchi's way of teasing people for their faith. So we thought we'd turn the tables on him. I came into the frat house one Friday night with the news that Hacchi was going to be operated on in the morning. We worked on our scheme all that night. It was all just a gag.

"But then he killed himself and the bottom fell out of everything. We tried to keep it quiet at first, but it wasn't working. Barry kept having bad dreams. Rich and I did everything we could with him. Then, last Tuesday he came back to the house and said a new teacher was in the Audiovisual office asking too many questions. I knew then he wasn't going to make it. Something would have to be done that night."

He smiled and shrugged, as if that explained everything. "It was only a gag, don't you see?"

"But what about your testimony in the Chapel service? I don't see how you could do such a thing," Kitteridge said, not with reproach, but simply in wonderment.

Harold had no answer for that, but Jason did. "If you are going to hide in the henhouse, it's a good idea to learn to cluck."

Rubber tires squealed on the sidewalk outside, and in the next second Annie from Audiovisual stuck her head into the small room.

"What's up?" she asked. "I just heard on my scanner there's a police car on . . . its . . . way."

She spotted the handcuffs on Harold, and her big brown eyes got bigger than ever. "Him? You mean he really did it?"

"Did what?" the sergeant asked.

"Did the killing?"

"What makes you say that?"

Annie frowned and shook her finger at Harold. "You

know, I had the funniest feeling about him. I thought all along maybe he did it, you know?''

''No, we don't know,'' the policeman said. ''Tell us about it.''

Annie said to Jason, ''You remember last Wednesday morning when we saw him on the steps, crying? I rubbed his shoulders and neck for him 'cuz I felt sorry for him. But his muscles weren't tight at all. Not like he was tense and worried about his friend. More like it was all an act, you know? I remember when my uncle died, my cousin Ramon's shoulders were tight, just like iron. Harold here was as loose as a goose.''

''What's that got to do with anything?'' Weir snorted.

But Jason was nodding in agreement with her. ''It all fits the pattern. I think if we had time to psychoanalyze the prisoner, we'd find he has a psychopathic personality, incapable of feeling remorse or guilt. How else can you explain his willingness to kill off two fraternity brothers, just so he could keep their secret? His display of remorse and sorrow had to be staged.''

Jason searched Harold's face for signs of remorse or guilt. Or something, anything, to indicate what was going on inside. But the curtain had gone down, and only the trace of a phony smile remained. He could have been an innocent two-year-old with his baby fat still showing. Harold had disappeared behind a childlike expression and showed no interest in Jason's harsh evaluation of him.

Jason gave up with a sigh, then snapped a playful finger at the brim of Annie's cap. ''You are quite a psychologist, Annie. I wish you had shared that with me earlier.''

She shrugged. ''Well, nobody asked me.''

The siren of a police car sounded in the distance, and

Weir put a hand under his prisoner's arm to get him to his feet. Then he turned to Jason.

"You want to ride along downtown? Maybe you'd like to see the lieutenant's face when I bring him in."

Jason smiled and stroked his bare neck. "No thanks. I gotta go home and feed my cat."

About the Author

Gaylord Larsen, media specialist for Ventura College, has taught audiovisuals in Los Angeles and Ventura, California. He was a writer for the television program "This Is the Life," and has produced scripts for educational and church films. He has four children and lives with his wife in Ventura. Larsen is also the author of AN EDUCATED DEATH and THE KILBOURNE CONNECTION.